Naked in a Pinstriped Suit

Naked in a Pinstriped Suit

Al Bowers

For the Browns
With best regards,

Als

Nov 16, 1997

Posterity Press

Posterity Press, Inc.
P.O. Box 71081
Chevy Chase, Maryland 20813

http:/www.posteritypress.com

Printed in the United States of America
Book Design by Krohn Design, Inc., Falls Church, Virginia

This novel is a work of fiction. Despite occasional references to actual places, the main characters and the setting in which the story takes place are entirely products of the author's imagination. Any resemblance of these characters to actual persons–living, dead or working in corporate America or the animal rights movement–is unintended and purely coincidental.

ISBN–1-889274-02-X

To my wife, Betts,

to my daughters, Christy and Cathy,

and to my little dog, Twee.

Chapter 1

"It's not just cream that rises to the top in big business," she laughed to herself, thinking about the singular collection of milksops, frauds, nitwits and toadeaters that peopled the upper management of Temeritus, Incorporated, the Fortune 500 cosmetics company. "And that's why I'm going to pull their pants down before this is all over."

She sat naked at her dressing table in her house in the Heights section of Houston, brushing her hair, talking to herself. "Yes, M," she said, "things are going better than you could have ever dreamed." She always used her code name, "M," before a meeting, the electricity of anticipation charging her mind. These meetings were the best part of her life. Here she was boss and no one told her what to do. The thrill of power was palpable.

She brushed her hair–luxurious, jet black and shoulder length–with long and careful sweeping strokes, holding the brush in her right hand and pulling her head to the side against the tug of the brush as it traveled downward. And as she stroked, relishing her reflection in the mirror, she weighed the changes in her life since joining the Animal Liberation Army–ALA, the super-secret animal rights organization that sought to put an end to all forms of animal subjugation.

Organizing a new cell in Houston had been slow and tedious. Recruitment problems and delays caused by the need for strict secrecy had plagued her from the start. But the cell now numbered twelve people and several "parties"–code for raids on animal testing laboratories and other acts of violence against the enemy–had been staged, all part of the systematic harassment of the worst of the worst in terms of animal abuse, the loathsome Temeritus.

Under M's leadership, a program of sabotage was underway–defacing the walls of Temeritus Tower and the insides of the elevators, slashing the tires of Temeritus vehicles, setting off smoke bombs in the lobby of Temeritus Tower, and other acts of vandalism designed to add to the pressure on the company to forsake its long-held practice of animal testing. The cell took as its model the "monkey wrenching" of the radical environmental movement. The spirit of the animal rights ethic, however, precluded the use of that term as being degrading to a fellow resident of the planet, the monkey.

M finished with her hair and began to dress–pulling old jeans over her slim hips and slipping into canvas tennis shoes and a denim shirt. No animal hides or fibers would ever touch her skin, just as no animal flesh or product would ever pass her lips–except when she traveled with the enemy wearing wool and silk, pretending to eat whatever was put on her plate to prove her disguise among the meateaters.

Her final task before leaving the house was to feed the animals. She had never intended to keep animals at home. She was against the human ownership of other animals, the notion of "pet-hood" being in her mind no different than the notion of slavery. But she had become attached to several of the animals liberated by an ALA cell in Dallas, ones that she had reluctantly agreed to keep while they recuperated from the wounds they had received in the labs.

She had Patches, a tired old beagle whose body still showed the scars left by his tormentors at a laboratory somewhere in the east, and three cats, Wynken, Blynken and Nod, also from an eastern lab. Of these her favorite by far was little Nod, a warm and friendly cat who had been, in the antiseptic terminology of medicine, "bilaterally deafferented"–her hind legs had been surgically "desensitized" to allow for the "painless and humane" experimentation on nerve regeneration. This poor thing still was deprived of the use of her hind legs so that she walked with her front legs doing all the work, the others trailing in lifeless drag behind her.

"Suppertime, gang," M sang out as she headed for the kitchen to begin the nightly ritual. Patches always reacted the same way, by waddling into the kitchen and baying with delight, his head turned up to the ceiling, "AHOOOOO, AHOOOOO." The cats remained unimpressed, except for little Nod, who dragged herself into the kitchen and waited next to her dish while M prepared the food.

"Yeah, Patches, old buddy, you're a good old dog," she said, squatting down and scratching the old beagle behind his ears. She turned her attention to Nod. "But you, little Nod," she said, picking up the deformed little cat and nuzzling her with affection, "you're the sweetest one of all."

She fed them all the same thing, lentils in a vegetable broth which she made in bulk each week and kept in the refrigerator. She put several scoops of the mixture in the two bowls on the floor for Patches and Nod and in the two bowls on the counter where Wynken and Blynken could get to them when they felt like eating. She had learned that an unprotected bowl of food would not escape the limitless appetite of the beagle.

M left for the meeting excited. On the agenda was a discussion of the next step in the campaign of harassment against Temeritus, the next logical step in the journey that would take them to their most daring adventure yet–the raid on the labs in The Woodlands.

Chapter 2

Casey O'Rourke couldn't wait for the speeches to end so she could go home. The awards banquet for one of the many business associations Casey belonged to out of necessity was now into its third hour. These things were always an ordeal, but tonight seemed especially bad.

Finally, the speeches were over. She walked out of the banquet room and into the lobby where she gave her parking ticket to the bellman and waited. When the car–a bright red Jaguar XKE convertible–finally appeared, she walked out of the hotel and into the soppy Houston evening. She gave the man a big tip and drove away.

Kathleen Callahan O'Rourke, known to her friends since her first week in college as "Casey," was the president and majority owner of a thriving public-relations/management-consulting firm and, at 35, a model of success. And she had done it all on her own, which made it even more rewarding. *I wish I had a nickel for every person who said I couldn't do it,* she thought as she eased into the traffic on Westheimer. *Oh, it's so hard out there . . . nobody ever makes it on their own . . . do you know the statistics on failures in small business? They didn't know me all that well or they would have known that nothing stirs me to action faster than someone telling me I can't do it.*

Her thoughts were interrupted when the music stopped and

the local news came on telling her of the continuing troubles of the city's largest employer, Temeritus, Inc. This company, once a model of corporate efficiency, had faltered in recent years and was now beset by problems which threatened its very existence. Embarrassing lawsuits, accidents, environmental problems, a series of inept management decisions—all had combined to create vast problems for this British-owned company. Any further difficulty it experienced was indeed important news in Houston—such was the impact of the company on the community through its payroll of 20,000 employees to say nothing of the money it contributed to local charities and the arts as well as the thousands of hours of devoted community service by its workers.

For several months Temeritus had been the target of a nationwide boycott of Temeritus products organized by a coalition of animal rights groups operating under the name CACTUS—the Coalition Against Cosmetic Testing in the United States. Earlier in the week CACTUS had begun to picket the Temeritus headquarters in downtown Houston. Tonight's news story was about the violence and arrests that had been spawned by picketing earlier in the day.

The news, weather and sports over with, music again filled the car and Casey's thoughts returned to herself. She was tired, as usual on a Friday night, but she was happy. She always enjoyed her weekends. She could sleep late, rest, and catch up on chores. But most important, she could spend time with Jake—John Jacob Gilligan, owner of a brew pub in the Village near Rice University, and the first man she had cared about in years. Yes, she thought, life is good. Maybe a bit slow and predictable lately—but good.

In the next instant a small bird broke her reverie—as it slammed against the windshield with a fluttering splat. "What's that mean?" she thought, shaken and slowing down for whatever might be ahead.

Chapter 3

The meeting had gone well, M thought. But not as well as she had hoped. Dissension was beginning to appear and she wasn't sure how to stop it. As she sat in her kitchen sipping herbal tea, she went over last night's meeting in her mind.

M had left her house and driven to a restaurant in the Montrose area that was to be the meeting place that night. Meetings were rarely held in the same place more than once, and never in a member's home. The size of the group and its dedication to the cause meant that the meetings could be held almost anywhere—usually in restaurants that could offer a private room or alcove but sometimes in a museum cafeteria or even in a park. Probably the most interesting place had been inside the Astrodome one night while a baseball game was in progress.

But regardless of where the meeting was to be held, the procedure was the same; M, the only person who knew the identities and phone numbers of the cell members, would call and leave a short message—"The book club will meet at the Blue Anchor on Fondren, 7:30, Friday night." Or "At the entrance to the Main Library at noon Saturday." Or, in the case of the Astrodome meeting, "at the first hot dog stand to the right of the West Entrance of the Astrodome Tuesday at 8:00."

If M needed to speak to a cell member, a more complex system was used. Each member had given M the number of a pay phone at a busy place that could be used for cell communications. That phone was identified by a code name. The time to be at that phone for a call was specified in code–"Later on" meant 7:00 p.m.; "Tonight" meant 9:00 p.m.; "Tomorrow" meant 7:00 a.m. the next day. So when M phoned a member at home and said, "I'll call you later on at Barbara's," the member knew to be at the "Barbara" telephone at 7 o'clock that night. Finally, to insure that communication could flow up as well as down, M carried a pager so that anyone in the cell could call her.

And so it was that last night the members of the cell began to arrive at the nondescript restaurant promptly at 7 o'clock. The ALA is in no way a social club and the period prior to the meeting did not include the banter and small talk usually found before most meetings. These members marched into the room and silently took their seats. Secrecy was of utmost importance to the security of the cell and its activities. Only M knew the real names and daylight identities of the members, all of whom were known to each other only by their code name–a single letter of their choosing. All social contact between members was forbidden, and as a result, meetings of the cell were gatherings of singular focus.

First on the agenda was a review of the activity planned for the week. A report was given by L, who was in charge of the "awareness program," as it was called. L reported that over the weekend he and two volunteers yet to be selected would break into the kitchen at the cafeteria in Temeritus Tower. There they planned to remove all the meat from the refrigerators and freezers. The meat from the freezer would be put in the ovens and turned on low so that it would be dried out and unfit for human consumption by the time it was discovered on Monday morning.

The meat that was not frozen would be spread around the kitchen, smearing as much as possible to make cleanup difficult. Small cuts of it were to be hidden behind the equipment in the kitchen–under the stove and behind the refrigerators and some of it even behind the walls in the dining area—so that by mid-week it would begin to stink and would be a lingering reminder of ALA's activity.

And of course they would make sure they got the credit for this by marking the walls with the various slogans that they favored— STOP ANIMAL TESTING; FREE THE ANIMALS; ALA STRIKES AGAIN; TEMERITUS NAZIS.

There had been a lengthy discussion of this proposal. Several members felt it was too risky for the little impact it would have and that it was time to move on to bolder measures. And although nothing specific was suggested, it was a reason for concern to M. She was fearful that some of the more intense members might become impatient and want to accelerate her schedule. Even worse, some of them might demand a turn to personal violence.

Chapter 4

Early Saturday evening, an hour late for the Blakes' party, Casey pulled her Jag into Rustic Pines, one of the many sprawling new subdivisions that span Houston's growing perimeter. Always the same, these parties—same people, same hors d'oeuvres, same chit-chat. She would much rather have gone over to the Village for a few beers with Jake. But Mary Blake had urged her to come, even if she only stayed a minute, to meet some bigwig from Temeritus who might be good for business.

Mary was the owner of one of Houston's finest dress shops and long-time friend. Of all Casey's friends, Mary alone had encouraged and supported her when she began her own business—instead of dishing her the usual crepe hanging: oh-you'll-never-make-it-on-your-own-you're-making-a-big-mistake-to-leave-the-security-of-a-big-company. I wonder what could be so special about this guy, Casey thought; Houston is crawling with Temeritus executives. But, it can't hurt and I'll be back at Jake's early.

She parked in front of the house and walked across the lawn to the front door. The house was a large two-story white brick mini-mansion with pillars that were supposed to make it look like Tara. It didn't. And even if it had succeeded, it still would have missed the mark because there were at least three others in the subdivision almost exactly like it.

Casey walked onto the front porch and up to the door. She could hear the buzz of conversation coming from inside so she opened the door without ringing the bell and walked in. Across the entry hall from the door was a large family room filled with people in small groups. She entered the room unnoticed and went to the bar where she asked for a merlot. She was savoring her first sip when Mary Blake spotted her. "Casey, you look wonderful; I'm so glad you could come. I want you to meet someone."

She grasped Casey's hand and dragged her off toward a small group standing outside on the patio. This group was gathered around a tall, well-built man who was explaining something in a confident but somewhat aloof manner. A handsome man with dark, medium length hair, perfectly styled and touched with gray at the temples. A large head with razor-sharp features, fine nose, square and jutting jaw, pencil-thin lips, his face tanned to perfection and offset by the palest and coldest blue eyes Casey had ever seen. His bearing aristocratic—arrogant, condescending and pompous, with the flared nostrils of someone who has just caught a whiff of something unpleasant. Every bell in Casey's considerable inventory of alarms began to clang.

Mary touched the man's elbow. "Proctor, I want you to meet my good friend, Casey O'Rourke. Casey, this is Proctor Philpott, with Temeritus." Casey and Philpott shook hands and exchanged the usual pleasantries. Mary continued, "Casey is in the public relations business—O'Rourke and Associates—you may have seen the article about them in the paper last month." Philpott admitted that he had and turned his gaze more directly on Casey.

Casey was stunned. So this is the great Proctor Philpott, she thought. This could be an interesting evening after all. She couldn't believe it. Proctor Philpott—the Crown Prince of Temeritus. This is fun, she thought. Should I tell him that I know more about him than he probably thinks, that I used to live next door to Charlie Abbott, one of his crack lawyers? That I know about his reign of terror at work and the awful things he has done to people in the name of his career? That I know about his endless reorganizations? That I know how despised he is in his company? No, much more fun to let this thing unfold naturally.

Philpott put his glass on the table next to him, quite pleased with what he had just said to the group before Casey arrived, and began an elaborate procedure the result of which was a lighted cigarette. First he produced from the inside pocket of his elegant blue blazer a silver case from which he extracted a long, thin, gold-tipped cigarette. He inverted the cigarette and tapped it three times on the side of the case with the sharp wrist snap of a dart thrower and stuck it at the very corner of his mouth. He snapped the case shut, returned it to its place and reached into the right side pocket of his slacks to produce a silver lighter identical in design to the case. He flicked open its hinged top, cupped it in both hands and activated the spark wheel, causing a small yellow flame to appear into which he thrust the tip of the cigarette. He sucked, filling his mouth with smoke and as he inhaled this mouthful, he sucked again preparing a second mouthful for inhalation so that when he finally began to exhale, he released a prodigious cloud of stinking smoke. He recaptured his wine glass and with smoke still escaping from both mouth and nose, he refocused on Casey. He rocked back on his heels and said, "So you're the little lady behind O'Rourke and Associates, are you?" And without waiting for a reply, "Tell me about it."

And they talked. Casey explained how she had started her company almost four years earlier after leaving a large company where she had extensive experience in public relations. "It's a small operation—nine people in all. We advise corporations and other organizations on specific problems they have difficulty handling in-house." Philpott had the beginning of a smirk on his face, a condescending tell-me-all-about-it-little-girl expression that Casey had seen so often from these superior men who could just barely contain their mirth at the thought that a woman could actually be very good at anything in a Man's World. "Yes, I'm sure. But tell me, Ms. O'Rourke, just exactly what is it that you do so well and why are you so good at it?" Casey detected a faint British accent, or at least a strained attempt at one, in his speech.

"We handle public relations on specific issues, and we handle internal problems, such as sexual harassment and sex discrimination. You mentioned that you had seen the article in the Chronicle on the sexual harassment awareness seminars we did for Exxon last spring." Casey paused to see if he was still listening.

"Yes," he said. "And I must say, I was rather impressed."
He pronounced it "raw-thur;" he was indeed straining at his accent.

"What sets us apart," she continued, "is that we work on very specific problems. And there are several reasons why we're so good. First, we are all owners of the business. We all have a stake in its success. We all like each other, so there is no backstabbing or office politics to get in the way of our work. And, second, all of us have worked for big companies and we know what it's like. And believe me, big companies aren't all that different from one another. So we can go into a company and interview the key people and begin to recommend things that will help solve problems that people in the company either can't or won't see. And we've solved some major problems."

The smirk that had begun to form receded in the face of Casey's spirited and confident statement. "I'll tell you what," Philpott said, sensing that Casey had further comments. "Why don't we have lunch sometime next week and kind of dialog this further? I can see that you're quite knowledgeable and I'd like very much to pursue it." He reached into another pocket for a dark-brown goatskin card case. He slipped a card from the case and handed it to her. "Call next week and set it up." She nodded and took the card. Then, shaking her hand with both of his, he concluded, "I'm really looking forward to getting to know you better. I might have a project for you." He gave her his best and most charming smile and was gone.

Very interesting, Casey thought as she drove back into Houston. Very interesting indeed to meet this man she had heard so much about. And surprising also because he did not fit the picture painted by Charlie Abbott. Rather than the snarling despot Charlie had described—the Father of Evil himself and bane of Temeritus, Inc.—Casey had seen a striking man whose bearing, while it did border on regal arrogance, nevertheless had a captivating allure. She'd have to discuss it with some of the Temeritus people she knew. She would call him for lunch. A consulting job with Temeritus would be very nice. But right now, all I want to do is see Jake and have a beer.

Chapter 5

Casey drove to Rice Village and parked in the first space she could find on Morningside. Midway up the block was the pub, its colorful wooden sign, hand painted in Old English script, hanging on two small lengths of chain from a beam that jutted over the sidewalk, its crimson letters gleaming in the wash of several floodlights. Some people called it Jake's, some called it The Horse. But its real name, as the sign so brightly proclaimed, was "One For Your Horse." Jake had explained to her that the name came from an old insult that he had heard in some long forgotten bar somewhere in the Philippines that goes something like this: "Well, I'll tell you what, pal, here's one for you, [gesture] and here's one for your horse [repeat gesture with other hand]!" Casey was not sure just exactly why this insult was so intriguing to Jake, but the name stood–"One For Your Horse."

Whatever name you chose, it was one of the great pubs in Houston, a city more known for ice houses and honky tonks than for traditional pubs. And it was one of the first brew pubs in town. Jake bought the old two-story brick building when he cashed out of the law firm and converted it into his dream establishment–an intimate brew pub with his living quarters on the second floor.

Casey hurried up the steps and walked in. The air was cool inside and the cool felt good after her short walk from the car. It was crowded, as usual on Saturday night, but even when crowded The Horse was never noisy. Only the muted buzz of a dozen conversations, punctuated with occasional flares of laughter. People talking and smoking and drinking, their features softened by the subdued lighting of Tiffany lamps. One For Your Horse had no juke box–just a sound system on which Jake played his jazz and blues CDs–and no television for people to shout over, and the result was a peaceful atmosphere rarely found in a place where alcohol is served. Someone was smoking a cigar and its earthy redolence took Casey for a moment through the time travel of memory for a brief visit with her grandfather in Arizona. Casey stopped to pet Serjeant Buzfuz, Jake's yellow Labrador retriever, the most regular of all the regulars who was always lolling around the pub.

Jake was behind the bar serving beer wearing a red-and-white striped long-sleeved T-shirt with the sleeves pushed up to the elbows. He was lean but muscular–the result of years of weight training, a habit that Casey had so far resisted despite his frequent urgings. Though she couldn't see the rest of him behind the bar, she knew what he would be wearing–faded old Levi's and leather, laced, ankle-top H.H. Brown hiking boots. And a white chef's apron folded at the strings so that the bib was tucked back under, with the strings wrapped around his waist and tied in the front–Jake's uniform while working the bar.

Jake was a former Marine and he looked the part–square jaw, neatly trimmed moustache, straight white teeth, dark brown eyes. His face had smile and squint lines that gave him a rugged and hearty look that women found attractive and men found impressive. His brown hair was cut short and a receding hairline added to his strong appearance. Unlike so many men his age, Jake made no attempt to hide the retreat of his hairline and his open acceptance of his fate only added to his aura of confidence and self-assurance.

It was always a treat to see him–the first man she had been serious about in the ten years since the death of her husband. He looked up as she approached, his face breaking into a smile. Casey stood on the brass rail and leaned over the bar. He took her face in both of his hands and kissed her on the lips. "Hiya, Case. How was the party?" Casey sat on a stool, pulled herself up to the bar and prepared to tell him about the encounter with Proctor Philpott. But first she wanted a glass of Jake's famous wheat beer.

Jake reached under the bar for one of the special Weizenbier glasses imported from Germany and filled it at the tap. He placed the extra tall, vase-shaped glass of pale and lightly carbonated liquid along with a slice of lemon on the coaster in front of Casey. She tasted the beer, savoring its fruity, malty bite and told Jake about the evening.

Jake listened, interrupting her only to serve beer to the others at the bar. "And so," Casey said concluding her story, "it was a very interesting experience and may lead to a contract with Temeritus. But before I do anything, I'd like to talk to someone at Temeritus and find out a little more about the company. And I'd like to find out more about Proctor Philpott. He was an interesting man, in a strange sort of way. Was he there when you were working on the cases for Temeritus?"

"No," Jake said. "He was on assignment in London during those years. Hardly anyone gets into a high level job at Temeritus without having to do a stint with the parent in London. The Brits have to check you out in person and make sure nothing's wrong before they send you back to the colonies for a big job."

"About the only person I know who knows him is my old neighbor, Charlie Abbott," Casey said. "I think maybe I'll give him a call."

Jake smiled as he tapped Casey a fresh beer. "Case, today must be your lucky day; it just so happens that Charlie Abbott is at the back corner table as we speak."

Casey spun around on her stool and looked toward the back of the pub. Sure enough, there was old Charlie sitting at the table with another man drinking a beer. She eased off the stool and walked with what remained of her wheat beer to the table where the two men sat drinking pints of what appeared to be Jake's own Noddy Boffin "Golden Dustman" Pale Ale. Charlie spotted her as she approached the table and jumped to his feet with a big smile, a profusion of greetings and a hug that almost caused her to spill her beer.

Charlie introduced her to his drinking companion who then excused himself, leaving the two of them alone at the table. "Casey, I can't tell you how great it is to see you. It's been so long, I was afraid you might've forgotten me."

"You old rascal, I was afraid you'd forgotten me."

And, of course, there could be little chance of that; no one ever forgot Casey O'Rourke. Five-foot-four. Bright red hair, naturally curly and cut in a short fluffy style. Creamy white skin with a natural blush to her cheeks and lips. Her face was a slender symmetry of flashing green eyes, smoky lashes, petite nose, high cheekbones and narrow chin and jaw. Her smile revealed straight and gleaming teeth with a slight gap between the front two that merely added to the feeling of sensuality that touched most men who met her. She had the build of a gymnast—taut, muscular, no fat—surprising in light of her eating, drinking and exercise habits. If you saw a picture of Casey, you would probably think her merely pretty. It was only when you saw her in person that she became striking. She was friendly, engaging; people were drawn to her. Her voice was husky—very sexy—and when she laughed, which was often, her head tilted back, her eyes crinkled up and she would unleash the lusty laugh that was her trademark. And yet there was something else in her personality, something in her composed assurance that said, "Back off, boys, I'm no broad to mess with." And you knew when you had seen her for just a few moments that she was delightful, funny, intelligent and tough. She was indeed unforgettable.

Seven years earlier, Charlie Abbott was in deep despair, living in a small apartment near downtown Houston, fresh from a divorce he didn't want, a lonely, miserable man. The only bright spot from those dark days was the friendship he formed with the young widow who had moved into the next apartment, a Marine Corps widow from Chicago. They shared wine and meals and many an evening of much needed conversation, but the friendship never crossed the line to romance. And that was probably what made the memory so special as the years passed. Shortly after Casey met Jake, Charlie married and left the apartment, and although he had lost touch with her over the years, the memory of her lingered—the memory of a beautiful young woman who had been such a help to him in trying times, unencumbered by sexual entanglement—simply the memory of a great friend. As Charlie gazed across the table at Casey, marveling at how the years had made her even more attractive, he regretted having lost touch with her in the press of his new life. And he swore he wouldn't let it happen again.

After ten minutes of reminiscing and catching up, Casey raised the matter of Temeritus. "You know, Charlie, that I'm a consultant now, have my own little company here, and I'm thinking about trying to get some business with Temeritus.

"I've been reading a lot about Temeritus lately—environmental problems, sales problems, profits gone. Now, with this animal rights thing heating up I thought it might be a good time to see if they could use the services of a good PR consultant. What do you think?"

"I think it would be great, Casey. Want me to introduce you to someone who could help?"

"That may not be necessary; you'll never guess who I met earlier tonight at a party—your old pal, Proctor Philpott."

Charlie groaned. "That must have been an awful party, Casey."

"Actually, I was impressed with him. He didn't come across as nearly the ogre you used to describe in our late night discussions back on Jackson Boulevard. He was very polished, and I must say, quite charming; pompous, yes–arrogant, yes–but charming nonetheless."

"Well, a lot of people think that. I guess a few years in London might soften the edges and who knows? But believe me, underneath all that English phoney-baloney lurks the same old Proctor Philpott. They don't call him the Prince of Proctology for nothing, you know."

"Charlie," Casey scolded.

"But seriously," he continued, "we all know the company really is on a downhill slide. Everybody knows that. And being in the Law Department we get an overview of the company that most other people don't. It would be a great time for you to ply your trade, if they will only listen to your advice. The way things are right now, upper management is so scared that they aren't listening to anybody and aren't really doing anything but reacting to the stuff that happens. Oh, sure, they have committees and study teams and all of that. And they still run around trumpeting how great the quality process is and how we are going to ride to victory on our so-called pathway to the future. But the fact is that the company is suffering from a bad case of managerial constipation and until somebody gets in there with some true vision, there aren't going to be any changes."

"How do outside consultants fit into this?" Casey said.

"Not very well. And it has created serious problems in the Law Department. And it's the same in the rest of the company. We have some of the finest professionals in the business. But for some reason, an in-house expert has no credibility with upper management. If they want to really know what the real story is–on a lawsuit or a legal problem or anything else–they go outside. The guy I work for, Harry Houdini, is one of the worst."

"Harry Houdini?" Casey was amused. "You really have a guy

named Harry Houdini?"

"No, that's just what we call him. His real name is Harold Hoare and he is the Vice President and General Counsel. I guess he must have risen from the ranks since the last time we talked about Temeritus; he's something to behold, I'll tell you. The reason we call him Houdini is that over the years he has gotten into so many scrapes and impossible situations because of his penchant for shooting from the hip, he has to be an escape artist in order to survive."

Casey laughed. "That's funny. But it sounds like the guy is already blessed with a name that's funny in its own right, especially for a lawyer."

"Yeah, it might have been funny at one time, but not anymore. Anyway, this guy is like the others–when he wants to get the true rule, he goes to the outside. I can take him an idea on a lawsuit and he treats it like it was a dead rat in his in-box. Then the next day he hears the same idea from outside counsel and the dead rat has become a mink stole. It's amazing; but it's good for lots of business for the consultants. So, I'd say that if you can get the right ear, you could do real well with Temeritus. And The Prince would sure be the right ear."

Chapter 6

George Downey had worked for Surveillance Security for almost five years. It was his best job ever and one in which he took great pride. Ever since his days as an Army MP he wanted to be involved in law enforcement. But his eyesight went bad on him and he failed the Houston Police Academy physical. So he went to work for Surveillance and grew accustomed to the idea that it was as close as he was going to get to real law enforcement.

That didn't keep him from imagining himself in the vanguard of the fight against crime. He read extensively in the literature of law enforcement and he presented himself as a professional—a legitimate member of the thin blue line, even if it was as a "civilian." His uniform was tailored to military perfection. His shoes were spit-shined and his shirts "boxed" with creases down the sides of the back just like they did it in the Army.

On Saturday night, at about the same time that Casey was talking to Charlie Abbott at The Horse, George Downey was driving into Houston to assume his duties at Temeritus Tower on the graveyard shift—midnight to eight. Most people couldn't understand why he liked this shift, and he figured if he had to explain it, the answer wouldn't make sense. He liked the quiet and solitude of the empty building. He liked being alone. He liked having long stretches of reading time uninterrupted by the human gnats and flies that were the constant aggravation of the day worker.

Not much happened in Temeritus Tower at night. Occasionally there would be some lawyers from one of the firms in the building working late. They seemed to work more than anyone else. And there was the time that he had stumbled upon two of those lawyers working off each other's briefs on a conference room couch. That was fun. But mainly it was the quiet that he liked. And the time-and-a-half the graveyard got him on payday was nice, too.

George parked his car on the street across from the building–another benefit of working the graveyard–and locked it. It was about ten minutes before twelve. As he crossed the street he heard a voice, "Help, help me, help!" He turned and saw, next to the van parked several spaces in front of his Mustang, a body stretched out on the pavement. He ran up to the man and knelt. The man moaned. "What happened? Are you hurt bad?" he asked straining in the darkness to see. As he reached out to touch the man's shoulder the man rolled over and grabbed him by the neck, pulling him with great strength onto the pavement, locking his head in a vise grip against the man's chest.

"What the hell. . ." He heard the van's door slide open. Other hands were on him twisting his arms behind his back, strapping tape across his mouth and pulling a cloth sack over his head. He felt himself being pulled back into the van. His surprise had been so complete and the force so strong that he had only given token resistance. He felt a sharp pain in his thigh. Blue and gold stars raced in chaos across the backs of his closed eyes and he fell into the well of drug-induced sleep.

Several minutes later a Surveillance-uniformed guard emerged from the van and walked across the street to the building, produced a security card and opened the locked door to the lobby of Temeritus Tower. He proceeded to the security desk at the far side of the building.

"Hi, George. You're late. I was beginning to think you weren't going to make it." The guard on duty looked up and realized that the man walking toward the desk, with flowing blond hair and bushy moustache, was not George. "Downey is sick. They moved me over here from my usual spot at Foley's." He smiled and held out his hand, "Bill Campbell. Glad to meet you. George said this was okay duty. Guess I'll find out."

The security guard stood up from the desk and grasped Campbell's outstretched hand. "Yeah, Mack Miller here. Nice to meet you." Jesus, he thought to himself as he shook Campbell's hand, Surveillance must be scraping the bottom of the barrel to hire this long haired slob. You'd think they'd be more careful who they hired and sent over to Temeritus these days. Especially since those animal rights nuts broke in and wrote all of that silly shit on the walls and jammed up all the crappers. "Well," he said, "It's real quiet. Not even the lawyers are here tonight." He gathered his things and prepared to leave.

"Yeah, great. That's the way I like it." Campbell placed his briefcase on the table. "See you around." Miller looked at him for an instant and then left without saying anything else.

Campbell looked around the deserted lobby. The only sound, except for the constant hum of air conditioning, was the clacking of Miller's shoes as he walked through the far side of the lobby, the sound fading with each step as he approached the door, paused to activate the unlocking device and left the building. Yeah, Campbell repeated to himself, this is the way I like it, nice and quiet. Now, I think I'll stroll over to the cafeteria and raid the refrigerator.

Chapter 7

Sunday morning. Jake was awake by 8:30, even though he had been up until 3:00 shutting down the pub. Sunday was his day with Casey–the best day of the week. Although he saw her almost every day, Sunday was the only day they could relax together and savor each other's company. And there was no time to waste.

He had never known a woman like Casey, and he had known many over the years–in the Marines, in college and law school, and during his seventeen years as a practicing lawyer. No one could match Casey. She was intelligent, beautiful and extremely feminine, but surprisingly she often ate, drank and talked like a man. And he loved it. She radiated a zest for life that Jake recognized the first time she came into The Horse, and he was immediately attracted to her. She was the most honest and unselfish human being he had ever met. And the more he was with her the more he realized that, for the first time in his life, he was in love. So it was with great excitement that he began to prepare for the day.

He showered, shaved and put on clean Levi's and a short-sleeved cotton no-name golf shirt. One of the many great things about no longer being in the white-collar world of downtown Houston was seldom having to wear a tie. Jake enjoyed being able to get up in the morning and put on whatever he felt like putting on. And so far, in the years since he left the firm, he was yet to awaken with an urge for neckwear. He slipped on a pair of deck shoes and went downstairs into the pub where he was greeted by Serjeant Buzfuz, who ambled over to the foot of the stairs as Jake came down from his apartment. Serjeant Buzfuz, the mascot of One For Your Horse during normal operating hours, became Sergeant Buzfuz, head of security, during off hours.

Jake patted the dog and went down the hall next to the stairs. He unlocked the door at the end of the hall and let Serjeant Buzfuz into the back yard. Then he unlocked the heavy wooden door half-way up the hall towards the pub and went into the brewery.

This room was Jake's retreat. He could spend hours there and often did. It delighted all of his senses. The sight of stainless steel tanks glistening under fluorescent lights; the sound of the refrigeration unit purring softly; the touch of the cool smooth surface of the tanks over which he ran his hand as if he were admiring the finish on a piece of fine furniture; the smell of fermenting beer, fruity and earthy; and finally the taste of beer drawn fresh from one of the four aging tanks. It was an experience he never tired of, and he repeated this ritual of the senses almost every time he entered the room.

After assuring himself that all was in good order in the brewery as well as in the pub, Jake and Serjeant Buzfuz left for Casey's. Sunday was Serjeant Buzfuz's day off; Sunday security was provided solely by the burglar alarm, which Jake armed as he left. He and the dog got in his truck—a bright red 1949 Chevy restored to mint condition—and chugged out onto Morningside.

A few minutes later he pulled into Casey's driveway. "Come on, Buz," he said as he got out. Serjeant Buzfuz jumped down from the cab and bounded up to the door. Casey had heard Jake's Bermuda Bell, which he had sounded as he entered the drive, and before he reached the porch, Casey opened the door and let her two-year-old Jack Russell terrier, So-So, charge out to greet her friends. While the dogs barked and rolled and tumbled on the lawn, Jake and Casey embraced. Every time he hugged her was as exciting as the first. She felt so good–solid and warm and padded just the right amount in just the right places. She was the most sensuous woman Jake had ever known, and he felt himself becoming aroused. "Control yourself there, Big Fella," Casey said with a laugh and a quick tweak as she pushed herself away from him. And he followed her into the house.

They went into the bedroom. Casey went into the walk-in closet and took off her clothes. When she came back into the room, Jake was standing beside the bed naked. They savored the sight of each other. She embraced him feeling with great excitement the full imprint of him on her stomach. She rubbed her hands across his back, over his shoulders and down to his hips.

"Oh, Jake," she said, her head turned and resting on his chest, "You feel so good."

They moved to the bed. His hands caressed her face and moved slowly down her body. "Casey, Casey. I love you, Casey."

An hour later they got up, showered together, put on robes and went into the kitchen, where Jake's favorite breakfast was waiting to be prepared–thick slices of French bread from the bakery in the Village, allowed to harden a bit, then soaked in a batter of eggs, heavy cream, Mexican vanilla and fresh grated nutmeg, and fried in butter to a golden brown. With hot maple syrup, crisp bacon and a glass of cold milk, it just wasn't going to get any better.

They ate and read the papers. When they were finished with the second pot of coffee Casey suggested that perhaps it was time for a "long nap." "I thought you'd never ask," Jake joked.

Jake and Casey made love for hours until they finally fell into the semi-sleep known only by serious lovers, surrounded by the smells of tender loving and raw sex they had just shared. "Damn, we're good," Jake said as he was easing into sleep. Casey couldn't have agreed more. They were.

Later, riding to dinner they talked about the people they were going to visit, Melissa and Craig Fellows. Casey knew them only through Jake, who had known Melissa for years, ever since he had worked on the Steers case as outside counsel to Temeritus. Melissa was in External Relations at Temeritus, and had worked with Jake in a futile attempt to keep the publicity of the case under control, and they had been friends ever since.

And quite a case it had been. It started one morning in the late '70s when a computer specialist, Percy Steers, had shown up for work at Temeritus Tower wearing a dress. Until then no one in the company had known that he was a cross-dresser. He had in fact been a highly rated performer who regularly received bonuses for his extraordinary service to the corporation. He was, however, summarily terminated when he refused to go home and change into something more traditional for a male Temeritus employee. Steers filed a complaint of sex discrimination with the Equal Employment Opportunity Commission on the grounds that women can wear pretty dresses to work and to prohibit men from doing likewise was unlawful sex discrimination.

Temeritus unwisely claimed the reason for the termination had nothing to do with the dress but in fact was a result of a sudden decline in performance on the part of Mr. Steers. The case became a local favorite with the press and caused Temeritus considerable embarrassment until it was finally settled, as were most Temeritus cases, on the eve of trial.

"Yes," Casey said, "I remember you telling me about that case but I had forgotten. Jake, was the General Counsel then a guy named Whore?"

"Yeah, how do you know about him?"

"Charlie Abbott talked about him last night. I couldn't believe that was really his name. What a perfect name for a corporate lawyer—or any lawyer, for that matter."

"Well, it's H-O-A-R-E, a perfectly legitimate English name."

"I'm sure. But do you know the guy?"

Jake laughed. "Do I know him! Hell, if it wasn't for people like him, I'd have never been able to have the money to retire so early. Here this guy sits, surrounded by a bunch of really outstanding lawyers, and whenever the company gets in serious trouble, he always runs to outside counsel to cover his rear in case something goes wrong. It's a stupid way to behave, but it has been great for me. Yeah, I know Harold Hoare. I'm his biggest fan!"

"Yeah, Charlie mentioned him always going outside. And I could sense a real hostility."

"He is detested almost universally. But the senior management sure likes him. He has a great legal mind. And he really is a nice guy except when his ambition gets in the way; then all bets are off. But he really is a whore. He does exactly what he thinks management wants in terms of everything—his legal opinions, his personnel opinions, even his political views. Everything is subject to frequent readjustment as he perceives the shifting tides of upper management opinion. What happened yesterday has no bearing on what his opinion today will be. And once he announces what today's opinion is, yesterday's ceases to exist. It is truly incredible. But somehow he gets away with it."

"That's why they call him Harry Houdini, I guess."

"Charlie told you about that, huh?"

"Yes, and that's why the thought of going on a contract with Temeritus is so enticing. I know the company is struggling and that the people who work there are getting more and more dissatisfied. It would be interesting to get up close to it and try to figure out what happened to such a strong company. I hope Melissa can enlighten me a bit on Proctor Philpott. After hearing about him from Charlie Abbott and then seeing him last night, I'm really intrigued by the man."

"Well, you won't have to wait long now." Jake pulled the truck into the driveway at the Fellows' small house in Bellaire. They got out and walked up to the door, Casey telling Jake how much better he looked now that he had changed from his scrufties into something more acceptable for Sunday dinner–tan slacks, open collar blue shirt, light Madras jacket and loafers.

Dinner was plain and good–grilled chicken, corn on the cob, potato salad and sliced tomatoes. They were well into the second bottle of zinfandel when Casey mentioned that she was considering going after a contract with Temeritus. She related the encounter with Proctor Philpott and, at the mention of his name, Casey noticed Melissa's eyes pinch and her mouth draw tight. "So, you met the Prince, did you? That must have been quite an experience."

"Yes, it was," Casey said. "What has been your experience in dealing with him, Melissa?"

The room seemed to chill a bit. Craig tensed in his chair and Melissa lost the glow of the wine. "All I can say is this . . . be careful." She paused. A loud breathless silence filled the room. "Be careful," she repeated. "Be very careful."

Chapter 8

"It was the most fun I've had in a long time. And it was simple. These people are easy. It's like taking candy from a baby." L seemed to be enjoying his report on the kitchen raid almost as much as he had enjoyed the raid itself. Several days had passed and, although M had been briefed on the raid immediately, the cell had not met since then and she had asked L to bring them up to speed. His description of the raid had people laughing–a rare thing for the ALA, not just because of their serious natures but also because their meeting places usually required a more secretive demeanor. Tonight's meeting happened to be in the private room of a large restaurant in west Houston near Sharpstown.

"Poor old George. He didn't have the slightest notion what hit him. All decked out in his uniform and coming to the rescue of a citizen in distress. Whap. He didn't even see us coming. And it worked just like we practiced. He came over, and bent down, and that was all she wrote. I already had my moustache and wig on, so as soon as we got him in the van and shot up, we got him out of his uniform and I put it on. Fit pretty good, too. All I had to do was get out his security card and put on the name tag we had made–W. C. Campbell. Yeah, he was a real guy. I got his name from the obituaries in the paper. Then as soon as the bozo on duty left, I went to the kitchen and started to work."

L then described what he'd done: some big cuts of frozen

meat left in ovens on 150° and the rest of it spread out and smeared and tossed into the dining area to rot; slogans on the walls; eggs, bacon, sausage–all piled up on the floor ready for breakfast on Monday. But the best part, he said, was taking an assortment of the smaller cuts–pork chops, steaks, hamburger patties, pieces of chicken–and walking around the building hiding them in places where they wouldn't be noticed until they started to stink.

"It was fabulous," he laughed. "Sort of reminded me of an Easter egg hunt, like when you were a kid and they'd hide all the eggs and things in the yard. Yeah, and I even hid a Golden Egg–a frozen chicken that fit real good in the coffee urn in that big room the board of directors uses, complete with a note from ALA. That should be a wonderful treat for them when they get ready for the next board meeting." He gestured in an exaggerated manner, depicting how the first person to peep into the reeking coffee pot would react.

By now almost everyone was laughing, taking advantage of the privacy offered by the room to let their hair down and enjoy themselves. This hilarity was, however, not shared by all.

One of those, unable to contain himself further, crashed his fist onto the table in front of him, rattling the dishes and sloshing the water in the glasses. The laughter stopped. "Goddamn it," he roared. "This is a crock of shit and you all know it." He rose from his chair and glared around the table. It was T, the biggest and meanest member of the cell. "How much longer are we going to pussyfoot around with this silly shit? We need to be getting on with the main reason we're here. We've got to get out to the lab at The Woodlands and free those animals, and we've got to force Temeritus to stop this testing. All of this other crap is just a waste of time, and the only reason we're doing it is because it's fun for assholes like L."

"Hey, hold it there, pal." L, still standing where he had been making his report, glared at T, but there was not much chance he would do anything physical. Not when he gave about 100 pounds, 7 inches and a mess of mean to T, the red-bearded giant who was renowned in the cell for his strength and his humorless intensity. "This raid was discussed and voted on, and it's too late for you to come in here and bellyache about it."

"That's right," said M, having risen from her chair and moved toward T, realizing she needed to assert her authority. And M was an imposing figure in her own right–tall, slender but muscular with long straight black hair and a spartan plainness that made her face esthetic, beautiful. There was never any doubt as to who was boss. All of the members of the cell were intimidated by her, even T, who sat back down at his place looking like a schoolboy who had just been scolded by his teacher.

"I'm sorry, M," he said. "I just get impatient. We need to get with it. All of this 'awareness' is getting old. How much awareness do these jerks need? We're just diddling with them; we need to sock 'em in the balls if we expect them to change."

"I know, I know," she said. "We all feel the same. But we must be patient. And we have to go about it in the right way."

"I agree with T." The other member who had not joined in the laughter now joined in the discussion. P, a scrawny woman in her mid-twenties whose main physical characteristic was her bushy dark brown eyebrows, spoke in a clipped and hurried manner as she expressed her opinion on the matter. "These little acts of harassment are getting old. Don't really do much. Just a mild aggravation to a big outfit like Temeritus. Like a low-grade headache–you notice it and it might slow you down until the aspirin kicks in; but it doesn't stop you from doing what you do. We need to start breaking some bones."

"Yeah," T spoke again, emboldened by P's support. "I say it's time to scrap this awareness crap and start some remodeling over there at Temeritus."

M blanched at the sound of the word "remodeling." She was afraid this would come up. It was ALA code for violent sabotage–bombing and arson–and that was something that she was dead set against. This had to be stopped, or it would spell the end of her work with the cell.

"Listen to me, you," M said, her blue eyes flashing. She walked to P's seat and pointed a finger into her face. "No more of this kind of talk. What we're trying to do doesn't include that kind of violence. We free animals and try to put an end to animal testing; we don't hurt people, and I won't stand for it. Keep this up and you'll be out of here. Do you understand me?"

P was not as intimidated by M as T was, but she was intimidated nevertheless. She decided to drop it, mumbling something no one could hear, shaking her head, rolling her eyes in disgust.

M continued, "And that goes for the rest of you, too. If you think you have a better idea, let's discuss it. But if you're thinking about bombs and fires, this is not the place for you and you should go elsewhere. And remember, I am the only person who knows your names. I can cut you out of this like I could pluck a hair from my head. I've worked too hard for too long for any of your violent ideas about basic strategy to derail me." She glared at the people around the table and continued.

"Let me remind you of something else. You all know the rules. This is not a social club. I organized it. I control the finances. I can dissolve it. There are to be no personal contacts. No names. No addresses. No talk of jobs or hobbies. Each of you is anonymous–for your own good and safety. This is imperative for the cell's security. Also for your own mental health. You cannot afford personal attachments within the cell. Our concern is for animals, not people. Find your friends elsewhere. Now, let's get back to our agenda and forget all of this other stuff."

There was a murmur of agreement around the table, and M continued. "The only reason we're here is to do just what they are talking about–free the animals. But keep in mind that this can be done in any number of ways. And a raid on a lab is only one of them. If Temeritus stops testing, we win. It's as simple as that. We're not here to do anything else but win. If we have to break down a few doors and bust up some equipment, fine; we'll do it; but that's not the end, only a means to an end.

"Under no circumstances are we going to hurt anyone. I mean, poor old George Downey may have had a little hole poked in his leg and he may have had a long nap that he hadn't planned on, but he's OK. But if we go around hurting people, we'll lose whatever public support we have. And you all know that there are a lot of people out there who are silently rooting for us to succeed. But if we get too violent, we'll lose them and ultimately the whole war." She paused and looked at the faces around the table. Most of them seemed to be in agreement. But T and P still looked unconvinced.

"Now, I'll bring everybody up to date." M spent the next thirty minutes describing her recent activities: gathering the things needed for the Woodlands raid–and a vast array of skills, equipment and information it was. M talked about her own training in England, where she had participated in a number of raids, and she stressed the global nature of the animal rights movement; this was not just an isolated, random act in Houston but part of a worldwide movement to end forever the oppression of animals. "In addition to the three or four people who will actually enter the lab and bring out the animals, we need a lookout, a driver, a locksmith and an electrician. And we need a veterinarian to tend to the animals after we rescue them and people to take them after they're brought out," she explained.

The list of equipment was even more extensive: a secure van, carrying cages, a small two-way radio set, medical supplies for the animals, uniforms and other disguises, and on and on. It was a logistical nightmare.

"And finally," she declared, "we need information. Lots of information about the enemy and its facilities. We need to know the floor plan of the lab and the schedules and practices of the security people. We need to know what kind of locks are on the doors and what kind of electronic security devices are in use. An encyclopedia of information is needed, if the raid is to succeed."

M hoped that by going into all of this detail–much more than she had planned for the evening–she could instill in the cell a renewed sense of patience for the tasks ahead. And looking around the room again–looking deep into the eyes of each person there–she felt that she had succeeded. Even T and P seemed to have mellowed to some extent. Well, she thought, you do the best you can with what you've got. She just hoped that would be good enough.

"Now," she said. "On that note, the meeting is adjourned."

Chairs scraped, books popped shut and the room was filled with the noises of people preparing to leave–except for the chatter of conversation usually found at the conclusion of a meeting. As M had reminded them, this was not a social group and all matters of a personal nature were forbidden. No one in the group knew who the other people were. Didn't even know their names. So when M adjourned the meeting all that was heard was the sound of people shuffling their things together and walking out the door. In the midst of this activity, no one noticed when P bumped T at the door and slipped a piece of paper into his pocket.

M stood in the empty room thinking. I've been at this far too long to let some hothead stop me now. Her mind wandered back to her early days in the movement and to some of the formative things she had witnessed, memories usually repressed but which in times of reflection bubbled to the surface: rows of rabbits, their heads poking through the restraining devices used in the odious Draize Eye Irritancy Test, their oozing and ulcerated eyes held open with clips so they wouldn't blink and dilute the strength of the substance being tested; cats clamped into steel frames that held their heads fast, assuring that the wires going into the implants in their skulls would not be disturbed by the cats' reaction to the agonies inflicted in the course of the testing; dogs, not unlike her own Patches, whose bodies had been cut, stabbed and broken in the name of science, prostrate in their own filth, chunks of their ears missing, nibbled away by the flies attracted to their urine- and feces-encrusted bodies.

An icy shiver danced up M's spine, and she brought herself back to the present. She walked into the main dining room, paid the bill in cash and walked out.

Chapter 9

The extravagant skyline, strutting its ultramodern fingers of steel and glass, gleaming and angular in the big Texas sky, rises out of the coastal plain like a mirage in the desert: Houston, Texas, pearl of the Southwest, glittering jewel of the Sunbelt. Dominating this skyline is the seventy-five-story Texas Commerce Tower, at 1,002 feet the ninth tallest building in the United States, second tallest west of the Mississippi. This ostentatious giant looks down on its vertically challenged neighbors in silent scorn as the city named for the first President of the Republic of Texas transacts its daily business.

In that cluster of lesser buildings stands what was once the proud centerpiece of the blossoming Houston skyline, Temeritus Tower, now dwarfed by a long succession of buildings that each held for its brief moment the title of Houston's tallest. Built in 1967, and the title holder for two years until overshadowed by One Shell Plaza, Temeritus Tower stands as a sad reminder of how quickly things change in late-twentieth-century America. But make no mistake. The faded condition of the building is in no way a reflection on the importance of the people working there or the significance of their work. The further up in the building one went, the closer one got to the nerve center of this corporate giant. In the paneled suites ringing the thirty-eighth, thirty-ninth and fortieth floors, some of the most talented executives in America dealt with matters of crucial importance to their world: the beautification of women everywhere.

"Mr. Slurry is here to see you, sir."

"Have him wait," Proctor Philpott growled into his telephone. He wasn't ready yet to meet with Sam Slurry, the head of security. He pulled open the lone drawer in his desk and took out a pale yellow file folder labeled "K. C. O'Rourke." A single piece of paper contained the following information: Kathleen Callahan O'Rourke, born November 30, 1957, in Flagstaff, Arizona; attended public schools in Flagstaff; BS, Communications, Arizona State University (1979); MS, Public Relations, Medill School of Journalism, Northwestern University (1985); work experience–1979-1980, Public Relations Representative, Sears, Chicago; 1981-1983, Assistant Base Public Liaison Associate, Camp Lejeune, NC; 1985-1989, Manager, Public Relations, Foley's, Houston, TX; and, finally, 1989-present, President, O'Rourke & Associates, Houston, TX.

Also in the folder were the notes he had taken during several calls he had made to some of his professional acquaintances in Houston, from whom he determined that O'Rourke & Associates, and Casey in particular, had an excellent reputation among the public relations community. And she received the highest praise from the president of Exxon, whom Philpott had known for many years. He didn't know any more than this and was unable to fill in the gap in the dates. That's where Sam Slurry came in. Philpott had to be certain that Casey was the right person to help him in his time of need. He picked up the handset once again and buzzed the intercom button, "Send him in."

Melville Higgins, Philpott's administrative assistant, rose like a stork from his desk and walked to the closed door of his boss's office. He opened the door and turned so that his back was flat against it. Then, with his chin elevated a few degrees higher than normal, he looked down across his nose at Sam Slurry and pronounced, "Mr. Philpott will see you now." Slurry walked past him and into the office where Philpott sat at his desk, pretending to be absorbed in the latest breaking financial news of the day. Slurry stood before Philpott's desk tweaking the lapels of his coat, and waiting to be recognized.

Slurry, at fifty-five years old, was short and pudgy, his stomach and face both showing the effects of a lifetime of sedentary pork-eating. His mouse-brown hair was in need of trimming and was combed back on the sides and top with the assistance of a leading cream-oil popular in the 1950s, which as the day progressed gave his hairline and forehead a greasy sheen that somehow complemented his porky flesh. Although he had taken readily to the pinstriped suit of the Temeritus executive suite upon his elevation to his current post, he was yet to achieve the élan with which his boss, Proctor Philpott, sported such apparel. On Slurry, a thousand-dollar suit remained ill-fitting and shabby–the sleeves were too long, the shirt collar too big and the tie poorly knotted and a touch off-center; the trousers bagging down onto unpolished and worn penny-loafers; the picture being complete if he removed his coat revealing both belt and clip-on suspenders and a short-sleeved shirt. Thankfully he seldom removed the coat.

Philpott looked up with a start as if in his deep thought he was unaware of Slurry's presence. "What did you find out?" No pleasantries, no invitation to sit down and be comfortable. Strictly business.

"Well, chief, I did just what you instructed. I placed the subject under surveillance, got a pretty good look at her. She's quite a gal. Lives in a little house in West U. Has this funny-looking little dog she takes with her a lot, shopping and all. She lives by herself. Has fairly regular hours. Spends lots of time at a bar in the Village called One For Your Horse. I went there a couple of times just to check it out and listen a little. It's a small place. Pretty nice, if you like that sort of thing. It seems like she's sweet on the guy who owns the place, a big guy named Jake Gilligan, but I'm not sure about the details."

Philpott grunted.

"But I established for sure that she's OK. Has lots of friends and doesn't seem to have any serious hang-ups. Doesn't do drugs, no booze problem, definitely not a lesbo. I checked her mail each day and there was nothing kinky or anything like that. Nothing radical. Her garbage checks out. She cooks. Drinks beer and wine. Has great taste. You should see the stuff inside the house–lots of fancy paintings and expensive furniture and cooking stuff."

"You didn't break into her house, did you?"

"No, of course not," Slurry said with mock indignation. "Let's just say that we had to do some up-close reconnaissance work. Nothing serious." Slurry was obviously well pleased with his skills as a clandestine operative.

"What about the time gap in the resume? What was she doing during those years?"

"I went over to Foley's, where she used to work. Somehow they thought I was an FBI agent doing a background check on her." He winked. "She's a widow. Was married to a Marine who was killed in Beirut. She went to grad school on her survivor bennies, took a job with Foley's and came to Houston."

"Well, good deal. Nice work, Sam. And remember, this is strictly between you and me." Philpott accented his words by canting his head to the right, arching his left eyebrow and almost closing his right eye. "Oh, and Sam. One other thing . . . Do you have to wear that damn gun when you come up here? It makes your suit fit worse than it already does. Why don't you leave it in your desk?" Slurry shrugged without responding.

Philpott dismissed Slurry by returning to his study of the financial report. Slurry left under the watchful eye of Melville Higgins, feeling, like most Temeritus employees, great relief at the prospect of being away from the thirty-ninth floor.

Alone again in his office Philpott rose from his desk, walked to the corner windows and stared out at the view, such as it was, being now mostly obscured by the newer and taller buildings. Alone with his thoughts, he reviewed his strategy for positioning himself as the only logical replacement for Wilfurd Timmons, the current President and Chief Executive Officer of Temeritus. He had to be certain he was next in line, and Casey was going to play a role in that certainty.

Yeah, I think she's the one, he thought. God, I hate to have to use a woman for this. Damn women seem to be taking over everything, and I hate it. But—he was now gesturing to his reflection in the window—she'll be under my control. She can give me all sorts of information. And she can do some work on a bunch of crap that won't make any real difference, then go back to her little company.

He walked back to his desk, looked at the file one more time and, congratulating himself on his superior intellect, left for his lunch with Casey O'Rourke.

Casey entered Philpott's club a few minutes early. She paused while her eyes adjusted to the darkness and then approached the maître d'. "Ah, yes, Ms. O'Rourke, Mr. Philpott has already arrived. Please allow me to show you to your table." She followed him into the dining room to a corner table where Proctor Philpott sat sipping wine. She extended her hand as she approached the table. "Mr. Philpott. It's so nice to see you again." He rose and took her hand. "Ms. O'Rourke. I'm so glad you could join me today. Please sit down." After the usual pleasantries, which included the ordering of wine for Casey and the agreement that first names should be used, Philpott began the business of the lunch.

"Casey, since meeting you at the Blakes, I've talked to several business associates about you. You have quite a reputation and may be able to help me out." He paused and began the cigarette lighting ritual that she had found so strange at the Blakes. Then, surrounded by smoke for which he never apologized, he continued.

"We've had lots of bad PR lately and we've lost several big

lawsuits and things just aren't the way they're supposed to be. And now this animal rights thing has gotten real bad and I'm convinced that if we are to move into the twenty-first century with our long-standing position as an industry leader intact, we're going to have to deal very effectively with this crisis. And I do not use that term lightly, Casey. Because I really do believe that we're in a crisis mode."

He shifted in his chair, drew a long sip of wine and continued, telling Casey about some of the things he had worked on in the past and how he had come to realize that in many ways the company was its own worst enemy. It was running scared, afraid to take bold stands, hoping problems would just go away, always hiring huge consulting firms long on reputation and short on performance, over-staffing to the point where nothing really gets done except a lot of meetings and hand-wringing and unnecessary expense. He wanted to use a different approach to the animal rights crisis by hiring a small outfit and keeping a tight control over the process. "I intend to shrink the beast," he concluded. "I am convinced beyond any doubt that I know better than anyone in the company how to deal effectively with this sort of thing, and I believe that with your help I can lead the company out of this crisis and into the future.

"I took it upon myself to commission a study on you, Casey. I had my research people look up your major clients and then I personally called and talked to a number of them and asked them what they thought. They were all very complimentary." He paused. "Everyone I talked to has told me that you're one of the best public relations consultants in the business. And that's what I am looking for." He paused again and looked at her as if he expected a reply.

"I appreciate your kind words very much, Proctor. I've always had the highest regard for Temeritus. When I was in grad school, it was frequently cited as an example of excellence in products and in management. I'm honored that you would consider me on such a volatile issue."

"It is assuredly our most pressing external issue." He paused as he shifted in his chair and continued, "There is a second issue–an internal one–that I would like to talk to you about. It's a problem I plan to address and correct–but in a manner that does not attract attention, which is to say with utmost discretion and effectiveness by a handful of chosen people . . ." He let the words hang for an extra beat. "I believe that we do not have nearly enough women in our work force, and the ones that we do have are not properly utilized. I think it is a national disgrace that industry has been so lax in tapping the management potential of more than half the population. And I'd like to enlist your help in correcting it at Temeritus."

He went into great detail about his long-held belief in equality for women and his commitment to the women's movement. He used all the correct words–empowerment, gender based, female role models–he even tossed in a statement of his admiration for Anita Hill and his gratitude to her for elevating the nation's conscience on the issue of sexual harassment. But in his overall demeanor Casey read somewhat less enthusiasm than the total commitment he espoused. It was, nevertheless, encouraging to hear a top executive raising this issue and her interest was peaked considerably, despite her initial pique at the arrogance of the man and his obvious assumption that she was simply dying to become associated with the organizational paragon currently in the capable hands of his dynamic leadership.

He finished the last of his wine and continued. What he proposed was that Casey come to work for Temeritus as a consultant on public relations on the animal testing issue and "other matters"–he raised his hands and flicked his index and middle fingers to indicate quotes around those words–as directed by him.

These "other matters," he explained, would be Casey's work for him–personally and confidentially–on the status of women in the company. He explained that this project had to be done behind the scenes. If he announced to all that Casey's mission was to investigate the status of women in the company, it would cause widespread fear and concern and would doom the study to failure from the start.

He reached into the pocket of his coat, took out an envelope and handed it to Casey. "Here's a draft of what I am proposing, including the compensation. I would like you to take this back to your office. Read it and think about it. Take a few days if you like. Then, call me with your decision. My only condition is that you keep the status-of-women part of the thing strictly confidential."

He paused and smiled, and with a note of finality, leaned back in his chair with self-satisfaction to repeat the cigarette ceremony. "Well, now, Casey," he said through his cloud of smoke, "I propose that we order our lunch and talk about other things. I want to get to know you better."

And talk they did in an interesting and animated conversation during which she ate more than she had planned and even had a second glass of wine. Philpott asked about her family and her background and accomplishments. He never talked about himself, which made him almost unique among senior executives of her acquaintance. Maybe this guy isn't so bad after all, she thought. And she already knew she would accept the job.

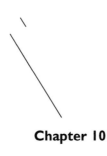

Chapter 10

T waited until the next day to call. He had not looked at the note P passed him until he got home. And he had thought all day before he acted on it. The note was simple–a mere phone number, scrawled out in pencil.

Was it a trap? Was it one of M's little tricks to trip him up? He had always suspected that she was capable of such a thing, always harping about the need for precious security and all. But the more he thought about it, the more he came to believe P's move was legitimate. Even M couldn't have staged that scene, with him getting pissed about the slow pace of the action and P coming to his side during the discussion. In the end he decided to call.

The phone rang six times. I'll hang up if I get an answering machine, he told himself. But she answered and, although he recognized her voice–husky and much deeper than you would expect from her emaciated appearance–he still felt uneasy. So he decided to play it safe. "This is Jerry Turner." He used his real name. "I'm calling from Southwestern Light and Power." He used his real employer. "And I'm checking to see if the matter you referred to last night still needed to be addressed."

She hesitated, and said, "I know this voice . . . Yes, the matter still needs to be addressed. If you believe it does, I'm willing."

"Good. Where can we meet?"

"The Hobbit Hole on Shepherd . . . tomorrow at one o'clock."

"I'll be there."

Chapter 11

Casey was up early Tuesday morning, ready to start as special consultant to Temeritus, Inc. She put on her newest and most sophisticated outfit from Neiman-Marcus–an Escada suit in her favorite color, emerald green. Accented with a gold choker and matching earrings, she was ready to dazzle them. She checked So-So's water supply, closed the kitchen door to keep her from roaming the house and left for downtown.

The elevator grunted and jerked and finally delivered Casey to the thirty-ninth floor. She had heard friends talk about how Temeritus Tower had deteriorated over the years. They complained about the carpeting (obviously the work of the Purchasing Division, which stressed price over all other factors), the cold off-white walls (more cost savings) and especially the pokey elevator service. Someone once told her that working on the upper floors of Temeritus Tower meant you were only ten minutes away from downtown Houston. Now she believed it.

The office suites of the top Temeritus executives, on the thirty-eighth, thirty-ninth and fortieth floors, were accessible only through the thirty-ninth, with stairways and a private elevator to serve them. The elevator opened on thirty-nine into a large reception area, called "the holding tank" by most because it usually contained nervous middle- and not-so-top executives waiting for an audience with one of the seniors. The room was paneled in dark oak and carpeted in thick gray. In the middle of the room a large round dark oak table was surrounded by four wooden chairs. Against each side wall, both to the right and to the left, stood a sofa covered in rich brown leather. And seated safely behind a panel of glass, in a cubicle not unlike those from which movie tickets are sold, sat a receptionist who had control over the sole door that gave access to the executive suites. Were it not for the receptionist, this would look like the lounge of an elegant men's club, an obvious renegade from the frugalities of Temeritus Purchasing.

She walked into the room and around the table to the ticket booth and told the receptionist who she was there to see. "Yes, Ms. O'Rourke, please have a seat and I will notify Mr. Philpott." Although she had been in Temeritus Tower before, she had never been to the executive floors, and she was surprised, despite what she had heard, at how much nicer they were than the rest of the building. She waited, her mind idling.

Her woolgathering was interrupted by a thin, well dressed man who entered silently through the door, stood at attention in front of her and announced "I am Melville Higgins, senior administrative assistant to the Office of the Executive Vice President. Please follow me." His face was rigid and his brown eyes never made direct contact with Casey's.

When Casey stood up she realized that Mr. Higgins was taller than he had first appeared. Almost six feet tall and whippet thin. His pale complexion was offset by a dark moustache, and a just-over-the-ears mop of dark hair. He wore a dark gray pinstriped suit–double breasted and precisely tailored–accented by a matching tie and pocket handkerchief and in stark contrast to his crisp white Egyptian cotton shirt. Very interesting, Casey thought, Proctor has a male secretary. She followed him through the door and down the hallway beyond, which Casey noticed was carpeted in the same luxurious fashion as the reception area.

Several turns and several doors later–each door requiring a magnetic key and digital code for access–they arrived at Higgins' desk guarding the door to Philpott's office. Higgins instructed Casey to sit in one of the two chairs near his desk. Casey sat. He picked up the telephone, put it to his ear and pushed a button on the console. "Ms. O'Rourke is here, sir." Pause. "Yes, sir." Without a word to Casey, Higgins began to read the magazine that sat opened on his otherwise empty desk. *Something tells me this guy doesn't like me very much,* Casey thought.

After a few moments of stony silence, the door to the office opened and Proctor Philpott walked out to greet Casey with a big smile and a hearty handshake. "Casey, it's so nice to see you. Come in, come in." And together they walked into the cavern that was his office.

The office occupied a huge corner of the building, with seven windows along each of the outside walls. Along the entire right side of the room, except for a door which Casey later learned went to Philpott's private bathroom, stretched a three-shelved bookcase holding books and small art objects. Over the bookcase a large piece of driftwood floated like an albatross between clouds of abstract paintings. The fourth wall was empty except for the door to the outer office and a single bronze sculpture. Angled near the corner of the windowed walls stood the large mahogany table that served as Philpott's desk. The office was dark–dark carpet, dark furniture, dark walls. Even the paintings were dark.

It was one of the biggest offices Casey had ever seen, with room for a large couch and three leather-covered chairs placed around a long mahogany coffee table. There were several small tables, each with a brass lamp and a three-way bulb burning at the lowest setting. The office was so big that even with all of this furniture, it seemed to be sparsely furnished.

Like the reception area and hallway, the office was almost

soundless, and although it was expertly decorated, it lacked warmth. There was nothing personal in it. No "me" wall boldly displaying pictures of all the important people the occupant of the office knows personally. There were no family pictures, no diplomas, no awards, not even the graduation certificate from the Temeritus Quality Improvement Training School, from which Casey knew all Temeritus executives had graduated. And something else was missing. Yes, potted plants—this office did not have a single potted plant. The combined effect was an atmosphere that made Casey shiver.

Philpott walked around the desk and sat in his chair, his elbows on the armrests and his hands clasped together as if he were playing the childhood amusement of "here is the church, here is . . ." He peered over the steeple at Casey and told her the details of her assignment.

She would report to him, and the work she was to do on women's rights was to remain confidential from everyone including the president. During her time with the company she would have "Senior Select" status, which brought all of the privileges of the fifty members of top management—parking under the building, access to the athletic facilities and executive lounge and, of course, use of the Executive Dining Facility, "the EDF."

The first part of her work was to consist of a tour of the company to include visits with the major vice presidents and several field trips—to the testing lab at The Woodlands and to the Washington Office. This would bring her up to speed on the organization and its operations so that she could not only evaluate the best way to handle the animal rights boycott but also observe the situation with regard to the status of women at Temeritus.

"Helping you with all of this is a man named John Stone. He is the general manager of Executive Services, which actually means that he does whatever the hell I tell him to do. He reports directly to me and I use him as my eyes and ears in the company. He has been around for a long time and, as they say, he knows where the bodies are buried. He will be your 'tour guide' as you take your orientation." Proctor repeated the two-fingered quote gesture she had observed before. "Unfortunately, he is out of the city today and you won't be able to start with him until tomorrow. So what I thought we'd do is go over and introduce you to Timmons and take you to lunch in the Dining Facility so you can meet some of the guys. Then you can take the rest of the day off and come in tomorrow ready to really get with it."

Before she could respond, Proctor Philpott had risen from his chair and walked towards the door. Casey followed him out of the office and down the hall through several doors and turns until they entered another large open reception area as spacious, elegant and sterile as the one they had just left. There were two desks, each occupied by a sour-looking woman. The top of each desk was bare, except for an open book on one and an open magazine on the other. These people looked like the others she had seen at the desks she had passed on the way from the other side of the building. It was as if there were a sign proclaiming THANK YOU FOR NOT SMILING. And it was as quiet as an empty concert hall.

Casey and Philpott entered an office similar to his–large and well-appointed–but this one was brightened by the personal touches that usually adorn offices–family pictures, mementos of the years spent in the business, personal and professional honors and membership certificates. It was reassuring to Casey to think that the president of the company might have the human qualities that Philpott seemed to lack. And she was not disappointed. Seated behind a large traditional desk was a distinguished man with silver-gray hair. He looks like an old version of Mr. Rogers, Casey thought as she watched him rise from his chair and amble around the desk to shake her hand and tell her how nice it was to meet her. He is such a kind-looking man, she thought, shaking his hand and assuring him that the feeling was mutual. He was of medium height, and stood with a slight stoop to his shoulders, as if he were weary. His face was heavily lined and droopy, with large dark bags under his eyes. The stoop to his shoulders was such that his head tilted forward, causing him to look at the people he was talking to with his eyes raised and his eyebrows drawn up, wrinkling even further his already furrowed forehead. His demeanor reminded her even more of Mr. Rogers, and for a moment she half expected him to break into "It's a Beautiful Day in the Neighborhood" while replacing suit coat and wingtips with cardigan and sneakers.

Timmons escorted his visitors to a couch, and when they were seated he eased into one of the two chairs facing them. He leaned forward and bounced the palms of his hands on his knees, slapping them twice and then resting them on his knees. "Well, Casey, I understand from Proctor that you are coming on board to help us deal with this animal rights thing."

"Yes, sir."

"Well, it's been a big problem for us lately for sure, and we really do have to do something about it. It's starting to hurt our reputation." Timmons went on to speak for ten minutes about the enduring reputation of Temeritus as a good corporate citizen and as a leader in the corporate community. Timmons reminded her of her father–gray, handsome, calm and scholarly. He looked more like a college professor than a high-powered CEO.

During the general conversation that followed, Casey was surprised to learn that this somewhat feeble appearing man was one of the top tennis players at the River Oaks Country Club and a low handicap golfer. He must be in much better shape than the looks, she thought.

"And so, Casey, I understand that you'll be working with Proctor on this, so I know you'll be in good hands; but if there is anything I can do to help, please let me know." He rose and escorted them to the door where he shook Casey's hand again and patted Philpott on the shoulder as they left the suite.

Philpott stopped outside of his office to read the discreetly folded note which Melville Higgins had placed on the corner of his desk. "Tell him I'll be there," he said to Higgins. He walked to his desk and picked up the three-ring binder covered with white plastic which Casey had noticed earlier was the only thing on the top of the desk. "Here is some background material I've put together for you—organization charts, our mission statement, the Quality Credo, a list of key executives." He thumbed through the pages. "A map showing our manufacturing locations and other facilities. Finally, there's a list of the main products in the Temeritus product line." He rose and handed her the binder.

"I have a very pressing schedule today, Casey. Why don't you take these materials with you and study them and come back tomorrow? Stone will be here and you can get started with your orientation. Sorry I can't take you to lunch today but something has come up. Be here at 9:00 tomorrow morning." He grasped her hand with both of his and smiled for only the second time during her visit.

Casey took the binder and left. She walked down the hall, through the doors and finally out into the holding tank, which now contained a small group of middle-aged clones who looked like they were waiting for vasectomies. She got on the elevator, which creaked and shimmied all the way down to the lobby.

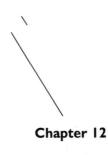

Chapter 12

The Hobbit Hole has been a Houston institution since the early 1970s when it was the only place in this carnivorous city where a person could get a decent vegetarian sandwich: whole-grain breads with heaps of avocado, bean sprouts and cheeses. Now such fare was called "Californian" and available everywhere, but once the Hobbit Hole was where you went if you wanted a great sandwich without the meat. And even today it still retained some of its "hippie" influence, which is why Jerry Turner, a.k.a. "T," felt conspicuous and out of place, despite his full red beard. He chose a table in the far corner, as far away from the other patrons as he could get, and sat down to wait.

Jerry Turner was a strange person to be involved in the activities of a radical animal rights group. He was a different kind of animal rights activist. Like the others, he was horrified at the thought of animal testing and had decided that he would break the law, if necessary, to stop it. But unlike the others, he saw nothing wrong with eating most kinds of animals. He was a hunter, a gun enthusiast, and a meat-and-potatoes man. In fact, the sandwich he contemplated–named, the menu advised, after a character in some science fiction book–was going to be the first sandwich he had ever eaten that didn't have some fowl, fish or other animal flesh in it since the PB&Js of his red-white-and-peanut-butter boyhood.

He was half-finished with the sandwich when P came in. She

looked different than at the meetings. She had on makeup and her hair was combed and she didn't seem as skinny. Even her eyebrows looked better–not as wild and bushy as he remembered them. She looks pretty good, he said to himself, feeling a tingle in his groin as he watched her approach the table.

She smiled and held out her hand. "Hi, I'm Nancy. Nancy Wade." He stood up and shook her hand. "Hi, Nancy. I'm Jerry. Sorry, but I had to order. I'm only supposed to take forty-five minutes for lunch."

She sat down across from him. After a long moment of awkward silence, she said, "I felt I had to call you and tell you how much I admired your stand the other night. I agree with you and I think M is full of baloney and all wrong."

Another moment of silence. She spoke again. "I know from the meetings that you don't like to say much. But I could tell that you were really serious the other night, and I wanted to ask you more about what you think we should do." She smiled and reached across the table, taking his hand in hers. "You can trust me, Jerry. You really can." She moved to the chair next to him and pulled it up close.

Jesus, he thought, she's looking better by the minute. He felt himself relaxing and feeling more aroused at the same time. Finally he spoke. "Yeah, I don't like to talk a whole lot. But when I get riled about something, I can't stand to be quiet. It's been a problem for me since I was little." She continued to hold his hand, and he continued to relax and soon he was talking more than he had in a long time.

They talked about their jobs and their past and all of the things that people who have just met and feel an attraction talk about. And all the while she held his hand, letting go of it to gesture or pick up her glass for another sip of tea, but always returning to it with a soft touch and squeeze when the task was complete. Jerry was captivated. And he was excited. The tingle in his groin had turned into a rigid erection which was now pressing in pain against the fabric of his

Levi's. Jesus, he thought, I can't believe this. My britches will be all stained when I stand up–if I can stand up.

Jerry often got erections in public. Ever since he was a young teenager, it was a source of embarrassment, especially if it persisted until nature's lubricant began to show through the cloth of his pants. Most men get past this stage by the time they leave their teens; Jerry didn't. And although he was in his late twenties, he still had the sex drive of a seventeen-year-old.

Things only got worse when Nancy's hand left the table and began to explore his knee and his thigh. Higher and higher on his thigh until at last she reached the damp bulge at the top. She ran her hand across and around it, squeezing with the softest touch.

"Oh, my goodness," she said in mock surprise, "what have we here! Why, you'll never be able to go back to work in this condition." Jerry was speechless. "I think we need to do something about this." She continued her gentle squeezing. "Why don't we go to my apartment and look into this?"

Jerry was still having difficulty figuring out just exactly what to say. His eyes bulged and what little blood not throbbing under Nancy's skilled hand rushed to his face where it turned his forehead, cheeks and nose the same bright red of his beard; sweat beaded his forehead. "Uh, yeah, I guess." He gasped. "But, I'm way over on my lunch break."

"I guess you'll just have to call in horny."

Chapter 13

Shortly before nine the next morning, Casey approached Melville Higgins' desk. Higgins raised his head from the paper he was reading, and without looking at her, said "Yessss, Mizz O'Rourke?"

"I have an appointment with Mr. Philpott at nine."

"No, Mizz O'Rourke. You do not have an appointment with Mr. Philpott. In fact, you have an appointment with Mr. Stone." He stood up. "Just follow me," he said as he walked down the hall.

Moments later Higgins stopped and knocked on the side of an opened door, peering around the door jamb into the office. "Mr. Stone," he said. "I have the young lady Mr. Philpott talked to you about yesterday." He ushered Casey into the room and introduced her.

John Stone was tall and square-shouldered. His face was tanned–the dark reddish tan of too much exposure to the sun–and lined with deep, weathered creases. A golfer or a sailor, she thought. His hair was blond and longer than she had expected in the executive suite. And it was combed back on the sides into what, with a bit more of a sweep, could have passed for a 1950s D.A. His hand was huge and enveloped Casey's with a firm and friendly grip. Although he smiled as he spoke–a distant and carefully controlled smile–his eyes remained passive and cold, untouched by the relaxed sound of his words.

Stone showed Casey to the round table across the office from his desk and asked if she cared for coffee. She did, straight–black, no sugar–and he poured her a cup from the chrome vacuum jug next to his telephone. When he placed the cup on the table in front of her, she noticed a small button in his lapel–a small triangle with slightly curved sides trimmed in gold, with a three-pointed white and black star, also trimmed in gold, on a red background. I knew there was something I liked about this guy, she said to herself–he's a Marine.

"Do you get together with your Third Division buddies often, Mr. Stone?" He looked at Casey as if she had just recited the names and ages of his three kids.

"You are very observant, Casey. How do you come to recognize the insignia of the Third Marine Division Association? And, please, call me John."

"Oh, I'm a big fan. My late husband was a Marine. I lived for several years on the base at Camp Lejeune and, of course, learned all about the Corps. And the man I'm seeing now is a former Marine. So I guess you could say that I have a thing about Marines. In any event, I'm familiar with the Third Marine Division Association."

John Stone's demeanor changed as she spoke, and his earlier distance turned into friendliness and warmth. A genuine smile crossed his face like sunlight washing the landscape after a summer shower, the lines around his eyes crinkled, as if he were telling himself, "Relax, this lady's going to be OK." Jake had told her many times that the Marine Corps was the greatest fraternity in the world and now she believed it. It had certainly broken the ice for her with Stone, who spent the next several minutes telling her of his experiences in the Corps.

Finally they got to the business of the day. Stone explained that he had been instructed by Proctor Philpott to devote several weeks to seeing that she got a first-class orientation. He was to escort her to see the people and places that Philpott had designated and to provide her with whatever materials and resources she needed to help Temeritus deal more effectively with the animal rights situation.

"Our first visit is with Pennrose Parker," Stone said. "He's the senior VP of Issues and External Affairs, what we used to call public relations. You'll like him. He's a very nice man. But, he's what I call a show dog–he looks great and you can dress him up real good in a nice suit or a tux and put a drink in his hand and he can dazzle anyone. The unfortunate thing is that he doesn't go any further than that. He's had a very successful career at Temeritus without having ever made a decision. He has an uncanny way of learning in advance the right way to line up on an issue, and he's always pointing in the right direction. He has perfected it to an art form. This trait is reflected in his nickname around the company–they call him 'Parallel.' Yes, old Parallel Parker, always lined up in exactly the same direction as the other cars around him. After you've seen him in action for a while, you'll get a better idea of why your services are so badly needed."

They walked into the hall and headed toward the stairs to the thirty-eighth floor and Parallel Parker's office. Casey noticed again how quiet it was. She followed Stone down the stairs, through a long hall and into another reception area. He brushed past the secretary sitting at attention at the desk immediately outside of the door and leaning in slightly, he tapped on the door frame. "Hi, Pennrose. Do you have a minute?" Without waiting for a reply, he led Casey into the office.

Rising to greet them as they entered the office was the most executive-looking executive Casey had ever seen. Pennrose Parker stood six feet tall, slim, perfectly manicured and coiffed. His hair was dark, peppered with just the right touch of gray, and cut in a medium length that, while neatly trimmed, was still long enough to comb back on the sides. Like Cary Grant, Casey thought. But the thing most remarkable about him was the soft, clear blue of his eyes; Casey had never seen such eyes. She had heard the term "baby blues" before;

now she knew what it really meant. This guy is gorgeous, she thought.

"Say, Casey. It's so nice to meet the person who can help us in our time of need. Please have a seat." He smiled and a boyish grin flashed across his manly face, exposing teeth that were as straight and white as if they had been handcrafted from the finest ivory.

Casey and Stone sat down, and Parker returned to the large leather-covered chair behind his desk. It was cleaner than either Philpott's or Timmons' had been. There was nothing on it at all. Not even a pen and pencil set. Nothing. And it had been polished to a high gloss. Parker reached into one of the drawers and took out a thin three-ring binder. He placed it in front of him and toyed with its edge as if he were making sure that it was perfectly aligned with the edge of the desk.

"Casey, over the years we here at Temeritus have developed probably the best system there is for issue management. That's the way we manage our issues, by issue management. And this little book I have here–he held the binder aloft, pausing and gazing at it in self-satisfied awe–"this little book is the best one we have." He lowered the book to his desk and stroked its cover with his opened hand. "It's on the A-T issue,"–he pronounced each letter separately–"Animal Testing, that is, and you'll see that it has separate sections for arm and farm."

"Arm and farm?" Casey asked.

"Oh, yes," Parker laughed. "That's A-R-M- and F-A-R-M; 'arm' and 'farm.' Those are our little words for the Animal Rights Movement and the Fanatical Animal Rights Movement. It helps to keep them separated." He chuckled. "Sorry for the corporate lingo, Casey, but it is the result of lots of hard work. Just like this book. And I want you to take it home and peruse it." He paused and grimaced, pondering what he had just said. "No, on second thought, you had better do more than that, Casey, you'd better read it carefully. And you'll see that this issue is caused entirely by them; it has nothing to do with what we're trying to do."

"Thank you, Mr. Parker," Casey said accepting the book.

"Have you ever worked on issue management, Casey? And please, call me Penn."

"Maybe we're only into semantics here, Penn, but my experience tells me that a company can't manage an issue; it can only manage its response to the way a particular issue is being played out in the press. You don't manage an issue any more than you manage the weather. What you do is try to develop your skills at forecasting what the weather is going to be and prepare what your response will be if you're right–and if you're wrong."

Parker pulled back in his chair in surprise. Casey almost laughed. Had she committed heresy? "But, Casey, we here at Temeritus do manage issues. It says so right in the Temeritus Issue Management manual. You don't think we'd have a manual on it if we didn't do it, do you?" He leaned back in his chair and smiled with obvious self-satisfaction.

"No, I guess not. And I'm looking forward to learning all about it. Tell me what we'll be doing."

Relaxed and in control once more, Parker told Casey what had been planned for her orientation. She was to be put under the tutelage of a young public relations representative, Elizabeth Stokes, who would bring her "up to speed on the intricacies of TIM"–he pronounced it as if it were a single word, 'tim'–especially as it applies to animal testing. "But, of course," Parker continued, "I plan to have daily contact with you when your orientation is completed and we get into the real management of this issue. You'll come to really have an appreciation of what it means to manage an issue Temeritus-style," Parker concluded with a condescending tone that Casey found almost laughable.

Parker stood and leaned over the desk to grasp Casey's hand.

"Say, Casey, it was great to meet you and I look forward to working with you. John, will you take Casey down to Liz Stokes' office? She's expecting you."

Parker sat at his desk for several moments after his visitors had departed, his smile replaced by a worried frown. He rose, went to the window and stared out into the hazy Houston morning, made to appear even hazier by the tinted windows. He had been concerned about this ever since Philpott had raised it in the staff meeting. Why did they need someone like Casey? Whenever they had gone outside before, it had been with one of the big national firms; why would he want to go with this nobody? Maybe she was his current punch. She certainly was a tasty little morsel, he chuckled to himself, and we all know what happens when Philpott's hormones start to kick in. But, no, she was a looker, but she also seemed to be very intelligent and that wouldn't register in the Prince's regal gonads. Oh, well, if he says to work with her, I'll work with her. But it sure seems strange.

Chapter 14

I look so good, I ought to dress like this all the time, Larry Mitchell said to himself as he went through the final inspection of his new look. Dark blue suit, wingtips, crisp white Oxford button-down shirt with rep tie. Right out of *Gentleman's Quarterly*. But the difference in his appearance came from the much more profound changes to his usual look–his normal plain-brown-wrapper look had been replaced by jet black hair, close-snipped moustache, black horn-rimmed glasses and two inches of height provided by elevator shoes. He didn't look at all like the humorous ex-cop, private businessman that he was. Yes, he said out loud to the mirror, you look just like an experienced FBI agent. He doubted if he would be recognized even by his fellow members of the cell, where he was known only as L, the Temeritus kitchen crusader. He adjusted the knot in his tie, and admired the vision in his mirror one last time.

In his driveway was a nondescript mid-sized bottom-of-the-line Ford–just the kind of vehicle used by the federal government. Pale gray, black side walls, zero frills. Finding such a vehicle at a rental agency had been difficult, but he had located a rent-a-wreck franchise on the far outskirts of the airport. The car was rented by one of the other members of the cell using a fake ID and delivered the night before to complete his disguise. After admiring himself further, he left the house and drove up Highway 59 through the center of town to the North Loop where he cut back to the west and hooked up with the Hardy Toll Road. From there it was a quick and straight shot into The Woodlands.

He had been to The Woodlands several times to visit friends and was always impressed by its beauty. In a city that took great liberty with the names of its subdivisions—a Rolling Forest had not a single tree or roll, and a Holly Hills sprawled on ground as flat and treeless as a coffee table—The Woodlands was indeed accurately named. Pines as well as hardwoods, many left standing in long green belts and other areas of open space with residential developments hidden throughout. In addition to the residential areas, there were numerous office parks and light commercial centers making The Woodlands a self-supporting community in which people could live, work and shop. And one of its landmark facilities was Temeritus Laboratories.

The facility was a large main building with several smaller outbuildings located on a sixty-five-acre tract that included the requisite trees and a small lake. The building was set back on the property, accessible by a long curved driveway, and looked more like a small college or a minimum security federal prison than a place of business. It was a pleasant addition to the community made more so by the lack of any form of signage. Nothing identified it as having anything to do with a major commercial enterprise and the unknowing passerby would have assumed it to be anything but what it was—a place for the testing of cosmetic products on cats, dogs and rabbits.

Even though he had been given a complete briefing, he was still surprised when he pulled into the long driveway leading up to the building. It looked so peaceful and quiet. There also appeared to be a total absence of security—no fences, no guardhouse, none of the things you would normally find at a sensitive business. But he knew this outward appearance was just a ruse.

He chuckled as he recalled the manner in which they had gained what little information they had about the inside of this building. The only senior citizen in the cell had showed up there a few weeks ago looking like Helen Hayes in *Airport* and conned them right out of their shoes. She drove up to the building and stumbled in saying she was trying to find her daughter's house and had gotten lost. Her imitation of what she had done had convinced even the most skeptical cell members of her skills as an actress. Fumbling, stuttering and me-oh-mying, she had gained entrance to the building, where she had been offered a seat while they tried to help her. She made a few calls and finally located her son-in-law who said he would drive over and escort her back to the house. Then, relieved that the ordeal had ended, she began to calm down and passed the time in light discussion with the security guards on duty.

From this duplicity they learned many things. First, that security here was provided by Surveillance, the same outfit that worked at Temeritus Tower. This meant that personnel, procedures and uniforms would be the same. Almost as important was the knowledge that from the inside, this pastoral retreat was a vault. The only entrance to the front of the building opened into a small room with a desk at which a security guard sat. The only other furniture in the room was a metal chair and a small table with a telephone. The walls were stark white and had no pictures or decorations. Behind the security guard was a large steel door with a small rectangular wire-reinforced glass window. This appeared to be the only means of access to the rest of the building. This room was no reception area; it was the primary security point for a place where Temeritus did not intend to entertain visitors.

And so, with the preliminary work having been done, Larry Mitchell drove up the long driveway and began Phase II of Operation Woodlands. He parked in the visitor's parking spot, walked to the door and entered the room. He knew what he would find and his command of the situation would enhance his authority. He opened the door with force and walked directly to the desk where he thrust his ID into the face of the surprised security guard. He was disappointed. He had hoped to find young George Downey on duty; it would have been great sport to diddle with that dumb-ass again. Instead he found a young man whose efforts to appear older had only made him seem younger. The man pushed his chair back as if he were considering flight.

"Special Agent Johnson, FBI," he barked. "Keep your seat." The guard froze. "This is a spot security check, and you are ordered to comply with my inspection requests under penalty of law. I want to inspect your records and check out the tightness of your security system and procedures. We'll begin with your records."

"Well . . . I, I . . . er."

"No, Corporal, there's no 'I, I' to it. You must do as I say, or you and your company will be in serious trouble."

"But I have to check this with my supervisor."

"Corporal. You don't seem to understand. This is an ORI, an Operational Readiness Inspection. It's done in secret and without warning and is required for the renewal of your company's federal license to engage in the security business. Any attempt to interfere with the progress of an ORI is a federal crime and could land you in prison. You are compelled to cooperate and you are commanded not to notify your supervisor until the investigation has been concluded. Do you read me, Corporal?"

"Yeah, I guess so." He had remained seated throughout this tirade and started to fiddle with the flap of his left pocket. Jesus, he thought, all I need right now is to get in trouble with the law. "What can I do to help?"

Man, this is fun, Mitchell thought. This poor slob has swallowed this whole line of crap. Where do they get these guys? "You will explain your procedures for logging someone into the building."

There followed a thirty-minute inspection during which all security secrets of gaining access to the facility were explained. His heartbeat quickened when they walked through the part of the building where the animals were kept in cages. This is what it's all about, he thought. But, to his surprise, he didn't see a single animal hooked up to a machine or in any other way appearing to be part of an experiment. Just people walking around and sitting in offices–all clad in white smocks and all looking proper and busy. It was all so clean and neat and businesslike.

Back at the security desk he made the final entries in the phony form he had used as a prop during the inspection and closed out the interview. "I have only one more question, Corporal. I noticed that none of the animals we saw seemed to be part of an experiment. Isn't the purpose of this facility to do experiments?"

"Oh, yes sir. But those are done in the lab downstairs. That's where the heavy stuff goes on. I guess. I haven't ever been down there. The security people aren't allowed down there. Nobody is, except for Dr. Flint and his staff."

"Why didn't you show me this when we were checking out the security points?"

"Well, sir, this isn't really part of our job. I mean, there's no security card or anything for that door. Just a key, and Dr. Flint has the only copy, I'm told. Security for the basement isn't our responsibility. Mr. Slurry is responsible for that and nobody goes down there–except for the Doc–unless Mr. Slurry is actually there with them. He's really goosey about the basement."

He couldn't believe it, a secret lab in the basement. What a fabulous thing that will be for us, he thought. "How do you get to this basement?"

"Come on, I'll show you." They walked back through the steel door behind the security desk and turned to the right. At the end of the hall was another steel door, this one painted green and labeled in large white letters, NO ENTRY. Unlike the other doors in the hallway, this one did not have a security device for allowing entry to card holders; it was secured with a heavy deadbolt lock. "I've never been in this room," he said, stopping in front of the door and gesturing toward it. "But I'm told that there is a freight elevator and a stairway inside, both going down to the basement. Like I say, nobody talks about it much and it isn't part of our job here during the daytime."

"What about at night?" he asked as they walked back to the front desk.

"Oh, that's a different story. At night—after the midnight shift has been posted—there's only one guard out here and he's at this desk. Everything else is shut down tight. There's no one else out here from midnight to eight. Not even in the offices. No one. It's all in the procedures." They went back through the heavy steel door and into the reception area. The guard sat at his desk and explained in more detail what he meant.

There were three shifts at the facility. During the day and up until midnight there were two guards—one at the desk and one at the parking facility. They came to work like anybody else—drove into the parking lot and went to work. The man on the midnight shift was driven out from Houston in a Temeritus van and posted with military formality by a senior security officer. There were regulations and procedures for everything. Only the most experienced people worked the midnight shift. And the instructions were simple: no one in the building at night—not even the people who work here—unless it's approved in advance by Houston. Everything shuts down. And it stays that way until eight o'clock the next morning.

"Yeah, they come out here and post the midnight shift like this place was a missile site or something. They quiz you about the duties and they reset the code to disarm the alarm on the green door. Then they set the alarm and leave."

Now we're getting somewhere, Mitchell thought. "The alarm?" he asked.

"Yeah. Most of the animals are delivered at night and sometimes that means they have to get into the basement. If they do, then the guard on duty has to make sure that the alarm is disarmed. Otherwise there will be a flap from Houston like you never saw, if they think there's been a break-in. So, you get a call from Houston saying that a delivery is on the way, you have to make sure that when they get here and want to go inside the green room, the alarm is off." He turned in his chair and opened what appeared to be a fuse box on the wall behind the desk. He pointed to the key pad inside. "If I put the right number into this key pad, the alarm shuts down completely. That way they can go down the hall and use their key to get into the green room. That's all there is to it. The alarm automatically resets itself after twenty minutes. So all you have to do is put in the number and sit here until they leave. It's really simple."

"That seems to be a very efficient system, Corporal. I'm sure the Bureau will be pleased and will quickly renew your license." He closed the notebook, placed it in the briefcase and snapped the briefcase shut. "I sure appreciate your help, Corporal. It's just too bad we can't take a look in the green room. Sounds like a fascinating place."

"Sorry I can't help you with that, sir. I guess you'll have to contact Mr. Slurry. He's in charge of corporate security and like I say, he keeps real close tabs on this basement."

"Yeah," he smiled. "I guess I will."

Chapter 15

Thirty floors beneath Pennrose Parker, in a small standard-issue Temeritus office, Elizabeth Stokes prepared for her meeting with Casey. She was reading for the second time the memo Parker had sent to the vice presidents of Issues and External Affairs, the action copy of which had been bucked down in the organization to her desk. It had been prepared and sent in response to the disclosure by Proctor Philpott at his weekly staff meeting that Casey had been retained to assist in the handling of the animal testing issue. The purpose of Parker's memo was to inform his vice presidents of Casey's hiring and to instruct the Vice President, Issues Management–Liz's boss's boss–to assign a member of the appropriate department to assist in her orientation.

This memo was then copied by the Vice President, Issues Management, and sent to the three general managers in the Issues Management Organization–Issues Identification and Classification ("II&C"), Issues Development and Modification ("ID&M"), and Issues Planning and Integration ("IP&I"). These groups handled all issues of importance to the company, including those merely suspected of potential importance. Although no issues escaped this process, there was a special group of individuals, created by Proctor Philpott and reporting directly to him, that handled issues of such importance that they required his special touch. Since its creation, this group had taken on a status in the Issues Management Organization not unlike that of the KGB–it commanded a fearful and begrudging respect. This group was known by the program it administered, the Proprietary Issues Management Program ("PIMP"). In the minds of many Temeritus employees, never had an acronym been so appropriately bestowed.

Designation of an issue for PIMP treatment was a matter of some mystery, often done at the direct command of Proctor Philpott but more usually by Pennrose Parker based upon his educated assumption that such special treatment was "what Proctor really wants." As Casey was to learn, decision-making at Temeritus was frequently based upon this assumption, often incorrect but never validated by an inquiry to Proctor Philpott himself. Such an inquiry was considered under the unwritten and unacknowledged Temeritus Code of Executive Manhood to be a fatal sign of both weakness and unsuitability for further advancement. The question of how best to handle Casey's assignment was decided by Parallel Parker based upon this assumption.

After he had signed and sent the memo to his vice presidents, Parker called Rex Childress, Vice President, Issues Management. "Say, Rex. Parker here. Just wanted to let you know that there is a memo headed your way on a new project on the AT issue, and Proctor wants it proprietaryised. You might want to think about giving it to Hancock." "Proprietaryised" was a word coined by Proctor Philpott and used by Parker always, and by others in the presence of Proctor Philpott, to refer to the designation of an issue for special treatment. Most people referred to this designation process as "PIMPed," a term never used by Parker because it would be contemptuous of Proctor Philpott's brainchild.

This transaction was handled over the telephone, as were all "this-is-what-Proctor-really-wants" instructions; in case it turned out to be wrong, a change in direction was much easier if there could be a misunderstanding of the spoken rather than the written. Upon receipt of the memorandum, Childress referred it to Jerry Hancock, Manager, Proprietary Issues Management Program, who in turn referred it to his top person on the animal testing issue, Ms. Elizabeth Stokes.

Liz Stokes had been with Temeritus for almost ten years, ever since her graduation from the University of Texas at Austin, where she received a degree in communications. She had been assigned to work on the animal testing issue her first day on the job and had been on that issue exclusively ever since. She was five-four, thin to the point of being considered skinny, and wore her jet black hair in a short businesslike style made all the more noticeable by a natural streak of white just above the right temple. This had for many years been a source of embarrassment to her, and during high school and college she had disguised it with the help of one of her future employer's leading products. But during her senior year at Texas she had decided to let it show the way it was, and since then had worn the white shock as a badge of distinction in a world where so many people seemed to be trying to look like each other.

Liz Stokes wasn't sure exactly what she was supposed to do with Casey O'Rourke. The animal testing issue had heated up substantially in recent months and, typically at Temeritus, the hotter an issue became the cooler top management got on discussing it in public. Now with "60 Minutes" threatening to do a piece on Temeritus, the issue had become so volatile that no one wanted to talk about it, even inside the building. No wonder this lady's orientation has been PIMPed, Liz thought. She looked at the materials attached to the memo—a brief write-up about Casey and about O'Rourke & Associates. She sure looks good on paper, Liz thought, as she poured herself another cup of coffee. I hope she's more help than the last one of the Prince's little elves.

Liz's musings were interrupted when Casey tapped lightly on the opened door and introduced herself.

After a few minutes of discussion, Liz suggested that they continue the briefing at her favorite Mexican restaurant just a few blocks from the building. Casey thought that was a great idea and they left for lunch.

Carmen's was dark and cool and filled with the lusty smells of Mexican cooking. They asked to be seated in a little nook just next to the bar. They ordered beef fajitas and drinks–Casey a Carta Blanca and Liz an iced tea.

"You do know about TAP, don't you, the Temeritus Alcohol Policy? " Liz said, after the waiter had left the table.

"No," Casey said, thinking about the wine she and Proctor Philpott had enjoyed at their lunch. "I didn't know that there was such a thing."

"Well, there is and it is vigorously enforced, at least among the rank and file. I'd suggest that you scratch that beer; one of Dewey's Darlings could be in here and even though you aren't an employee, it could create an unpleasant scene if you got TAPPED."

"Dewey's Darlings?"

"Yeah, that's what we call the little band of spies from the Internal Affairs Organization that Dewey sends around to make sure that all of the policies of the company are being followed."

"Who's Dewey?"

"Dewey is Dewey B. Shivers, the Senior Vice President of Internal Affairs, what most companies call 'Employee Relations' or the trendier 'Human Resources.' He views the company's policies as religious dogma and he is always on a jihad to find and punish Temeritus sinners, at least those below the level of Senior Select. I'm surprised that you haven't met him or at least heard about him. The guy's a real nerd."

Casey called the waiter and changed her drink order. Then, over big glasses of sweetened iced tea, they began to discuss the Temeritus handling of the animal testing issue. Liz explained that Temeritus, like a large number of manufacturers, tested its products on laboratory animals to ensure the safety of those products for human use; in fact, for new products for which no safety data was available, such testing was required by federal law.

"Most organizations, obviously including the United States Government, consider this practice to be in the best interest of the American consumer," Liz said, pausing only long enough to sip on her tea. "But, it's being attacked by an increasing number of so-called animal rights groups. Some of them deal in mostly above-board lobbying and protesting but others are just wacky, like the ones that want to outlaw rodeos, horse races, zoos; some of them even want to ban the ownership of household pets. These people are harmless for the most part and you deal with them the same way you deal with any other specialized group of people urging a limited agenda.

"But some of these folks are really scary. Like the ones you read about that harass women who wear fur coats and throw paint on them and things like that. They like to call anyone who doesn't agree with them on the subject of animal rights a Nazi, which is terribly ironic since Mr. Nazi himself, Adolf Hitler, was a strict vegetarian."

"I didn't know that," Casey exclaimed.

"Yeah, he was. Isn't that a riot? Anyway, the really scary group is the one that calls itself ALA–the Animal Liberation Army. These people are terrorists. They use economic sabotage and personal intimidation to further their goals, and they also do things like raid animal testing labs for the purpose of 'freeing' the animals held 'captive' there. They are similar in tactics to Greenpeace. And, of course, the animal rights movement dovetails nicely with the environmental movement and with the '90s interest in healthful eating, you know, vegetarians and all."

The waiter served the fajitas, smoking and sputtering, filling the air around them with the spicy aroma of skirt steak, onions and green peppers, sizzling in a shallow almost red-hot skillet which he carefully placed on a wooden trivet in front of them. Casey and Liz each filled a warm flour tortilla with beef, onions, peppers, guacamole and pico di Gallo, and rolled the entire thing into a tube and ate in awed silence. Casey laughed as she reached for the tortilla basket, "Damn, these are good. I don't know about you, Liz, but I don't think I'm interested in becoming a vegetarian quite yet." Liz nodded her silent agreement and they ate.

Over cinnamon-laced coffee, Liz's briefing continued. "So, a lot of cosmetic companies have given in to this pressure and have stopped animal testing. Or at least they stop doing it themselves–if tests are legally required, some product manufacturers will have the testing done by the ingredient manufacturer; then they can truthfully say that they don't test on animals. In any event, it's certainly the politically correct thing to do, and as in the environmental area, a lot of companies are using their stand on the issue as a marketing tool. 'Buy our product because we . . . you fill in the blank–we recycle, we shun fluorocarbons, we don't test our products on animals, whatever." Liz sipped her coffee.

"Our problem is that Temeritus has chosen as a matter of corporate policy to continue to engage in animal testing. So it's become the symbolic target of this increasingly vocal and active effort to end it. The boycott is just the latest manifestation of this. It hasn't hurt our sales. So it doesn't seem to be doing much good. But it's an easy way for the politically correct to show how concerned they are about the issue. Sort of like not eating table grapes a while back. Or the protests in the late '80s against companies that did business in South Africa; divestiture of the offending stock didn't do a damn thing for the folks in South Africa, but it sure made a lot of sanctimonious jerks in the U.S. feel good. This issue is the same.

"What makes this problem so hard to deal with is the pitiful leadership–really a void in leadership–in the company. Temeritus prides itself on how 'good' it is. Any publicity is bad, even if it's good. And for years the company prospered with this no-profile approach to PR. But times have changed and that just isn't possible any more, especially for a company that has done all of the dumb things that Temeritus has done lately. Maybe the fact that you've been hired to work on this means that we are finally going to change with the times. Who knows? But we can talk about all of that later. Tell me about yourself."

Casey spent the rest of the lunch telling Liz about herself—her background, her professional experience and how some of the things she had done before might be helpful now.

Chapter 16

The call came in to M's office phone at 11:15 Friday morning. "The party was a success. Please call the caterer." That was the entire message delivered over the phone by one of M's many "hands," people who were not in the cell but who were sympathetic to the cause and wanted to help when they could. This hand was a trusted old friend who had agreed to be a "telephone drop" for M on special occasions. Getting word about Larry Mitchell's "inspection" of the Temeritus laboratory was one of those occasions, and M had given him the telephone number of the hand with the instruction to call and report on the operation. If there was something that needed urgent attention, he was to add the part about the caterer and M would call him at a designated convenience store near The Woodlands.

M left her office and went to a pay phone several blocks away and dialed the number of the convenience store. "Woodlands Catering," L said when he picked up the phone. There followed a pre-arranged exchange of passwords.

"All animals are equal," M said.

"But some are more equal than others," Mitchell said, finishing out George Orwell's famous quote from *Animal Farm.* Now they could talk.

"It was a piece of cake, M. Candy from a baby and all that. But there is something we hadn't planned on. According to this bozo on the security desk, all of the serious testing—he called it 'the heavy stuff'—goes on in a lab in the basement. And he says that even the security people don't have access to it. There's a locked room with a freight elevator and a stairway going down into the basement where the lab is. I thought you should know this as soon as possible."

"Just as I suspected," she said. "I knew there was something fishy going on. Listen, this changes things a lot. Can you meet me tonight for dinner somewhere? I think we need to discuss this in more detail."

Mitchell was not sure what to say. He knew that M was death on social contacts between members of the cell. Could this be a test? No, not considering the circumstances. "Sure," he said, "That'd be fine."

"Great. How about Butera's on South Shepherd? If the weather holds we can even sit outside. Seven o'clock."

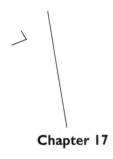

Chapter 17

T and P were not the only ones dissatisfied with the direction of the cell. Carl Winokur, a.k.a. "C," sat alone in a small apartment in Houston's most eclectic and diverse neighborhood, Montrose. For over a week he had been haunted by the memory of the dispute at the last cell meeting. Every time he thought about the hulking and violent T, he quivered. Maybe this whole thing is all a big mistake, Carl thought, as he reflected on his recruitment and quick disenchantment with ALA.

Carl was a Temeritus brat; he had grown up in the closed society of Temeritus as the son of an engineer whose various assignments had taken him to numerous places in the United States and Europe. He was thirty years old and had never held a full-time job for more than a matter of months. For the last several years he had been a graduate student at Rice University living in a garret in Montrose on the income from his father's trust fund. He was an intellectual, a dreamer and a slob. Skinny to the point of emaciation and as unkempt as a pile of dirty laundry.

Everything about him was thin–his body, his face, his eyes, even his light brown hair, which was thin in two ways: it was fine and silky; and it was missing from the top of his head, which was as hairless as the top of a mushroom. What hair he had grew out in a fringe starting above one temple and passing around the back of his head to the other, hanging below his ears limp and straight, giving him the appearance of wearing a French Foreign Legion hat without the crown.

Several months after he began his graduate studies at Rice, he became involved in an animal rights group on campus known as The Animalis Society. It was a small group that met on an irregular basis to discuss the classic writings of the animal rights movement–Jeremy Bentham's *Introduction to the Principles of Morals and Legislation,* Henry Salt's *Animal Rights Considered in Relation to Social Progress,* Tom Regan's *The Case For Animal Rights* and, of course, what is considered by most to be the bible of the current animal rights movement, Peter Singer's *Animal Liberation.* The group didn't do anything but talk. It had no agenda for action, and it really was nothing more than an intellectual club of gabfesters who liked to meet for beers at The Ginger Man on Morningside, just up the street from The Horse, and talk about the philosophy of animal rights.

At one of these gatherings Carl met a man who claimed to have contacts in the most radical of the animal rights groups, the ALA. To a member of a wimpy group like The Animalis Society, the mere mention of the name "Animal Liberation Army" could ignite romantic fantasies in the imagination. It had the dark allure of the Irish Republican Army–sinister and dangerous, secret and deadly; armed men and women so dedicated to their cause that they would give their lives, if needed, to further the ends of the group. Yes, he told the man, I would be interested in talking to someone from the group.

Finally, after months of telephone interviews and questions that would put an FBI background check to shame, he met M and learned the rules of participation. His value to the cell was in his linguistic skills–he was fluent in Spanish, Portuguese, French, German, Italian and Dutch. For the first few months of active membership he enjoyed himself. He translated papers and other documents and provided interpretation when needed by M or others in the cell. But as the activities of the cell began to escalate in violence, he began to lose his zest for the group.

Now, through his lifelong friendship with a fellow Temeritus brat and current Temeritus employee, he had learned a terrible secret about the labs at The Woodlands certain to cause serious problems if it became known by M and the more aggressive members of the cell. For days he debated what he should do. A small piece in the gossip column of the *Houston Chronicle* provided the answer.

He picked up the folded newspaper and read for the tenth time the item that had by chance caught his attention.

GRAPES FROM THE VINE–We hear that Temeritus, Inc. has hired local PR biggie Casey O'Rourke to help cure their mounting woes on the animal rights front. Could it be that the Big T is finally getting ready to address this matter head-on?

Carl tossed the paper onto the table in front of him and went into the kitchen where, after a frantic search through the piles of debris on, under and around his kitchen table, he found the Houston phone book. O, O, Olson, O'Malley, O'Rourke . . . here it is, K.C. O'Rourke. Hmm, the paper said "Casey." Well, this must be it. Anyway, it's worth a try. He dialed the number.

Casey picked up after the third ring. Oh, Jesus, Carl thought, I really don't know yet what I want to say. "Er, is this . . . K.C. O'Rourke, the public relations lady?"

"I'm the president of O'Rourke and Associates, yes. May I help you?"

"I saw about you in the papers, your job with Temeritus and all. And I have some information you may be interested in. I can't talk about it on the phone, but trust me, it's something you'll want to know. Where can I meet you?"

Casey was skeptical. But she figured she could use all the information she could get. "I'll be at One For Your Horse in the Village Friday night. If you have something to tell me, you can meet me there. Ask the bartender. He'll point me out to you." She paused.

"And you are . . . ?"

"A friend of Temeritus. And I'll see you there." He hung up, stumbled back to the living room and collapsed on the couch in the midst of a week's worth of newspapers and unfolded clothes. Jesus, what am I going to say to her?

Chapter 18

The Horse was crowded and noisy, as always on Friday night, when it took on a special atmosphere of its own. Friday was the top business day of the week. Friday drew the biggest crowds; Friday sold the most beer; and Friday smoked the most cigars.

Casey could sense all of these Friday phenomena at work as she walked up the steps. Through the opened door she could see the packed house, hear the buzz of conversation accented by bursts of alcohol-lubricated laughter, and smell the smoke of fine cigars. It was Friday night at One For Your Horse.

She walked through the crowd to the bar where Gabe, Jake's assistant manager, was busy serving beer. He looked up as she approached. "Hi, Casey. Jake's back in the brew room. Some problem with the feed lines. What'll you have?" Casey ordered a pint of Steel Hook Porter and looked around the room. A darts game was underway, and a group of people had pulled several tables together for what appeared to be a farewell party for one of their colleagues. Casey finished her survey of the room and turned back to the bar, hardly noticing the man who had slipped onto the stool beside her.

"Are you Casey O'Rourke?"

She looked at him for the first time and affirmed that she was indeed that person. "You must be the friend of Temeritus."

"I am." He paused, and then continued. "And what I'm doing here is very dangerous."

Casey turned on the stool to more fully face this friend of Temeritus. Seated at the bar she could not tell how tall he was, but she could see that he was thin. And bald on the top. This guy needs a serious haircut, Casey thought, looking at the limp fringe of hair hanging from the sides of his otherwise bald head. At least, he doesn't try to camouflage the bald spot by combing the hair from the sides up and over and around on the top.

"Dangerous?" Casey said.

"Extremely," he said pushing his rimless glasses up on his nose. "Could we go over to one of those tables where we can talk without being so conspicuous? I want to tell you what I mean.

"My name is Carl. Last name doesn't matter. I'm a member of a group called The Animalis Society. I don't know if you're familiar with it or not, but it's a group dedicated to the principle that all living things are equal in terms of their right to live on this earth, and in an ideal world no one animal should exercise any dominion over any other. Our ideal would be a world in which there was no such thing as animals being raised for slaughter and no animals being used for the testing of human products. Or even being kept as pets, for that matter. Have you heard of it?"

Casey had not.

"Well, it is an obscure organization," he said. He fidgeted in his chair, sighed, and continued. "My father worked for Temeritus for thirty-five years before he died, and it was the Temeritus stock that was bought out by the English when they acquired Temeritus that paid for me to go to college and to live in the style that I now do. So I have a soft spot in my heart for the company and certainly have no wish to see it hurt."

He stopped, pushed up his glasses again and signaled for another beer. "Now," he continued, "I have some information. And I won't tell you where it came from—only that it's extremely reliable—and I want to give it to you so that maybe you can use it in the work you're about to do." He paused and Casey waited in silence. "You see, you're being lied to by the people at Temeritus. They may take people to the lab and show them all the great things they're doing and how much they love their so-called non-human employees. But they're lying. There's another lab–in the basement–and that's where they do the real testing; that's where they do the things to the animals they don't want anyone to know about. You need to somehow get in to see it and then do something that will make them stop." He sat back in his chair and drank, gulping almost half of the fresh beer in one long pull.

Casey wasn't sure what to say. Who was this guy and why was he doing this? None of it made any sense, and Casey's natural skepticism was fully activated. "That's very interesting, Carl. How do you happen to know about this?"

"I told you. I have a good source of information. I'm not at liberty to disclose it, but I guarantee what I've told you is true. You can take it to the bank."

"OK. But assuming it's true, why don't you use this information in the activities of your group, this Animalis thing?"

"That's the key point, Miss O'Rourke. And that's why it's so important for you to act quickly. You see, Animalis has become radicalized. It's been taken over by people who've lost touch with the peaceful origins and purposes of the founders. They're becoming more like the ALA–the Animal Liberation Army. Raids and violence and confrontations and stuff like that. I fear that if the radicals at Animalis find out about the secret lab, there will be a wave of violence that may be the undoing of Temeritus. And that would be tragic. And that's why I'm telling you this. I can't tell anybody at Animalis because I know how they'd react. In fact, if you ever accuse me of having any contact with you or of telling you anything about any of this, I'll deny it. I'll deny ever even knowing who you are." He sat back in his chair again and finished the rest of his beer.

Casey was still skeptical. "One more question. Why do you feel that telling me this is dangerous?"

Carl pushed his glasses up on his nose and leaned even closer, his voice lowered to a whisper. "Because these nuts would try to kill me if they found out."

Chapter 19

"This guy can be a charmer when he wants to be," Stone said as he pulled a chair up to Casey's desk and sat down. "But he's a real snake.

"Actually, 'chameleon' would be a more appropriate reptile to describe him. He can change colors in the middle of a sentence. He's awful, a lot like Parker in that regard except he is openly aggressive about it, not slippery like Parker. He's confrontational. And he knows the answer to any question you can come up with; If he doesn't really know it, he'll make something up. I've never seen anything like it–frequently wrong but never in doubt. A hip shooter and his hip shots cause problems all the time."

"I've heard of this guy," Casey said. "Jake's pub is popular with some of the lawyers from Temeritus and I've heard them talking about him. I understand they call him 'Houdini' because he's so good at escaping from the traps he gets himself into."

"Yeah, isn't that great?" Stone laughed. "I don't know how he gets away with it. But it really isn't funny. He will literally do anything he thinks Philpott wants. And that's true on personnel matters as well as legal matters. If he thinks a particular lawyer has fallen out of grace with Philpott, he will go out of his way to screw the guy, even if it's a longtime friend. But then he can turn around later on and reverse himself if he thinks that Philpott has changed. And when he changes his mind on something, it's as though he has always felt that way and what he did or said yesterday is irrelevant. He is reviled by everyone in his organization and by almost all of his peers. But they seem to love him at the top."

"Sounds charming," Casey said. "When do I get to meet him?"

"Right now," Stone said rising from his chair. "I'll tell you more about him on the way down to his office."

As they walked down to the thirty-eighth floor, Stone told Casey that Hoare had been general counsel for ten years. He had been a disciple of J. Wardman Buffington and even though many of the things which were hailed as works of genius at the time had turned out in the harsh light of hindsight to have been colossal blunders, Hoare still clung to the traits and characteristics that he had so admired in Buffington. He fancied himself to be another Buffington—not just a lawyer but a leading industry expert who would someday take his rightful place as the CEO of the company. And he tried to emulate Buffington—he was bold, decisive, no work by an associate was good enough and no decision went unchallenged by his razor wit. He practiced Buffington's brand of management by fear, never being satisfied with results that always "could have been better" and always questioning the opinions and recommendations of his managers, not knowing that although this could work wonders in the short term, it caused long-term devastation to the morale and productivity of the organization. But somehow top management couldn't see through him and he remained the darling of the Board. "Simply amazing," Stone concluded.

Casey and Stone entered Hoare's office, not unlike Pennrose Parker's in size and furnishings—a couch against the wall inside the door, a round table with four armless straight-backed chairs around it, and a long cabinet that extended almost all the way down the other wall. The main feature of the room was the large wooden desk, different than any Casey had ever seen—it was two feet taller than a regular desk, and it dominated the room the way that the Texas Commerce Tower dominates the Houston skyline, towering above everything. And standing behind this fortress of a desk was H. Harold Hoare, equally towering and imposing. This intimidating scene was made even more so by a large portrait hanging behind the desk which showed in stark black and white the stern visage of General George S. Patton, Jr., in full battle dress–helmet, ivory-handled pistols and all–gazing down upon the room.

Somehow, Stone had failed to mention the one feature about Hoare that was unique among Temeritus employees: He had a stand-up desk and conducted almost all of his business with subordinates while standing behind it. No one knew for sure why he did this, but there were several theories–that he had a bad back, that he had served with an officer in the Coast Guard who used this as a technique of intimidation. No one knew for sure. But one thing was certain–it was intimidating. A person summoned to meet with Harold Hoare for the first time did not soon forget the experience.

Hoare came out from behind the desk and greeted them with a nervous smile. He was not as tall as he had seemed standing behind his elevated desk; he was, in fact, quite short for a Temeritus officer. He was completely bald with only a hint of eyebrows, and his complexion was a pasty white. "Casey, it's nice to meet you. I've heard so much about you," he said, shaking her hand with both of his. Strange, Casey thought, that such an important man would have such soft and wimpy-feeling hands. They are as soft as a baby's and as cool as the room.

They sat at the round table and while Hoare's secretary was serving coffee and sodas, Casey looked around the office. Casey had long been a student of the little things that people did to personalize their offices. Some offices, like Wilfurd Timmons', were filled with family and other personal items that could tell an observer much about the occupant of the office, while others, like Proctor Philpott's, were as barren of personal intelligence as an unoccupied hotel room. Hoare's was closer to Philpott's, but there were a few telling things. A plaque with a quote from Wilfurd Timmons was displayed on the wall. And on the long cabinet displayed in matching chrome frames, were an old *Time* magazine cover featuring J. Wardman Buffington and a glossy black-and-white portrait of Proctor Philpott. But other than these items of homage to senior management past and present, the portrait of Patton, and, of course, the stand-up desk, there was nothing to differentiate this office from one that was waiting to be occupied. There were no family or personal items anywhere in the office. The office had all the warmth of a dentist's waiting room.

A final thing that Casey noticed about Hoare was his hands. The hands that had seemed so unnaturally soft and cool were as white and flawless as if they had been carved from Ivory soap. They were the palest hands she had ever seen with neither hair nor scars nor wrinkles nor any other markings on them to give them the character that most men's hands have developed over the years. And they were small, out of proportion to the rest of his body as if they had been put on in haste several sizes too small on an assembly line with no quality control. The fingers were the most unusual features of these unusual hands–cone-like, fat and porky at the knuckle, tapering to normal at the large joint and tapering further to a small point at the tip, each tip accentuated by a tiny fingernail, clipped, buffed and coated with clear polish. Casey could hardly keep her eyes off of them as they caressed his icy glass of sugar-free Sprite.

"Proctor has told me all about you, Casey, and has instructed me to help in any way I can. As you will come to learn, Proctor is so good at what he does, he's just a treasure–a virtual treasure–to this company, and if he says that you are the person for the job, that's all I need to know. What can we do to help?"

"Tell me about your organization, Mr. Hoare."

"Well, it's one of the best. We spend less money on outside counsel fees than any of our major competitors by far. And that means less overhead and more to the bottom line." Hoare smiled with the pride of a gushing parent.

"Can you show me a chart of the department?"

"Not at the moment. You see, we are going through a reorganization—oh, excuse me—a re-engineering, er, redesigning of the Law Department. So I can't show you exactly how it's going to look. But it doesn't make much difference because everyone here works for me and I have cut down all of the bureaucratic infrastructure that gets in the way of effective delivery of our services to the client. We have less infrastructure than any other corporate law department and, if you really want to know the truth, less than any other part of the company as well.

"I like to think of the Law Department as a fraternity. And I am the chapter president. That's how we keep everything crisp." With the word "crisp" he held up his right hand and pinched his chubby index finger and thumb together, as if he were squeezing a bug. "Yes, crisp." He pinched the air again. "That's the word that Mr. Buffington liked so much and I think it's a great one, too. It describes so well the effect I achieve through my streamlined approach.

"And it is streamlined. Why, I don't even have a general manager here. Don't need one. The only place in the company that doesn't have one. Keep down those costs. That's what I say, Casey. And, besides, general managers just aren't all that important. I don't pay much attention to them myself. I mean, don't get me wrong, some of them will become vice presidents, so you do need to be careful. But I just don't want one around here."

"Will there be a lawyer assigned to this issue that I can call on if I have a legal question?" Casey asked.

"Oh, no," Hoare replied. "This issue has been proprietaryised and no one works on those but me. If you have a question, call me. I handle all the really important issues. That's the way Proctor wants it."

Hoare fondled his glass in awkward silence for a brief moment and then said, "I understand you'll be working mainly with Pennrose and his organization, so I don't really know what we can do to help. If you really want to know the truth, this boycott is really not a legal matter. Of course, we are ready to jump if needed with a request for a restraining order or something like that if the crazies get out of hand. But so far nothing like that has happened, and we're trying to concentrate on those things which will help on the bottom line." Casey wondered just exactly what those things might be.

"And, as you may know, it has not been a good time for the company. So we're always looking for better ways to do more with less. And for the animal rights nuts to come after us at this point in time is just ridiculous. So I sure hope you're able to help us put an end to this stuff, Casey. And if there is anything we can do to help, just let me know," he said, rising from his chair and heading towards the door. This interview is over, Casey thought, as she and Stone also got up to leave.

As she reached Hoare's door she turned to him and said, "By the way, I think you know a good friend of mine, Jake Gilligan, used to be with F & W. He tried some cases for Temeritus."

"Jake Gilligan?" His eyes jerked into sharp focus, a look of apprehension on his face. "Sure, I know Jake. We worked on lots of things together. He was a hell of a fine lawyer. I heard he had dropped out of practice. What's he doing these days?"

"He has a pub over in the Village where he brews and sells beer."

"A pub!" Hoare looked at Casey as if she had just told him that Jake had become a nudist and took a daily romp through the central business district in the buff. He laughed. "Why is he doing that?"

"I guess he thinks selling beer is better than selling himself, Mr. Hoare," Casey said.

Casey and Stone walked out and Hoare closed the door behind them. Stone looked at Casey and they both burst into laughter. "Yeah, that was something, all right," Casey said as they walked away from the suite.

Chapter 20

Butera's: an upscale delicatessen that features fancy salads, sandwiches, trendy pasta dishes, wine by the glass and imported beer.
Cafeteria style, with tables inside and outside on the sidewalk. An
unrushed place where people linger over their meals and enjoy an
extra glass of wine or cup of coffee. Many of its patrons sit alone por-
ing over a recent purchase from the gigantic bookstore that fills the
old Alabama Theater a few doors away. A soothing place filled with
the buzz of pleasant conversation and polite laughter.

M sat at an outdoor table. She had stopped at the bookstore
for a half an hour of literary grazing and had emerged with a copy of
the Penguin edition of Aristotle's *Ethics*, why she wasn't sure. She was
thumbing through it when L appeared at the table.

"A gift for your friends at Temeritus?" L asked, as he eased
into the chair beside M.

"They could sure use it," she laughed. They chatted for a few
moments and then went through the line selecting their salads and
drinks. "Now," she said when they returned to their table, "tell me
everything."

And he did, starting with the brilliance of his disguise and
ending with his report to her over the phone. "So it all boils down to
this," he concluded, "they have a fortress out there where they are
pulling off one of the great deceptions of our time. They tell the public all of the humane things they are doing all the while engaging in

vivisection in the secret lab in the basement."

M pondered this for a few moments. "I think it's time for the raid," she said. "For something as sensitive as this is, they really don't have as much security as you would expect. I think we can breach it and find out for sure what's inside. If it's what the security guard told you, there are innocent animals in there and we should get them out. Besides, what a fabulous thing it would be to catch Temeritus in a lie." They discussed this at length–the pros, the cons, the risks and benefits.

"I'll call a meeting of the cell for Sunday," M said. "At the statue of Sam Houston in Hermann Park. Three o'clock. We'll have a picnic." She smiled and paused for a moment, "Won't it be nice to finally get on with it." He agreed, and they both got up from the table to leave. "Now," she said in closing, "I'd better get home and read my Aristotle."

Chapter 21

By 10:30 Saturday morning Casey was up and in the kitchen fixing pancakes. She cooked two stacks of four. These she augmented with country sausage, a pot of coffee and a glass of milk and sat down to eat. As she ate, she reviewed the events of the week in her mind. It had been quite a week, one surprising thing after another. Surprising because, in spite of all she had heard about Temeritus being in trouble, she had still been under the impression, built over time, that it was one of the great corporations in the country. It had been cited and awarded and feted so often and for so long that inertia alone had kept it on top in the minds of the public—at least of the public that followed such things, a much smaller public than the senior management at Temeritus would believe.

The most surprising thing was the isolation of the executive suite. If these people were aware of the mood on the lower floors, it was not apparent. Casey had spent most of Thursday and Friday on the floors near Liz Stokes' office talking to people and overhearing the conversations around her. What she found was a general mood of gloom and desperation, a cynicism similar to that exhibited by Stone but more desperate because those expressing it did not have the financial safety net that Stone's time and position in the company provided him.

Everywhere she went outside the executive cloister she found the same thing—the talk of rumored staff cuts, the feeling that no one in top management really cared or understood, the disgust over the hypocrisy of the senior management spending thousands of dollars and hours trumpeting the merits of Quality Improvement but not practicing it themselves. But most of all, the feeling of betrayal–the feeling that in tough times the people who were expected to provide leadership were in fact living in splendid isolation and not honoring the basic unwritten but very clearly understood contract of employment: If you come to work here and do a good job, we'll take care of you; you may not always get what you think you deserve, you may not always have the position you think you want, but you will always have a job and you will be treated fairly. It was obvious to Casey that the troops at Temeritus felt that the contract had been breached.

As to the "secret project" for Proctor Philpott, Casey had been able to discern that the amount of progress was so minimal that it didn't really exist. Discussions with a number of the women and a perusal of the published materials about the company showed that almost all of the company's women were in low-level positions traditionally held by women–secretaries and clerks. In the so-called "professional" jobs, women appeared mainly at the bottom of the salary grade levels with very few in managerial or even supervisory positions.

In all of the Senior Select there was but one woman–Abigail Siefer who, although she carried the impressive title of Senior Vice President, International Relations, was widely known to be merely a figurehead, a high-level gofer for the senior management in its dealings with the parent company. And despite her lofty title it was widely believed that she was the lowest paid officer in the company.

The company had no special policies or practices that would put it into a separate league as far as attracting or retaining exceptional women was concerned; and when Casey had asked Proctor Philpott for copies of the corporate strategy for recruiting and advancing women, he had responded with hostility. "Goddamn it, Casey. That's why I hired you. So I wouldn't have to worry about this crap!" His response had been even more vigorous when she repeated what she'd heard about Gail Siefer being the lowest paid officer in the company. "That's what's wrong around here. People worry about the wrong things and not about how they can help the company. Siefer may be the lowest paid officer in the company, but did anyone tell you that she started out here as an assistant librarian? Yeah, everybody forgets about that. And I'm telling you, for a librarian she's doing great."

Casey's first visit to the Executive Dining Facility, generally known as the "lunch room," was a vivid example of how far out of touch the management seemed to be. Stone, in his usual cynical way, had briefed her prior to her first visit. "This is the best show in town, Casey," he had told her. "Careers are made and destroyed here. You'll never see such a collection of wishy-washy, weak-kneed wimps in your life. There are two long tables. Timmons sits at one and Philpott sits at the other and they hold court. Attendance isn't mandatory, but it's strongly encouraged unless there is a compelling reason to be elsewhere. For most of the people there, it's an hour or so of sheer terror. It's like a gangster movie where all the mobsters sit around and hope they are responding right to the Godfather—got to be careful; it's as bad to not laugh when you should as it is to laugh when you shouldn't. But the worst thing is when someone gets a question from Philpott that causes him to seem not up-to-date on something. Then the sharks circle and everyone is free to join in the feeding frenzy. It's amazing, as you'll see."

And see she did. The first thing she noticed was the elegance of the room—silver settings, crystal and china. In between the main reception area and the dining tables was a large buffet area—a round table filled with cold shrimp, crab claws, oysters on the half shell and other delicacies. Off to the side was the wine table that Stone had warned her about—it was there only for decoration; drinking any of the wine would be frowned upon; not prohibited, he pointed out, because Temeritus management did not have to comply with the rules they imposed on everyone else. So the Temeritus Alcohol Policy did not apply in the lunch room any more than it applied to the executives when they were dining anywhere else. In fact, the hands-off policy regarding the daily wine display had preceded the TAP by several years. No one knew why the wine was still presented each day. But there it was—chardonnay opened and chilled in a silver ice bucket, cabernet sauvignon opened and breathing next to the bucket, appropriately shaped glasses at the ready—calling to the innocent passerby to be sipped and savored.

The highlight of the lunch was meeting Dewey Shivers, Senior Vice President of Internal Affairs. He had been in the lunch room when she and Stone got there, fussing and fidgeting and making sure that everything was in order for the lunch. Stone had told her they would find him there. "He's the advance man at anything Timmons or Philpott might attend. So he goes every day and farts around making sure that all the doilies are lined up and that the silver is polished and all of that. It's a joke. I think he counts the blueberries in the executive muffins each morning. The guy's supposed to be in charge of personnel and he runs around like a scared rat worrying about crap like the lunch room. My secretary calls him 'the frightened fawn.'"

He was short, much shorter than most of the Temeritus executives, and hunched over at the shoulders—even more than Wilfurd Timmons. His dark hair was balding in an irregular pattern that gave him a mangy look and the hair that remained was slicked straight back on the sides and the top. He wore large round eyeglasses with black metal frames held together with a gold band which fitted tightly across the bridge of his nose. Casey couldn't tell whether it was his natural expression or whether it was the magnification from the glasses, but his eyes were bugged-out as if he had just been startled.

His face was long and narrow and seemed at first glance to be out of proportion to the rest of his rotund little body. The man's body was in the shape of a triangle–starting with the pointy top of his head and widening as it went down. The face itself was narrow, but it rested upon one of the most spectacular double chins that Casey had ever seen. This glob of flab appeared to melt downward into a pair of scrawny shoulders almost devoid of muscle and then down further into a sagging belly. The triangle effect was completed by a puffy rear end perched atop flabby and bulging thighs.

Dewey had been checking the placement of the hors d'oeuvres forks next to the oysters when Casey and Stone walked into the lunch room. He looked up nervously thinking that someone important had come to lunch early, before he had finished checking the setup. He appeared to be relieved to learn that it was not, and after muttering a few words of greeting, he excused himself. "I still have an awful lot to do, you know," he said as he scurried over to the wine display to check on the ice bucket.

This image of Dewey Shivers flitting about like a bee in frantic pollination, and everything else about the day, vanished at the sound of the phone ringing–Jake calling to ask about plans for the banquet. Proctor Philpott had invited Casey and her guest to attend the annual J. Wardman Buffington Golden Circle of Quality Awards Dinner. She had learned during the week that while the dinner was considered by upper management to be a thing of singular importance, it was generally regarded by the rank and file as a matter of high hilarity. Liz Stokes had expressed it best. "All of these self-important stuffed shirts get together and tell each other how wonderful they are to have put the great quality process in place. Fact is, that they haven't got a clue as to what the process is all about and wouldn't recognize it if they stepped in it. It's Alice in Wonderland with the Prince of Proctology playing both the Queen and the Mad Hatter. Most people call it the Golden Circle Jerk. You'll love it."

Casey spent the rest of the day doing chores and tending to all of the little things that needed her attention. At seven o'clock, she went to The Horse for Jake. As much as she liked Jake's truck, she refused to go to a fancy place–defined by her as any place with valet parking–in a pickup truck.

She parked on Morningside and went into The Horse. Jake was pretending to be a customer tonight, sitting at a table talking to one of the regulars. He rose when he saw Casey come in and gave her his usual big hug and kiss. "Hiya, Case. Wow, do you ever look sharp!" And she did. She had on a strapless turquoise sequined dress by Victor Costa, with matching heels. The dress fit her to perfection and there was a slit on one side that went almost to her thigh. Fabulous.

Casey, however, was not the only elegant person at The Horse. Jake cut a splendid figure himself. Christ, he looks good in a tux, Casey thought. I can only imagine how fabulous he must have looked in his dress blues.

Jake introduced her to the man he was seated with and they each had a pint of "Golden Dustman." Then, amid applause from Gabe and the small group of regulars, they left for the banquet.

Chapter 22

By the end of the weekend Jerry Turner was in love, or at least he thought he was. Nancy Wade laughed when she thought how easy it had been. Her aggressive approach in the restaurant had worked. And when she got him back to her apartment and showed him some of her special tricks, he fell completely under her spell. And each day since—over a week—they had been together.

For months Nancy had watched M and her super-cautious approach to Temeritus. All the planning and calls for patience. It was all hot air and cold feet. Things like the kitchen raid. Big deal. We liberated some dead animals. A lot of good that will do. All something like that accomplishes is to make our enemies mad and confirm what they already suspect—that we're a bunch of loonies. Well, that's about to change. She looked over to where Jerry was sleeping off another round of sex. Yeah, she thought, and this big lunk is going to be a key player.

Jerry stirred. He rolled over and looked at Nancy propped up in bed reading a book. "Argh," he growled, "I think you're trying to kill me, Nancy. I won't be able to walk for days."

"Nah, you'll get over it, just like you have before. It's amazing the recuperative powers of that little pecker of yours. It just bounds back to life. What a trooper." She laughed and reached under the covers to touch him.

"Oh, no you don't," he said bounding out of bed. "I've got to get out of here and go to work." As he had ever since they had met, Jerry had stopped by Nancy's for a nooner—"funch" they called it. But unlike the first day, he now made it back to work, even if his lunchtime had expanded well beyond the allotted forty-five minutes.

Nancy sat on the side of the bed and watched him dress. "What do you say to some Mexican food tonight?" she asked. "There's some stuff about the cell I think we should talk about. Have you been to Paradisio?" He hadn't. "Great. Then I'll meet you there at 7:00. On Fairview, a couple of blocks east of Montrose."

"Sounds good to me," he said. He finished dressing, gave Nancy a quick kiss and left for work. Funny, he thought, that's the first time she's mentioned the cell. Wonder what she has in mind?

Chapter 23

"This is the first time I've seen these people up close," Jake said as Casey pulled up to the site of the J. Wardman Buffington Dinner. Standing behind a police line fifteen growling and snarling protesters were waving signs decrying Temeritus' animal testing. Jake hadn't seen anything like it since the Vietnam War protests of the late '60s, and the sight of this group of unhappy people chanting their contrived slogans took him back to San Francisco in 1967 and a young Marine buck sergeant stepping off an airplane to be greeted by a similar group screaming insults at him. For an instant Jake felt the urge to dash into the group and unleash thirty years of pent-up hostility. Casey reached across the seat and touched his leg. "Easy, Baby. Easy." She gave his thigh a pat and a squeeze. Jake drew in a long breath, looked at Casey and smiled the slightest smile, as if to reassure her that he was under control. "Right," he said and opened the door to get out.

Jake and Casey walked past the small group of protesters, trying without success to look as if nothing out of the ordinary was going on. Hard to do. "ANIMAL KILLERS!" –"TORTURERS!" – "NAZIS!" –screams of hatred. These are not nice folks, Casey thought as they walked into the hotel. She had seen the protesters outside Temeritus Tower each day during her short stay with the company, but had not seen them up close before. The ones downtown were more peaceful–merely marching back and forth displaying signs and handing out their literature. This group was scary and the uneasiness she felt followed her into the hotel. Shake it off, she told herself, nobody said this was going to be fun.

The ballroom was magnificent–a sea of starched linens with silver and crystal glistening. The centerpiece of each table was a replica of the J. Wardman Buffington Golden Circle of Quality Award, a small lucite pyramid with a gold-colored ring attached to its top. Towering over this assemblage of opulence was the elevated head table from which Proctor Philpott would orchestrate the evening's activities.

Casey also noticed the red and gold balloons held aloft by netting, awaiting their release at the ceremony's conclusion. Casey knew all about these balloons having heard earlier in the week about the preparation that went into this dinner. Scores of people were taken off their regular jobs to work on it, many having been placed on "balloon duty." When Casey asked about this, she was told that as a cost-saving measure Dewey Shivers decided to have the balloons inflated "in-house."

A detailed schedule had been prepared under which each department in the Internal Affairs and Issues & External Affairs organizations would send "volunteers" to the balloon room to do their share. Casey had been assured that the logistics of filling, transporting, and installing thousands of balloons was no simple matter. And there they were–pendulous sags high above the readied banquet tables, probably unnoticed by all, except those who were aware of the effort that went into placing them there, awaiting their call to action by the beckoning tug of the release string.

Casey and Jake wound their way to their assigned table, introduced themselves to the people already there and sat down to await the start of the evening. The man next to Jake turned to him. "Jake, I'm with Monarch Minerals. Who are you with?"

"I'm with Casey," Jake said, starting the game he loved to play.

"Casey? I'm afraid I'm not familiar with them. What do they do?" At least this guy is honest, Jake thought. Sometimes people would fake it–make believe they knew that Casey was the name of an organization or an acronym for a foundation of some sort.

"They don't do anything. Casey is the beautiful woman on the other side of the table. She's my special friend and I'm with her."

"Oh." The look of confusion, momentary disorientation. "I see. Well, what do you do?"

"I run a brew pub down in the Village. Maybe you've heard of it–One For Your Horse. On Morningside."

"Oh." Again, the look of confusion, but this time accompanied by an expression of "how the hell am I going to get out of this?" And the conversation wandered off in the same manner these things usually did, with the man acting like he was talking to someone who had suffered some deep personal tragedy and needed to be treated with extra care and sensitivity. Since he left the nine-to-five world of the dark pinstriped suit, Jake found that most of those who dwelled there had no notion of another world nearby, one that, without demanding conformity and regimentation, offered unfettered opportunity for personal challenge and growth. Sometimes he found a dinner partner who was genuinely interested in what he was doing but it was rare, and Jake knew from the uneasy demeanor of Mr. Monarch Minerals that tonight was not one of those times.

Philpott entered the room like a politician, smiling and waving, going from table to table greeting everyone and welcoming them to the event. He went to the podium where he repeated his greetings over the sound system, reminding them what the award was all about. He invited them to enjoy their dinner and to be prepared for a wonderful evening of tribute to the honorees. Salads were served, and everyone began to eat and visit.

Jake had been to many banquets over the years but had never enjoyed them until he started to attend them as an observer–a "noncombatant," he called it. He was here merely as Casey's guest with no clients to impress or business to transact. It made a big difference. The best thing about these events now was watching Casey in action. It was always a treat to see how tablemates not familiar with Casey would change as the evening passed.

Most people—and surprisingly, women as well as men—formed an immediate impression of Casey: Someone so beautiful could not be both intelligent and personable. They were on guard—is this woman a dummy, successful because of her good looks, or is she a militant bra-burning overachiever? No one ever thinks this way about a good-looking man. The only way that guy ever got where he did is because he has such a great set of buns! So it was fun for Jake to sit across the table and watch Casey shatter stereotypes one more time. He could see it working again tonight. The faces of those around her began to mellow and take on a relaxed tone—more open, warmer. Their humanity would blossom, not unlike time-lapse photography of a flower blooming.

Another common occurrence was the assumption that Casey was with Jake; he was the man and the man is always the head of the delegation, so to speak. When they learned otherwise he would be immediately dismissed as unimportant and could spend the rest of the evening observing. Occasionally he would see someone from the firm or someone else from his earlier life, but they would avoid him and he could practice his observations in peace.

The main course was served—a "surf and turf" atrocity that featured a fist of beef with a rubbery curl of frozen lobster tail. Awful. Yet the dinner proceeded.

By the time the formal part of the evening had begun, Casey had charmed all of her neighbors and the entire table was having a much better time than was usually the case at these functions. Then Proctor Philpott returned to the lectern and the table talk ceased.

There were speeches and tributes and a video about the recipient of this year's award, all choreographed to perfection. The only thing remaining was the finale, the much-prepared-for balloon drop. The band was to strike up a rousing version of John Philip Sousa's "The Thunderer" and after a few bars, Proctor Philpott would pull the release string, covering the crowd with the colors of Temeritus, Inc., cascading from on high. A glorious ending to a glorious evening.

But somehow the release string for the balloons had become entangled with the automatic sprinkler system's manual release lever. Several bars into "The Thunderer," triggered by Proctor Philpott's tug on the string, those assembled to honor the recipients of the highest quality award Temeritus could bestow were cascaded, not with balloons bearing the Temeritus colors but rather with a cold shower of the primary ingredient of most of Temeritus' products. Pandemonium ensued.

No one in the room was spared. The torrent was as instantaneous and thorough as a Texas thundershower. The attendees rose as one and scampered out of the ballroom in near-panic. Soaked, Jake and Casey dashed out through the nearest exit into the anteroom, which was filled with the similarly soaked. Hairdos fallen, clothing sodden, moods ranging from hilarity to ire. Everyone was shouting and looking down upon their wet clothing in disbelief.

Back in the ballroom, a small band of Temeritus functionaries, under the panicked leadership of Dewey Shivers, leaped into action trying to find someone who could turn off the sprinkler. By the time this had been accomplished, the ballroom was vacant except for Proctor Philpott and some of the Temeritus people who had not been in the ballroom and were as dry as they had been when they arrived. Philpott stood at the lectern in a pool of water, his Italian silk tuxedo reduced to a stinking rag, his expertly coiffed hair twisting in strands down his face, his usual demeanor of studied arrogance substantially diminished. It's hard to be imperial in a wet tux.

A frenzied Dewey Shivers appeared with the hotel's general

manager in tow, a small man who looked as if he had just had a bucket of ice chips packed into his shorts. "Mr. Philpott, Mr. Philpott. What can I say? I'm so sorry. I don't know what happened." Proctor Philpott's rage smoldered on his face. "You son of a bitch, you'll be hearing from our lawyers on this one, you can be assured of that." He stalked out of the room, leaving behind him the shambles of what had been the Annual J. Wardman Buffington Golden Circle of Quality Awards Dinner.

Casey and Jake dried off as much as possible. And headed home. "This is some quality company you've gotten yourself involved with, Case," Jake laughed as they drove through the darkened streets.

Chapter 24

People were talking about the banquet fiasco when Casey got to work Monday morning. The irony of the incident was not lost on the men and women of Temeritus, all victims of Proctor Philpott's application of the Golden Circle of Quality Program. The incident had already been given a name–The Golden Shower–and it was the topic of much gleeful discussion.

Almost everyone at Temeritus had a favorite Golden Circle story illustrating the woeful misunderstanding of Total Quality Management on the part of Proctor Philpott and his lackeys. Everyone in the company received formal training–even those whose departments were being eliminated by "downsizing." The members of one such department received their framed Golden Circle initiation certificates the week before their departures. Another favorite was the Fiftieth-Year Anniversary T-shirt–FIFTY YEARS OF AMERICAN QUALITY emblazoned on thousands of shirts, all of which had been manufactured in Korea.

There were so many false starts and reversals and second guessings that the real motto of the Total Quality Management program–"Do it right the first time"–had gone through several mutations in the minds of the troops. First it was "Do it right the second time," but the fumbling and second-guessing of senior management resulted in the far more accurate–"Do it right the next time," thus providing the flexibility needed by the Senior Select.

At one point, a statement of "Temeritus Guiding Principles" had been issued. Fourth on the list was "dedication to the application of Total Quality Management." This led many to the sarcastic boast—"At Temeritus, quality is job four."

And so it was with great amusement that the many victims of Philpott's painful applications of Total Quality Management learned of yet another application—the literal hosing of a roomful of customers and fellow employees. Instead of welcoming them to the Golden Circle of Quality, Philpott had doused them in its golden shower. Wonderful.

This amusement did not, however, find its way to the Executive Dining Facility where the banquet was not even mentioned.

By Wednesday, Casey had gotten a better feel for the mood at Temeritus. It was worse than she had suspected. People were demoralized. The years since the big layoffs had been bad ones. The staff had been downsized, but not the workload. And since all Senior Select remained intact, so too had their insatiable appetite for the mindless detail they felt necessary to fully prepare for the continuous cycle of pre-meetings, meetings and debriefings that clogged the decision-making process. People were weary.

Now morale was further burdened by rumors of yet another round of staff cuts. Although there was nothing to support this, the continuing poor performance of the company had caused renewed concern that Temeritus management would again feel the need to cut overhead in the only way that it knew how—by getting rid of people below the senior management level.

Aggravating this situation was the unconcerned attitude of senior management, most of whom sneered at any thought that people might be over-worked. Proctor Philpott told Casey that statistics showed the average Temeritus employee was paid substantially more than the average worker. He seemed offended that people were not more appreciative.

Harold Hoare was even more callous. He told Casey that the last round of layoffs were "mere prunerizing," simply getting rid of deadwood in the ranks. "Besides," he told her, "most of these people don't really have enough to do anyway. They waste time and effort on things that just aren't important. So when we give them more than they think they can do, it forces them to be more selective in how they allocate their time. It's good for the health of the organization."

Philpott's blindness to reality became more obvious to Casey when, in one of his usual lunch room monologues, he detailed his decision to participate in a management magazine interview for an article on "The Absolute Best Companies in the USA to Work For." He was sure that Temeritus would be chosen as one of these companies, but he wanted to stress the importance of properly screening the interviewees—only those with "the proper Golden Circle attitude" were to be included in the survey. "Even though we have done a splendid job in removing our malcontents there may still be a few left, and it's up to you to ensure none of them participate in this study." He paused a moment and concluded, "You know, this really is a great place to work, if you just talk to the right people."

All present at the table agreed that any list of great employers that did not include Temeritus would hardly be legitimate. The hypothetical "visitor from Mars" would have thought Temeritus to be the model employer of the Quality Era. Casey wondered if the others in the room really were unaware of the mood in the company or were merely protecting their rears by admiring yet another article of clothing from their Emperor's expanding wardrobe. Casey had been told that kissing ass at Temeritus was an acquired taste; she was beginning to appreciate the wisdom of that remark.

After lunch Parallel Parker had called and asked Casey to come to his office. Parker sat behind his desk as perfectly dressed as ever, looking as though he could participate in a photo session for a magazine article entitled "Executive Fashion on the Cutting Edge." He was magnificent—a double-breasted wool suit in classic gray plaid, wide black-and-silver rep tie, white pointed collar shirt and white silk pocket square. This guy was definitely a book that you were tempted to judge by its cover. The discussion that followed, however, verified the opinion of everyone she talked to outside of the Senior Select—this book was all blank pages.

"Say, Casey, I'm beginning to feel some pressures on your project, and I'd like to sort of have you tell me what you think you plan to recommend to Proctor." Casey gave him a summary of the things she was considering to counter the rising tide of adverse press coverage.

"Yeah, that's what I was afraid of. I mean, you may have to kinda soften that a bit because I don't think that's what Proctor wanted us to be doing, you know, being so, like, proactive."

"I don't agree, Penn. In fact, I'm sure it's exactly what Proctor wants."

"What makes you think that?"

"Well, for one thing, that's what he said."

"Oh, sure, that may be what he said." He paused and called up his most earnest face. "But I assure you, that is not what he wants . . . And I see him all the time." Parker leaned forward and placed his open palms flat on the desk. His eyes squinted. "And I know what he wants."

"Did you ask him what he wants?" Casey said. Parker, whose responses up to this point had been quite confident, was speechless. His eyes bulged and he stared at Casey in disbelief, as if she had just asked if he had inquired into Proctor Philpott's sex habits.

"Ask? Er, um, well, . . . no, of course not. I don't have to. I just know, Casey." He fumbled with his hands and fidgeted in his chair. "And besides, you don't just walk into Proctor's office and ask him to explain what he wants. That's what I get paid to do—to know what he wants."

"But isn't that contrary to the basic notion of Total Quality

Management? Isn't there supposed to be an understanding as to the requirements of this project? And if we don't understand what the requirements are, aren't we bound by the quality principles to ask? I mean, really, Penn, all of this stuff is right out of the Temeritus quality manual."

"Yeah, that's all well and good. And easy for you to say, I might add. But I know what happens to people who do that. Quality may be great for the rest of the company, but up here in the suites it'll get you in a heap of trouble."

"Well, in that case I guess I'll just ask him myself," Casey said.

Parker looked at her as if she had just said she was going to leap out of the window and bring back a double order of crispy tacos. "No. No. You can't do that. I'm telling you, I know what he wants." He raised a fist into the air and brought it down in front of him stopping just before it hit the desk so that it made no noise, a gesture as void of substance as the man himself. Casey almost laughed. "And if you go and ask him, he may change his mind and all of our work will be down the drain."

"What work, Penn? I thought I was supposed to be doing this project."

"Well . . . like . . . sure. But I just sort of had a little work done to, you know, kind of set up the parameters of where I thought you should be. But, yeah, sure. You're doing the study. I just won't be able to be on it with you, if you know what I mean, unless you listen to what I say. But, sure, you want to talk to Proctor, go right ahead."

He extended his left hand and pulled his cuff away from the face of his thin black wristwatch. "Oh, I have to go to a meeting." He jumped to his feet. "But, we can kinda talk about this some more when you get back from your trip to Washington and actually get something put together, OK?" And with that he walked out.

"Yeah," Casey said to herself, sitting in the slight breeze Parker's abrupt exit had created. "Kinda."

Chapter 25

Northern Virginia is beautiful in the autumn, especially after an early cold snap, and Casey's view as the plane began its descent into Washington National was spectacular. From her window seat she could see sparkling in the distance the buildings and monuments that make Washington, D.C., unique among American cities. No skyscrapers here, thanks to a planning commission's amazing foresight which years ago decreed that no buildings were to detract from the grandeur of such things as the Capitol and Washington Monument. From the air the slashing wheel-spoke diagonals of Pierre L'Enfant's two-hundred-year-old design take on a beauty and sense of symmetry lost on those unfortunates who must negotiate them by car, whereupon L'Enfant's dream becomes the motorist's nightmare. It is, nevertheless, a magnificent sight, particularly on a bright fall afternoon.

She was apprehensive. She had not been to Washington for over ten years—not since her husband's funeral. God, what an awful thing that had been. Just about this time of the year and just about as beautiful a day. She tried to put it out of her mind as the plane banked to the right and slowly back to the left, beginning its final approach.

The plane finished its arc and headed straight down the path of the river, its wings now leveled, flaps lowered, losing speed and descending. Just as the plane passed over the Watergate, Casey, now facing away from the city, saw rising into view the beautifully manicured rolling hills of Arlington Cemetery, thousands of headstones in perfect alignment–"the gardens of stone," Nicholas Proffitt had called it. Oh my God, she thought, as it all came pouring back into her memory.

The drums. That was what she noticed the most, the drums. BrrrdaRAP . . . brrrrdaRAP . . . brrrrdaRAP . . . Monotonous, ominous, chilling because you knew down deep in your soul what they meant. Anyone who was within the age of memory on November 22, 1963, knew exactly what those horrible sounds meant–the military funeral of a fallen hero.

Casey had been six. A first grader in Flagstaff. It was just after lunch. Miss Wilcox was called to the principal's office and made a big pitch for the maintenance of decorum in the classroom while she was out. There was the usual cutting up, especially by the boys. But when Miss Wilcox came back everyone knew something awful had happened. She was crying, sobbing so hard she could barely talk. "Oh, boys and girls, it's so terrible. President Kennedy has been shot and killed in Dallas. What are we going to do!" And then everyone began to cry and hug each other and wonder, as Miss Wilcox had–what are we going to do!

There followed a weekend of national agony and mourning never seen before or since as the nation watched on TV. There was Jackie, so beautiful and tragic; and Caroline, so little and pretty; and John-John, returning the salutes of the military. Caroline was not even as old as Casey at the time and Casey kept thinking how terrible it would be to have her own daddy shot and killed. And throughout it all, the drums–brrrrdaRAP . . . brrrrdaRAP . . . brrrrdaRAP. . . And then they took the flag that had been draped over the casket and folded it and gave it to Jackie . . .

Now here was Casey, many years later, on a cold and sunny day–just about the same kind of day–and there were the drums and she was standing at an open grave, and strong young military men in dress uniforms were folding a flag and handing it to her. Oh my God, this can't be happening to me. Please tell me it's not happening!

"Are you all right?" the flight attendant asked, bending over Casey and touching her gently on the shoulder. "Yes . . . yes, I'm fine, thank you." The sight of the cemetery had shaken her, and she had not noticed the landing.

She exited the empty plane and looked for the person who was to meet her. Since she was traveling alone her name would be on whatever sign was prepared to catch her attention. She knew from experience that this would not be the case if she were traveling with a man–for no matter how much she might outrank a male traveling companion, his name always appeared on the sign.

Casey saw a young man holding a sign that said "MS. O'ROURKE-TEMERITUS, INC." Scottie Pettigrew from the Washington Office was young–twenty-four years old, one year with Temeritus, coming there from Capitol Hill, where he had been an issues staffer to a one-term Congressman from the Midwest. In the wake of his boss's unsuccessful re-election campaign, he parlayed his experience into a position as a Junior Legislative Representative at Temeritus. And there he stood, as earnest and fresh-scrubbed as when he emerged from the Midwest upon his graduation from college.

"I'm Casey O'Rourke," she said, extending her hand to the young man. "You must be Scottie Pettigrew."

"Yes, Ma'am, Ms. O'Rourke . . . at your service." He smiled a weak and nervous smile. "Welcome to Washington." Ma'am, she thought. Jesus! This guy makes me feel even older than I thought he would.

"Hi, Scottie. It's nice to meet you. And, please, call me Casey."

They chatted as they walked to the baggage claim area. One thing Casey did not do was travel light. She hated the hassle of squeezing a carry-on bag into the ever-decreasing overhead storage areas, and she hated to be away from home without the things that made being at home so pleasant. She needed her stuff–like her own coffee maker and special blend coffees, her CD player and CDs, and a wide variety of reading. And, of course, anywhere Casey went, she required a large wardrobe of both business and casual clothing. Unless it was a one-day trip, Casey traveled heavy. So they headed for the baggage claim to retrieve Casey's two-piece set of Hartmann Tweeds, for which her attaché was the perfect complement.

Casey enjoyed the ride into the District. Up George Washington Parkway and across Memorial Bridge and the Potomac River, made even more serene this day by the presence of a crew from Georgetown University sculling on the river—pull, glide, pull, glide—rhythmic and hypnotic. And finally, around the Lincoln Memorial and into this most continental of U.S. cities.

"Mr. Weakly said to express his regret at not being able to meet you at the airport. But he'll be able to meet with you tomorrow. He also asked me to take you to dinner, if you don't have any plans."

"Thanks, Scottie, but I have plans. I'm having dinner with an old college friend of mine. You may know her, Theresa Moorehead. She works for Senator English from Arizona."

"Terry Moorehead!" Scottie seemed surprised. "Of course, everybody knows her. She's the Senator's AA, one of the most powerful staffers on the Hill. Wow, I can't believe you're having dinner with her tonight. That's great."

Jake had told her to be wary—everyone who works in Washington is always surprised to learn that someone from outside the Beltway, especially someone with no Hill experience, has a contact of importance in the government. "It's really funny," Jake had told her. "I'd go to D.C. for a client, and when the people in the client's Washington office found out I was a close friend of some senator or one of the many other people in government that I'd known in the Marines, they'd react as if I'd just told them I'd been selected for the next moon shot. Even worse really, because my selection screwed them out of their rightful seat on the spacecraft." Casey laughed to herself at the accuracy of Jake's words.

Ten minutes later they pulled into the driveway of the Hay-Adams Hotel where Scottie restated his offer of whatever assistance he might provide. She assured him she was fine and said she would see him at the office the next day.

Chapter 26

At 8:30 the next morning, Casey entered the nondescript building that housed the Temeritus Washington office and took the elevator to the third floor. Being aware of the company's desire for a low profile, Casey was hardly surprised to see that the door to the suite did not disclose the name of its occupant. Nothing but the number of the suite–340–in small brass numbers above the mahogany framed double glass doors and a small brass plaque on which the raised letter "T" was barely visible. It could be a doctor's office, she thought as she waited for someone to respond to the buzzer and let her into this dim and quiet sanctum.

Finally, Scottie Pettigrew appeared and opened the door. "Hi, Casey. Come on back." Casey followed him past a number of well-appointed offices, most of them vacant, and into an office in the corner of the suite. The man behind the desk looked up and smiled as Casey entered. He stood up and walked around the desk, a big man, dressed in a dark blue–almost black–double breasted, pinstriped suit with matching silver-and-navy tie and pocket handkerchief. From the mirror-like shine on his black wingtips to the touch of white French cuffs peeking out from under the sleeves of his coat, he was the picture of studied elegance. "Hello, Casey. I'm Travis Weakly," he said extending his hand to her. "Welcome to Washington."

After several minutes of small-talk, he escorted her to the conference room where for the next two hours, Casey was briefed on the intricacies of representing Temeritus in the nation's capital. After the briefing and a short visit with the members of the staff, Casey and Weakly left for lunch.

A short walk later, they entered what Weakly described as his favorite restaurant, the Bombay Club, one of the best in Washington. Quiet, elegant, tasteful in its decor, it offers some of the finest food and service to be found anywhere. Casey felt as if she had been transported back to the Raj. Lots of brass and dark wood, ceiling fans turning at the lowest speed, and pictures spaced throughout the restaurant depicting scenes from India. A small bar to the left and a large dining area to the right. A lovely setting.

With an animated flash of recognition the man at the reservations stand rushed up to them. "Mr. Weakly, it's so nice to see you. How have you been?"

"Fine, Ashok, just fine. Ashok, I'd like you to meet Casey O'Rourke from our Houston office. Casey, this is Ashok Bajaj. He owns this place." Ashok took Casey's hand and bowed slightly and, after brief conversation, escorted them to their table. He's as elegant as his restaurant, she thought as she took her seat.

Weakly ordered for them. For starters, dahi papri–dollar-sized crispy tortilla-like pastries topped with little cubes of boiled potatoes, onions and chick peas in a mint sauce with a light touch of date and tamarind, and an order of onion kulcha bread. Then the house salad and finally the trademark item of the Bombay Club, tandoori salmon–tender fillets of fresh salmon, marinated in yogurt, garlic and lime and cooked on skewers in the tandoor oven. Fabulous, especially when eaten with the great tandoor breads, mint paratha and more onion kulcha. Then, over coffee and light dishes of rice kheer, the discussion took on a more serious turn.

"Casey," he paused and looked as if he were debating with himself whether to say something or not, "I have to tell you in all candor that what you witnessed this morning back at the office was mainly a load of eyewash. I thought earlier I'd just give you the standard dog and pony show and let it go at that. But I got to thinking that if you're really going to help on this project, you have to know what the situation is. All of this stuff about categorizing issues is just so much fluff. Fact is, we work on whatever is hot at the moment and that usually means whatever burr is under Proctor Philpott's saddle at the moment. It shifts and changes and usually has to do with some mention of the company in the press or something one of the overseas directors has asked about. It's like going to a restaurant, there's an issue of the day, right there on the menu; except in the Temeritus restaurant you don't always get to look at the menu.

"Oh, sure, we put these fancy issue books together and we do all sorts of research. But you know what? It doesn't make any difference because the Issues Book, which is supposed to be our bible in lobbying Congress starting in January each year, doesn't actually get put together until June or July. It's unbelievable!"

"That's what I've heard." Casey said. "But you're the first person in management who's wavered from what seems to be the company line. And I appreciate your candor. What . . ."

He interrupted her. "Ha, let me tell you something, Casey. I'm the furthest thing from management there is in the entire company. Sure, they give me a fancy title and a fabulous office and all that, but when it comes to authority, I have less than the newest clerk in the mail room. I can hardly go to the bathroom without having to check with Houston. And they are afraid to do anything. It's wait and delay and 'Oh, no, what if someone notices us?'"

"What I don't understand," Casey said, "is why, with this approach to public relations, Proctor Philpott would have hired me and started this project. It just doesn't make any sense."

"Well, I don't know for sure. I can tell you one thing–he's the only guy in the management who even begins to understand Washington. And he doesn't know squat. He was a Senate Page one summer when he was a kid, and he thinks he wrote the Constitution. But at least he's interested in the political process. And, of course, Harry Houdini puts on a great show of being interested, too. But that's just because he knows the Prince likes it and he'd develop an interest in anything he thought would help him kiss the Prince's regal rear. I'll tell you what, if the Prince got interested in doilies, that phony Hoare would start taking crochet lessons." He stopped and laughed at his feeble joke.

"Have you met Houdini?" he asked. Casey nodded. "Then you're familiar with the problem. He stands there all puffed up and self-important behind that goofy desk of his harping about the bottom line, with Old Blood and Guts staring down on the room. Man, he's really something. If Philpott were to stop real quick, there would be a terrible accident." He chuckled. "Have you ever seen Hoare when he gets around Philpott? It's unbelievable. He's raised ass kissing to a fine art."

"Yes," Casey said, "I understand that it is an acquired taste."

Weakly's head tilted back in a loud and long laugh. "That's a good one, Casey. And I'll tell you what, for people like Hoare, they do it for so long it becomes addictive." He shook his head and laughed again. "Man, it's just too funny for words." He pulled a handkerchief from his hip pocket and wiped his eyes. "I haven't laughed this hard in a long time."

He put the handkerchief back in his pocket and continued. "And you know what, that's one of the things that's wrong in the company—we don't laugh enough. It's all so sad. This used to be a great place to work. Used to be fun. But not anymore. We're suffering from a chronic case of what I call 'regalitis.' These guys at the top get to feeling regal and they start to believe that they really are smarter than everyone else. They isolate themselves and guard access to the top so carefully that people like Timmons never have the slightest hint as to what's happening in the real world.

"If you could somehow convince them to loosen up a bit and even smile or laugh once in a while, it would be a great step forward, I'll tell you. You go up on those top floors and you get the idea that it is against the company bylaws for anyone to smile, or laugh, at least not during normal working hours. It's all so serious, like they were doing God's work or something."

"It sounds grim," Casey said.

"It is, believe me. I guess my advice to you is to be careful. Except for Wilfurd Timmons, these guys are a bunch of snakes and they will do anything it takes to protect their own hides. If Timmons or maybe the directors from across the waters would ever wake up and smell the coffee, maybe something could be done. Maybe you could . . . " He paused as if he were trying to decide whether to finish what was really on his mind or not, and then he laughed, "Oh, well, Casey, just do the best you can. And, good luck. Now, we better get on back to the office."

Chapter 27

"National Airport," Casey told the cabbie. Casey settled into the seat and looked out at the day, which was turning darker and colder. She was still debating whether to go to Arlington or not.

Her debate continued as the cab wound its way through central Washington onto Constitution Avenue. Despite her new life in Houston and her new love for Jake, the memory of Ken's death and all of the events surrounding it still haunted her, dormant but always ready to pounce in unsuspecting moments when her guard was down. Maybe if she returned to the scene of the most dreadful of these memories, she could finally elude this unwanted intruder from the past.

Maybe. But there was also the possibility that such a visit would kindle new fires in her memory that would be even worse than the ones that had smoldered for so long.

The cab started across Memorial Bridge. When Casey saw the Memorial Gateway to Arlington National Cemetery at the end of the bridge, she knew she had to go. She leaned forward in her seat, "Sir. I've changed my mind. Please take me to Arlington Cemetery first."

The cab turned into the parking area next to the Visitors Center and stopped and Casey sat motionless, staring straight ahead. "Yes, I've got to do it," she said out loud. She opened her purse, took out a big bill and handed it across the seat to the cabbie. "Here's fifty dollars. Wait for me. I'll be back in a while, and I'll pay you to take me to the airport." She got out of the cab, put on her trench coat and walked towards the cemetery.

She walked past the Visitors Center onto Eisenhower Drive and stopped. It's still not too late, she told herself. I can just turn around and walk back to the cab and go home. A uniformed civilian guard at the crosswalk saw Casey standing alone and deep in thought.

"Can I help you find something, Ma'am?"

"Oh, no," she said, surprised. "I know the way." How could I ever forget, she thought as she turned to the left and started her slow walk down Eisenhower Drive.

When she reached McClellan Drive, she stopped. Yes, this is it. Section 59. And she stepped over the curb and began to walk across the grass toward the middle of the section. In a few moments the cedar tree came into view—a cedar of Lebanon tree planted as a living memorial to the 241 servicemen killed in Beirut. The memorial was dedicated exactly one year after the bombing—on October 23, 1984—and although she had been invited to attend the ceremony, she had not. She didn't think she could bear the agony of reliving Ken's funeral. Now, seeing the cedar tree for the first time, she regretted she had not attended the ceremony, that she had not come here sooner.

Casey stepped up to the flat marble slab and read its inscription:

"LET PEACE TAKE ROOT"
THIS CEDAR OF LEBANON TREE GROWS IN LIVING
MEMORY OF THE AMERICANS KILLED IN THE BEIRUT
TERRORIST ATTACK AND ALL VICTIMS OF TERRORISM
THROUGHOUT THE WORLD.
    DEDICATED DURING THE FIRST MEMORIAL
CEREMONY FOR THESE VICTIMS.

GIVEN BY: NO GREATER LOVE
OCTOBER 23, 1984
A TIME OF REMEMBRANCE

It's so peaceful here, she thought. She looked up into the cedar of Lebanon and beyond. You'd never know from this vantage point that you were anywhere near Washington. You can't see any of the buildings across the river in the District. Even the Washington Monument is blocked by the foliage. If it wasn't for the roar of airplanes taking off and landing at National, you'd think you were in the country.

Casey walked slowly through the grave stones around the memorial. There were so many more of them than she had remembered but, of the twenty-three bombing victims to be buried at Arlington, Ken had been one of the first. Finally, when she was ready, she stopped at headstone number 59 530. She walked to the front of the stone and looked down.

KENNETH

DAVID

O'ROURKE

CAPT

US MARINE CORPS

LEBANON

AUG 15 1956

OCT 23 1983

So many years, so many memories. But somehow Casey didn't react as she had feared she might. It was so tranquil. What had been a raw and ugly wound in the earth awaiting the casket of her husband was now a soothing patch of grass. She recalled Carl Sandburg's words—"I am the grass; I cover all . . . I am the grass. Let me work." She could hardly imagine the scene of agony and sorrow that had played out here that day over ten years ago. The horses and the honor guard and the rifles firing and the drums. The crying of Casey and her parents and Ken's father and sisters. And the young Marine in dress blues bending to her and handing her the folded flag which had covered Ken's casket. She had felt so lonely and so cold, clutching that flag and wondering how in the world she was going to bear it all.

She had tried for so long to close these memories out of her mind, but somehow the passage of time and the changes in the setting had filled her with a strange sense of peace and calm. Maybe this was what it was like when an old soldier returns to a battlefield and finds it so changed from the place of carnage he had known. I guess I'll never know, Casey said out loud as she walked away.

She walked back to the street and into the older part of the cemetery and up the hills, eventually stopping at the John F. Kennedy gravesite. During her slow walk through the cemetery the weather had worsened still further, and by the time she stopped it was gray and cold and almost dark. The air had the sharp and musty smell of deep autumn and promised a harsh winter to follow close behind. She stood for a moment gazing at the Eternal Flame, and then turned and walked to the circular terrace at the foot of the gravesite and the low wall on which are inscribed some of Kennedy's most famous remarks. Among them she read:

LET EVERY NATION KNOW WHETHER IT WISHES US WELL OR ILL
THAT WE SHALL PAY ANY PRICE—BEAR ANY BURDEN . . .

She raised her eyes from these words and gazed across the river. Her thoughts turned to the Vietnam Veterans Memorial, which she knew was hidden behind the trees near the Lincoln Memorial, the awe-inspiring monument that honors the men and women who served in the Vietnam War. Its polished black granite walls bear the names of those who gave their lives and of those who remain missing–over 58,000 souls–the very legacy of President Kennedy's bold words. She wondered if he had known when he uttered those words how high would be the price, how heavy the burden.

The rain began with a drizzle, soft at first then increasing in intensity until it became a downpour. It pelted the White House and the Capitol and the Pentagon. It pelted the National Cemetery at Arlington and the graves of twenty-three young men who were murdered in their sleep. And it pelted a young woman standing near the JFK gravesite, weeping, her face buried in her hands as she sobbed in the cold gray dusk.

Chapter 28

The plane thumped down onto the runway, causing one of the over-head bins to pop open and flop down bouncing, until one of the flight attendants could fasten it. The landing roused Casey from the twilight sleep of flying—not deep enough to be restful but soothing enough to let the mind roam free—and caused for a split second the focused terror that sudden noises or motions will bring out in even the most seasoned of air travelers. Is something wrong? No, just a rough touchdown.

The plane taxied to its gate at the terminal and stopped with the gong that signals a storm of activity as people struggle to retrieve coats and hats and carry-on baggage. She left the plane and started up the jetway. Humidity, always a prominent member of the Houston welcoming committee, greeted her well before she reached the gate. Welcome to Houston—a great place to live, but you wouldn't want to visit there. She retrieved her bags and with skycap in tow, headed for the parking lot. Finally, she began the long drive into the city, glad to be home, glad it was Friday.

She was exhausted from the trip and from the emotion of the visit to Ken's grave, and all she wanted to do was have a cold beer, play with So-So and go to bed. When she finally got home—almost ten o'clock—So-So greeted her at the door by barking and dancing and tearing up and down the hall so fast that her forward movement carried her crashing into the wall each time she tried to change direction. Everything seemed to be in order. Whenever she was out of town, Jake would check the house each day, feed So-So, and bring in the mail and papers.

She went into the kitchen to get a beer and found the usual note from Jake on the refrigerator. "Case, I'm SO glad you're back. Call me ASAP. Love ya', Jake." I wonder what's so urgent, she thought as she poured herself a Pub Draught Guinness, the one in the tall black and gold can that somehow makes the beer as rich and creamy as Guinness from the tap in a good Irish bar. She went to the phone and pressed the preset number for The Horse as she took a first long satisfying taste of the stout.

Jake's message was simple—lots of Temeritus people had been at the bar and there were an unusual number of rumors flying. What had been merely an undercurrent of innuendo regarding another round of layoffs had become a tidal wave of paranoia. And several people, including the animal rights nerd, had been in The Horse asking if Casey was there. But most surprising, Melissa Fellows, whom Jake had not seen since the night they ate dinner at the Fellows' house, had come into the bar looking almost distraught and asked Jake to tell Casey she needed to talk as soon as possible, but not to call her at work.

Casey told Jake about the trip and about her discussion with Travis Weakly. She decided to save the visit to Arlington until they were together. "So that's about it, Baby," Casey said, "I better get going. Really pooped. And I guess I'd better call Melissa before it gets any later."

Craig answered. "Oh, hi, Casey, Melissa was hoping you'd call tonight. Listen, she's in bed. But she said to get her up if you called, so hang on."

Casey waited for what seemed like several minutes before Melissa came to the phone. "Casey? Thanks so much for calling. I hate to bother you and to sound like such a neurotic, but there are all sorts of things going on at work that you really need to know about. And I don't feel comfortable talking about it at the office. Can I take you to lunch tomorrow?"

"Sure, but what's happening? You sound terrible."

"Well, I feel terrible. But I really don't want to talk on the phone. I need to see you and discuss it in person, if that's OK with you."

They agreed to meet at Calypso, one of Casey's favorites in the Village, not far from The Horse on Morningside. "Oh, and Casey," Melissa said, her voice almost at a whisper, "you can't tell anyone we are meeting." She paused. "Promise?"

"Sure, Melissa. I promise."

Chapter 29

Thirty minutes before she was to meet Melissa Fellows, Casey sat on the terrace at Calypso. She had long thought that the outdoors as a general rule was much overrated and usually preferred to be indoors, but even a confirmed indoorsman would have wanted to be outside on a day like this. Houston is not blessed with many days of meteorological beauty, but when one does come along it is indeed a thing to treasure. And this was one of those days. Bright sunshine in a cloudless sky, warm in the sunlight and cool in the shade with a low humidity rarely felt in Houston. The air was clean and bracing. Casey ordered a Red Stripe Beer and some conch fritters. It was a great day to be alive and well in Houston, Texas.

A few minutes before noon, Casey saw Melissa crossing Morningside. She stood up when Melissa reached the table and they hugged and each exclaimed how wonderful the other looked. Melissa's statement was true because Casey did indeed look her usual stunning self; Casey's was a lie–Melissa looked awful. She had lost weight since Casey last saw her and she looked distracted and tired. Her eyes were red and the skin under them was dark and puffed.

"Oh, Casey," she said as she was pulling her chair up to the table. "No wonder you are so good at public relations. I know I look awful. But thanks anyway. How are you?" Melissa ordered a glass of wine and listened as Casey told her how busy things had been. In the course of her discussion Casey mentioned the rumored staff cuts.

"That's why I wanted to talk to you, Casey," Melissa said. "It's more than just a rumor. And it's driving me crazy. Craig isn't much help on this sort of thing, and I simply must talk to someone about it. As you'll see, I could hardly discuss it with anyone at the company and someone who isn't familiar with what's going on in the company wouldn't understand what I'm talking about. So, in desperation, I'm turning to you for a friendly and understanding ear." She paused and finished the wine. "And I must swear you to secrecy."

"Of course," Casey said. "Except for Jake."

"Except for Jake."

Melissa ordered another glass of wine and began to tell Casey her story. Several weeks ago she had been called to Proctor Philpott's office. He told her that a staff reduction—a "timely right sizing," he had called it—was going to be announced in November. But this time he wanted it done right. Not like the last time, when the plan to cut was announced months before the target personnel were identified. There had been unnecessary publicity, and the company had received far more attention than he liked. Melissa's job was to help plan this project so it could be announced and implemented with military precision. To that end she had been put on a top secret special assignment, reporting directly to him.

Her assignment was composed of two things. First, she was to go through the ranked performance listings for each major organization in the company and identify the bottom fifteen percent of each. And, second, she was to prepare for Proctor's approval all of the notices, press releases and other things that would be needed in the implementation of the plan. No one other than Proctor Philpott and she were involved in the project. And it was about to drive her out of her mind.

"It sounds awful," Casey said. "But I don't understand why such a monumental effort would be undertaken by a single person working directly with Philpott? What about the rest of his staff? What about the employee relations people?"

"He feels that one of the problems the last time was there were so many people working on it. It got too emotional and he wants to avoid that. 'Just do the bottom fishing and get on with it,' is the way he phrased it to me. He said that getting rid of fifteen percent of a company just isn't that big of a deal and if we do it right, it will hardly be noticed in the press. We get it done in November so it's not on the books for next year, and it will be out of people's minds by Christmas. And maybe he's right." She sipped her wine.

"But that isn't the problem. What bothers me is that I know–in a way that he never could–the horrible toll this will take on the people involved. And it's tearing me apart inside. I see these lists and the names of people I know and have worked with over the years. And I think about their families–wives and kids and college bills and all of the things that make us human beings. But he doesn't see any of that. To him it's just another step on the way to becoming president of the company. And he's so cold about it. It's like he was talking about switching coffee suppliers or something. And I feel horrible having to be a part of it."

Casey could see that Melissa was distraught, but she had a hunch that Melissa had not yet told everything she really wanted to, everything about why she was so upset. "But there is one thing I still don't understand, Melissa. Why, of all the people in the company, did Proctor choose you for this project?"

Melissa looked down at her glass, twisting it between her fingers. "I was hoping you wouldn't ask that question, Casey." She paused for almost a minute, sipped her wine and continued. "No, really, I'm glad you did. Fifteen years ago, when I had been with the company for just a short while, Proctor and I had an affair. He was such a handsome man and so charming and I fell for him like the proverbial ton of bricks. He was single at the time and I was in love and hopeful that we would get married. He strung me along for several years. And it was all very discreet.

"Oh, I guess there were people who suspected something, but we were very careful. Never went out in public and all of that. There was a strict policy against people in the company dating at the time, so we were careful. But then, when his career started to soar, he must have decided that he needed more of a trophy than I could ever be and that was the end of that. I was crushed. I would have left Temeritus, but I had a good job and I needed the money real bad. So I stayed. But it was awful. Haven't really gotten over it. Probably never will." Tears began to well in Melissa's eyes.

"But it's much worse than you can imagine, Casey. I was young and just out of the constraints of living at home with my parents. And Proctor was the first man with real sexual maturity that I had ever been with. And he was a great lover, I'll tell you. We did things that I'd never even dreamed of. But like a fool, I let him take pictures of me doing things that he liked to watch me do. He was pretty kinky, and the pictures are really bad. And he made sure that he was never in them, just me.

"Well," she paused, and her lips tightened across her teeth, "when we broke up, it was real ugly. I was desperate. I thought I couldn't live without him. I threatened to disclose our affair and ruin his career. And then, in the argument that followed, he got out the pictures and told me that if I ever said a word, he would leak them out into the company and send copies to my parents. So I didn't say a word. And I've been under that threat ever since. And now that I'm married, of course, it's even worse. So that's why he chose me for this project–he has to have total secrecy and he knows he can get it with me. You can't imagine how terrible it is, Casey. I have to have someone to talk to." Melissa covered her face with her hands and sobbed.

Casey sat silent and still while Melissa struggled to regain her composure. Finally, after several tissues and several sips of water, Melissa looked at Casey and managed a feeble smile. "Thanks for listening, Casey. I've been living with this all by myself for so long now. And having him use it on me again in the context of a sneak attack on the good people of the company is just more than I can bear."

"Jesus, Melissa, everyone has something that they've done in the course of their life they wish they hadn't. That's the way it is. But for that slimy snake to blackmail you with pictures that were taken years ago in the utmost of confidence is really unbelievable to me. The son of a bitch should be crucified for what he's doing to you."

Melissa sighed and leaned back in her chair. Although her eyes were still red, her face had the look of relief that often follows an emotional outpouring. "Now," she said, "you can see why I'm not able to discuss this with Craig. He still gets jealous when he hears about any of the guys I used to just date before we were married. I don't even want to know what he would think about my torrid affair with Proctor Philpott."

She paused a moment and then lifted her glass. "Let's drink to the soul-cleansing effects of a good friend and a good cry."

"I'll drink to that," Casey said raising her glass. "Let's eat lunch and talk about this some more. There's got to be a way for you to handle this."

They ordered lunch. While they ate, they continued to discuss the situation at Temeritus. Melissa confirmed that there was to be a big meeting of the Senior Select on Thursday at which time the details of the scheduled "right sizing" would be disclosed. It would be quick, and ruthless, like the stealth bombers of the Gulf War–fly in under the enemy radar, drop your bombs and get the hell out of there before anyone knows what's happened.

"Are any of the Senior Select on the target list?" Casey asked.

Melissa laughed her first real laugh of the day–of the last several weeks in fact. "You've got to be kidding. The Senior Select? That's rich. Casey, haven't you learned yet that one of the basic rules at Temeritus is there is never any suffering at the top? The only way that would happen would be if Proctor felt challenged by someone and wanted to get rid of him. But they're all far too crafty to ever do that. So they're safe."

"The only difference between this one and the last one is the stealth. It's the same thing in substance. The ship has run aground and the captain calls all the officers to the bridge and says, 'We've hit the shoals, men, and we've got to do something about it.'" She spoke in a mockingly low voice, her chin pulled back. "'Let's throw fifteen percent of the crew overboard so we can back off the reef and continue on our voyage.'" She coughed and continued in her normal voice, "No thought given to the incompetence of the navigators who steered the damn thing. Last time the officers got to pick the sailors who were thrown overboard; this time Philpott will do it for them. All they have to do is pass the word. And none of them will do that themselves. They'll delegate it and hide in the lunch room until it's done. I mean, this is a real company of cowards."

Casey shook her head in disbelief. "I would never have believed that a major corporation could be so screwed up by a single person. But it seems to me that everyone there is so afraid of him they seem to have lost their will to fight. And poor old Wilfurd Timmons has abdicated his power to Philpott; and the rest of the management team, if you could even call it that, focuses on whatever it takes to stay on the good side of the Prince."

Melissa nodded. "You got that right, Casey. It's unbelievable, isn't it?"

They ate for a while in silence. Then Casey continued, "You know what, Melissa? If he's doing this to you, he's got to be doing something similar or just as dishonest to other people. We just need to find out what it is and be clever enough to beat the bastard at his own game."

Melissa smiled. "Yeah. Wouldn't that be sweet."

Chapter 30

"Do you want me to call the cops or what?"

"No. Not yet. But it sure pisses me off. I was only in here for about forty-five minutes. I guess you just never can tell." Eddie Mason shook his head in disgust and disbelief. "Come on outside and I'll show you where I parked."

The bartender came out from behind the bar and followed Eddie into the parking lot. "I parked it right over there," Eddie said, pointing to the vacant spot among the various vehicles, mostly pick-up trucks, parked outside the building. "Just an old beat-up Dodge van. Don't know why anybody would want to steal it."

"Can't help you, pal. Like I said, I'll call the cops if you want. Other than that I guess it's just tough shit."

"Yeah. But it might have been one of my kids or a joke or something. I'll call home and get a ride and see if I can figure out what happened. Then I'll call the cops if I think it really is stolen." He handed the bartender his card. "Call me if you hear anything, OK?" The bartender stuffed the card into the pocket of his T-shirt and walked back into the bar, looking back at Eddie with a why-is-this-guy-wasting-my-time look on his face.

Eddie walked to the pay phone in front of the building, dropped a quarter in the slot and dialed the motel. "Mrs. Murphy's room, please." He waited. "Mrs. Murphy, this is the nursery calling. I thought you'd like to know that the seeds have been planted." He hung up and walked two blocks down the street, got into his van and headed for the motel he had just called.

Eddie was another one of M's many "hands"–people sympathetic to the cause of animal rights but not directly involved in the day-to-day activities of the cell. He had agreed to let M use his van for the raid and his call was the last thing on M's pre-raid checklist–"plant the seeds" for an auto theft, should that become necessary. This was standard procedure: take the raid vehicle to a tavern or restaurant and make a scene about how it had been stolen from the parking lot; make sure that enough is said so that someone in the place will recall it; if something went wrong during the raid, the owner would be notified, he would report the theft, and his connection to the cell would remain hidden.

M was excited by the thrill of planning and executing a raid. Since Saturday afternoon–a little more than a week ago–she had been operating under an assumed name out of a cheap motel off of Crosstimbers in North Houston. She still went to work each day and did as much as she could there, but most of the activity was at night. And now, Saturday evening, M sat poised in the motel room ready for the raid to begin.

The on-site work by Larry Mitchell plus the surveillance done earlier in the week had convinced her that security at the lab would not be a problem. There appeared to be only one guard on duty from midnight to eight. His post was at the desk inside, and he left this post every hour or so to walk around the building. Four nights of surveillance had failed to show anyone else at the location. It should be easy, much easier than M's earlier ones had been, because they would gain access to the building through subterfuge rather than through the usual stealth or violence. The plan was simplicity itself. Drive into the facility pretending to deliver a shipment of experimental animals. Once the guard on duty disarmed the alarm, he would be incapacitated and they would break into the green room and free the animals. All the arrangements–for both people and equipment–had been worked out by M during the week.

The people part was the easiest. M would lead the raid and be assisted by Larry Mitchell, dressed again in his security guard uniform, and four other cell members–a van driver, a lock expert, a veterinarian's assistant, and a lookout. Others from the cell in support of the raid were the driver of the delivery van, who would take the animals from the transfer point at Lake Conroe to their new home in Dallas, and the person who would prepare the materials for dissemination to the press. And finally, from outside the cell, there was the veterinarian in Conroe who would provide whatever treatment they might need.

The equipment was more difficult to pull together. In addition to the van she had arranged through Eddie Mason, M had to rent and outfit a van to deliver the animals to Dallas. The delivery vehicle was not as sensitive as the one used in the raid and did not require anything more sneaky than the use of a false ID in its rental. During the week it had been fitted with cardboard pet carriers, food, water and other necessities.

She also had to procure a number of the items that would be needed in the raid–security guard uniforms for Larry and the driver and white coveralls and cheap canvas shoes for everyone else; two-way radios for communication between M and the lookout; carrying bags for the animals; chemical Mace; a high-power rechargeable drill with carbide bits. One of the most important was a supply of a mild anesthetic that was often used in veterinary hospitals and grooming businesses to calm animals without actually putting them to sleep, and the necessary syringes to administer it.

And now, finally, it had all come together and the cell members who would be involved in the raid both directly and indirectly were gathered in M's motel room for last minute preparations and instructions. The six people going on the raid had changed into their costumes, and the people in support had been briefed on their roles. The syringes had been loaded and the gear checked, rechecked and packed in the appropriate canvas carryalls. Eddie's call meant that any minute now the van would be parked in the lot outside the motel room and they would be ready to go.

They waited in the room, some of them sitting on the bed, some on the floor leaning against the wall. No one spoke. The only sound was the hum of the ventilation unit under the window. This must be what it's like for soldiers before a battle, M thought. We've done everything in our power to prepare and now we're just waiting for the word to begin the campaign. And in the pre-battle calm, the adrenalin flows, the focus tightens and the normal sense of time's passage is dulled.

M knew that once the raid began, many things would be out of her control and she could only hope that the preparation had been good enough. Too late to worry about that now. But never too late to worry about the workings of the law named for the person whose name she had, with her characteristic sense of irony, chosen as her alias in the motel—Murphy: Anything that can go wrong will go wrong. Just hope for the best, she said to herself.

The tense quiet of the room was pierced by three loud knocks on the door, a full second's pause between each RAP–RAP–RAP! Eddie's signal that the van was in place. "Let's do it," M said. The raid was on.

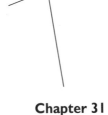

Chapter 31

Eddie's van was fitted with curtains on the sides and behind the front seat so that no one outside the vehicle could see what was in back. Larry Mitchell and the driver, Jerry Turner, dressed in their security uniforms, sat in the front. It would appear to the casual observer to be nothing more than a couple of security guards going to work.

They stopped at a gas station north of Houston. Mitchell went to the pay phone and dialed the number of the special phone at the Woodlands Lab, the one he had obtained from the guard on duty during his FBI caper.

"Yeah, Jackson here," the guard answered.

"This is Ivers," he said. Through his contacts in the Houston Police Department he had obtained the name of the top guard on duty for Surveillance that night. "Listen, I got a load of animals to deliver tonight . . . in about a half an hour."

"Fine. I'll be ready for you." You don't know the half of it, Mitchell thought to himself as he walked back to the van.

Jackson took his hourly walk of the building perimeter. He didn't want to be out of the building when they showed up with the animals. This night shift could get real boring and a delivery would be a nice break in the routine for him. Must be an important one, too, he thought for them to call twice on it. Should be fun.

He went back to the building and continued reading his magazine until he heard the alarm announce a vehicle on the facility's long driveway. The lack of a security gate had been troublesome to some of the guards who worked the night shift and in response to their suggestions, Temeritus had installed an electronic device that could be activated at night to let the guard on duty know when a vehicle had turned into the driveway and was heading up toward the main building. The driveway was so long and winding that an approaching vehicle could not be seen until it had come almost all the way to the building. When Jackson heard the bong, he knew it would be a matter of minutes until his guests would be at the door. He got up and went into the bathroom to fix himself up. He wanted to look fit for the boss. And besides, frequently on these night-time deliveries there would be some bigwigs from Temeritus.

Back at his station, Jackson looked out of the window and could see the lights of a vehicle coming up the road. It was a van. Funny, he thought, I don't ever remember them using a van like that before. Oh, well, nothing ever stays the same for long.

The van stopped in front of the building. Mitchell, dressed again in the flowing blond wig and bushy moustache of the kitchen raid, got out and walked toward the office while the van was being turned around and backed up to the front door. He walked into the room and approached the desk. "Hiya, Jackson. How they hanging tonight, Babes. Got a big load of live meat for the basement. How 'bout coding in the green room for me, old buddy."

"You bet," Jackson replied. He turned around in his chair, opened up the control box and entered in the number that his posting supervisor had given him that evening. "That ought to do it," he said as he spun around in the chair to face his visitor. But instead of the smiling face of his visitor, Jackson was staring into the working end of a canister of chemical Mace. PAROOSH. A stream of chemicals hit his face, causing immediate blindness and violent coughing. He fell to the floor gasping for breath, clawing at his eyes to stop the pain. M, who had been waiting outside the door, rushed in with a syringe loaded with 5 cc's of the hypnotic drug Ketamine, which she jabbed into his thigh. "Sweet dreams, my prince." She laughed as he fell into unconsciousness.

M went back to the door and signaled for the others, who grabbed their tote bags and ran into the office, leaping over the unconscious Jackson. She retrieved Jackson's security card, opened the door into the hall and raced to the green room door. There the locksmith took out a heavy duty cordless drill and, in a single expert movement, drilled its carbide bit into the core of the lock cylinder. He crammed his "nutcracker" into the hole, jerked the cylinder out of the lock and opened the door. I hope this thing doesn't have a silent alarm on it, M thought to herself as she raced into the room.

Inside was just as they had been told—an elevator and a stairway. They took the stairs to the basement, where they found another heavy locked door. Again the locksmith came forward with his drill, and at last, they burst into the lab.

M's years of experience in the animal rights movement had brought her into contact with many things ghastly and abhorrent. She was callous to the sights sudden entry into a testing lab could produce. But in all her years, nothing had prepared her for what she saw inside this lab. As Dickens said of Scrooge when he awaited the arrival of the second of the three spirits, "being prepared for almost anything, he was not by any means prepared for nothing." So it was for M as she gazed in astonished wonder at an empty room.

Yes, there were built-in cages. And, yes, there were the stainless steel tables used in animal experimentation. But there was not an animal to be seen. Just a big room full of empty cages and cold tables. The room had the smell of recent occupancy—a fetid mix of sour feces and pine-scented cleansers, of dried urine and stale air. There had been animals in here not long ago. But what had happened to them and where were they now? A careful search of the room failed to uncover any hint as to where the recent occupants of the room might be. Furthermore, diligent search of this basement area failed to show anything else in the basement but this one room.

"This is crazy," M said. "There must be something in here somewhere. Let's go back upstairs and look around." M turned and ran up the steps. As she passed the door to the reception room, her radio squawked–"Mayday! Mayday! Temeritus truck in driveway heading your way–get out of there fast!"

"Quick," M said. "Everybody back in the van. We've got to get out of here. Now!" They raced through the reception room. Someone tripped over Jackson's still unconscious body causing several of the others to fall into a confused pile. They jumped into the van. Just as before, everyone in the back except Mitchell and Turner. M was squatting directly behind Mitchell hidden by the curtain. Breathing hard, she whispered to him, "What do you think?"

"I don't know," he said as the van pulled away from the curb. "The truck is about halfway here and there is no other way out. We'll get caught for sure if we try to race past them. I'll have to try to bullshit our way out."

They continued down the driveway. M could feel the fear in the air as all of them sat with their thoughts–capture, arrest, some of them would lose their jobs. They knew the risk involved in what they were doing and all were prepared to accept it. But none of them thought they would pay such a heavy price for a raid that didn't free a single animal. Well, it was out of their hands now. And they remained motionless in the back of the van, hiding in fear behind the curtain, hoping that somehow they could avoid capture.

In the Temeritus truck, Sam Slurry and one of his underlings, Mike Freeman, were halfway to the main building before they noticed the van heading in their direction. "What the hell is that?" Slurry said.

"I didn't know there was anybody else out here tonight."

"Neither did I," Mike said. "Maybe it's the cleaning crew fixing up the green room for its new occupants."

"Naa," Slurry said. "Can't be. Philpott told me that was done last night. That's why we couldn't get out here any sooner with these healthy ones. Had to clean it up and let it air out a bit. Flash 'em down and we'll see who it is."

Freeman flashed his lights and signaled out the window with his hand for the van to stop. The van pulled up alongside of the truck and stopped. Slurry and Freeman could see that the two men in the van had on Surveillance uniforms. The man on the passenger side got out of the van and walked around the front and up to the driver's side of the truck.

"Howdy," Mitchell said as he walked up to the truck. "Suppose you boys show me a little ID and tell me what you're doing here." The best defense is a good offense, he thought to himself.

"You asshole," Slurry yelled, leaning across Freeman and glaring through the rolled down window. "Don't you recognize a Temeritus vehicle when you see one?"

"Can't say that I do. All I see is a truck driving around out here where nobody's supposed to be at night. Now, how 'bout that ID?" Slurry got out of the truck, slammed the door and stomped around to the front.

"Do you know who I am, Sergeant? Here's some ID for you." He shoved his ID card in front of Mitchell's nose. "I'm Sam Slurry, director of corporate security for Temeritus, and I could have you fired for this. We called out here and told the man on duty we were coming, and I don't expect to have to put up with any shit from a piss ant like you."

Mitchell stood motionless, his eyes staring straight ahead, braced at attention. Slurry's anger subsided and he looked at Mitchell as if he were seeing him for the first time. This jackass is really scared, he said to himself. I think I'll have a little fun with him. "Who are you anyway? I don't think I've ever seen you before. Why don't you show me a little ID." Mitchell fumbled with his wallet. Slurry continued without waiting for the ID, "And what the hell are you doing driving around in this old van? Why aren't you in a Surveillance vehicle?" He walked to the side of the van. "What a piece of shit this is," he shouted. And thumped the side of the van with his fist.

Inside, everyone was frozen with fear–breathless, muscles tensed–expecting the door to be opened in the next instant. They could hear the bite of Sam Slurry's voice getting closer to the van. What a piece of shit this is! Then the sound of Slurry's fist pounding on the side of the van. The locksmith, whose deft fingers had only moments ago drilled out the green room locks, felt a stab of warmth in his crotch which spread like the ripple of a small stone in a still pond as his bladder emptied. His body began to shake in terror and the van filled with the sharp sniff of urine.

But Slurry did not open the door. Instead, he walked back to Mitchell and resumed his harassment. He put his face nose to nose with Mitchell and screamed, "OK, you little peckerwood. Are you going to say anything or are you going to just stand there with your thumb up your butt? What are you doing here?"

Struggling to regain his composure, Mitchell stammered, "Well, sir, me and Henry in the cab there, we're just going off duty from over in Conroe where we got a job, and we stopped out here to see how ole Jackson was doing, and I guess we just got carried away when we saw your truck. Sure didn't know it would be somebody important like you, Mr. Slurry. Honest, all I want to be is helpful." No one spoke for a moment. At last, Slurry thought, this little shit is giving me the respect I deserve. "So," he continued, "if you don't mind, Mr. Slurry, sir, we'll just mosey on our way and leave you folks alone." He backed away from Slurry towards the van.

"Wait just a minute," Slurry said, "I may not be finished with you yet. In fact . . . "

"Hey, Sam," Slurry was interrupted by his driver, who called to him through the window of the truck. "Ivers wants to talk to you. Says its urgent."

"Christ," Slurry muttered. "This is all I need tonight." He looked at Mitchell again. "OK, Mr. All-I-want-to-be-is-helpful, you and your buddy just wait right here while I get this phone call, you hear?" Slurry glared at Mitchell a final time before he walked around the side of the truck and got in, cursing the falling employment standards at Surveillance. "Yeah, Ivers. What can I do for you?"

Mitchell continued his slow walk around the van until he was standing next to the door. Without taking his eyes off of Slurry and without making a sound, he opened the door and got in. "OK, T. Let's ease on out of here–slow and easy. Try not to make any noise. If I see them turn around, I'll let you know and we'll try to outrun them. We got to get as much of a head start as we can. When we get to the main road, haul ass." Jerry Turner put the van in gear and pressed the accelerator just enough to start the van forward.

"What!" Slurry screamed into the phone. "Can't you get Jackson on the phone? . . . The green room? You got to be shitting me . . . yeah, we're almost there. I'll let you know what I see." He hung up the phone and said to Freeman, "We better get on up to the lab. There's a problem of some kind." Freeman put the truck in gear and started to drive up the hill. "What about the guys in the van, Boss?"

"Damn." Slurry looked back to where the van had been. "I told that shit head to stay put." Slurry turned around in his seat just in time to see the van creep out onto the main road and then speed off into the darkness.

Chapter 32

At least we didn't get caught, M thought to herself. That's about all you can say good about it. It could have been worse, but by almost any standard the raid had been a disaster. We bungled it—didn't even free a single animal. But at least we didn't get caught.

M sat in front of her dressing table mirror brushing her hair. Some people work crossword puzzles to relax, some play solitaire; M's relaxation was this ritual brushing of her hair. And after the last two days she needed some relaxation.

She had gone over the whole thing many times and it always came out the same—about the only thing you could say was that they hadn't been caught. Even that was far from certain when the van had been stopped. M shuddered when she thought how close they came. She and the others huddled in the darkness of the van straining to hear what was happening outside. Barely breathing, pulse pounding in her ears. And then, a wave of relief as Mitchell got into the van. "OK, T. Let's ease on out of here . . . "

When the tires hit the main road a cheer went up from the back of the van. They were laughing and slapping hands and all talking at once, the adrenaline of fear turned into the adrenaline of elation. But this soon gave way to a feeling of depression and then to anger. And by the time they had reached what was to have been the transfer point for the rescued animals, the mood in the van was sullen and angry.

The second-guessing began with Nancy Wade. "This is ridiculous," she had shouted. "We go to all of this trouble, all this fiddle farting around with planning and coordinating"—these words spat out in mockery—"and all we get out of it is the chance to pee in our pants"—she gestured to the stain covering the locksmith's white coveralls—"while we wallow around in the back of a van. All I can say is it's a good thing stud muffin here"—she gestured again, this time at Mitchell—"is such a great bullshit artist or we'd have been busted." She paused and glared around the room. "Or worse. I say this was poorly planned and poorly executed and it's all your fault, M."

During the arguments and recriminations that followed, M had tried to explain that there were always things that couldn't be planned for and that over time it would prove to be a mild setback at the most. But she had the feeling that, despite the vigor of her defense, her words were not well received. After much frantic discussion they had all agreed on a cooling-off period—no one was to do anything until the next meeting. Let the dust settle and see exactly what Temeritus was going to do. Then they could regroup and plan their next course of action.

M walked to her bed and lay down with her head propped up against the overstuffed pillows she enjoyed. She picked up the folded copy of the *Houston Chronicle* that was on the bed and read for the third time the article about the raid.

TEMERITUS LAB RAIDED, NO ANIMALS RELEASED

A Temeritus, Inc. laboratory at The Woodlands was broken into early Sunday—perhaps by a radical animal rights group, Temeritus officials said yesterday. One security guard was overpowered and forcibly drugged. The break-in was discovered by other security officers after 1 a.m., the company said.

Officials at Temeritus, the American subsidiary of British Temeritus, International, Ltd., said they believe the attack was conducted by an underground group, the Animal Liberation Army or ALA. The basement lab was broken into but none of the 12 animals inside were harmed or released.

Temeritus has been the target of a boycott by a coalition of animal rights groups and has been the repeated target of vandalism. Anonymous phone calls to the news media have frequently attributed such attacks to the ALA. No such calls were received regarding this break-in, however.

What's going on, M thought. This is crazy. What are they talking about—the twelve animals in the lab? There weren't any animals in the lab.

Chapter 33

"I still can't get it out of my mind." Nancy Wade stomped across the room for the third time in minutes. "And now, when I see what those rotten bastards are trying to do, it really pisses me off."

Jerry Turner finished his beer, belched and wiped his mouth with the back of his hand. "Yeah, me, too." He was seated in an over-stuffed chair in the living room of Nancy's apartment eating popcorn. "But what are we supposed to do? We haven't heard from M yet and there's no need to get all worked up about it."

"Well, maybe not. But I can't see how we can just stand around and let them get away with it." She sat on the arm of Jerry's chair and reached for the popcorn bowl. She sat lost in thought eating the popcorn one piece at a time.

"I think we should look at it again." She walked across the room and turned on the TV and VCR. The screen flickered and blinked and then presented one of the local news anchors looking out in earnest good humor at the TV audience.

"And finally tonight, we take you back downtown where Temeritus, Incorporated, held its first press conference since the incident at its Woodlands laboratory last Sunday. Channel 2's Julie Rodgers was on hand." The scene shifted to a shot of the Houston skyline as seen from the Buffalo Bayou. Then, as the audio began, giving a quick summary of the Temeritus troubles with the animal rights groups, the camera zoomed in on Temeritus Tower, a difficult shot due to the new and taller buildings that had grown up around it over the years. " . . . and in a rare showing of public profile, Proctor Philpott, a senior executive with Temeritus, held a lengthy press conference that covered not only the incident at The Woodlands but also the company's recent troubles with animal rights activists."

The video then switched to a shot of a distinguished fifty-something man standing in front of a lectern and a cluster of microphones. The camera zoomed to a close-up, and the audio cut into his words, " . . . and this most recent act of terrorism was committed, as you all know, last Saturday, really early Sunday morning. Through destruction of personal property and infliction of personal injury to one of our security people, this person or persons forced their way into the laboratory only to discover that the facility housed twelve very healthy beagles. I have brought one of these little beagles with me today." He looked into the camera just as he had been taught at the Temeritus TV school and said in his most earnest manner, "We at Temeritus like to think of our laboratory animals as non-human co-workers, and we treat them with the same dignity and respect that we do all of our other employees."

The camera cut to Rodgers. "This press conference was rare for Temeritus, a company which usually communicates through its official spokesperson. In addition to Mr. Philpott, Temeritus also had on hand the veterinarian who had been hired to inspect the dogs from the lab."

The camera cut back to the news conference itself and to a young beagle who had been placed on a table next to a man in a white laboratory jacket. Rodgers continued off-camera, " . . . and the veterinarian, Dr. Thomas Wilson, went into the details of his examination of the twelve dogs. He pronounced them to be in the best of shape." On camera Dr. Wilson continued to pet the beagle, who stood wagging his tail and trying to jump up on his handlers. In the background, Proctor Philpott stood beaming with smug pride.

The camera returned for its closing shot of the reporter. "According to authorities, there have been no leads as to the identity of the people responsible for the break-in at the Temeritus labs. This is Julie Rodgers, Channel 2 News, reporting."

"It makes me sick," Nancy said, as she pushed the rewind button on the VCR. "You were there. You know there weren't any animals in that room."

Jerry laughed. "I think it's a riot. Reminds me of the old Johnny Carson Show. Too bad that beagle didn't crap on the table like some of those zoo animals used to."

"Well, I don't think it's funny myself. We know there were animals in there before we got there. And we know they wanted to keep it a secret. Now they trot out these healthy little beagles and say "Oh, aren't we the greatest. Just look at these cute little puppies." She paused in disgust. "Non-human co-workers my ass. Give me a break."

She walked back to the armchair. "I guess it just proves what old George Bernard Shaw supposedly said. 'Those who do not hesitate to engage in vivisection, will not hesitate to lie about it.' It's disgusting."

"Yeah," he said, "but what I'm really wondering is what is M going to do. It's been two days and we haven't heard squat."

"M," she said. "I'm getting tired of M. I've felt all along that we're moving too slow. But, oh no, listen to M, the world expert, trained in England and full of knowledge. I say she's full of crap."

Jerry got up and went into the kitchen for another beer. "So what do you plan to do about it?" he asked when he got back into the room. He sat back in the chair and grabbed another handful of popcorn.

"Well," she said, "I have an idea. You're going to think I'm crazy, but hear me out on this before you reject it, OK?" Jerry nodded and she moved over close to his chair and began to spin out her idea. True to his word, he waited until she finished before he spoke.

"You're right," he told her, "I think you're crazy. In fact, I know you're crazy. But then that's one of the things I like about you. 'Cause I've been called crazy, too." He got up from the chair, walked to the window and stared out into the street. "And you know what I think? It just might be crazy enough to work."

They both laughed.

Chapter 34

"Mr. Philpott will see you shortly," Melville Higgins said with the reserve that seemed to be his trademark. "Please be seated."

Casey obeyed and sat outside the door to Proctor Philpott's office. This has been quite a week, she thought, as she reviewed the things that had happened since Pennrose Parker called on Sunday and asked her to participate in the handling of the Temeritus reaction to the raid at the lab.

Parker's call had come in before breakfast and ruined what had been planned as a day of rest and relaxation with Jake. "Casey, there's been a break-in at the lab and we sort of have a major crisis to address. Proctor asked me to call you and see if you could come in to the Tower and help us out on it." How could she refuse?

Soon, Casey was on her way into the so-called "issues" conference room on the eighth floor of Temeritus Tower. The room was small, windowless and covered with a fabric-type wallpaper that had been fashionable at one time but was now as dated as shag carpets and Nehru jackets. This paper was either beige or so aged that its true color had faded.

Gathered around tables arranged in a horseshoe were Sam Slurry and an assortment of people from Issues and External Affairs and from the Law Department. Casey was introduced to the people she didn't know, and they waited for Parker to arrive.

At 11:15 Parker entered the room and took his seat at the top of the horseshoe. He was wearing a suit that had the same pallor as the wallpaper, and Casey thought she would burst out laughing when she recalled Liz Stokes' description of Parallel Parker as being "just one of those beige sort of men who you never really notice." When seated at the table he blended into the wallpaper and the only thing that stood out was his perfectly groomed head. It's amazing, Casey thought, this guy blends into the background even when he chairs a meeting. And why would he be all decked out in a full business suit to work on a crisis on a Sunday, Casey thought. Maybe he was on his way to church.

Parker turned the meeting over to Slurry, who described the situation–a routine check of the facility at The Woodlands late Saturday night had uncovered a break-in. The guard on duty had been overpowered and a door had been broken, but other than that nothing had been destroyed and the intruders had fled without free-ing any of the animals in the lab. He reported that there were twelve beagles in the lab and they were untouched. Slurry said he had been on the scene and could verify that what had been reported was true.

Parker asked Slurry a series of questions and concluded on the basis of the answers that Temeritus should be able to keep this raid a secret, thereby thwarting the ALA in its desire to get publicity. Casey balked. "This sounds like a raid that failed" she said, and then a domino series of questions, "Why would ALA want to publicize a failure? Why not use this as a means of taking the offensive on this issue? If the company isn't doing anything to be ashamed of, what sense did it make to be so secretive? Why don't we put out a press release saying that we've been broken into and we're clean? Why don't we hold a press conference and let them see what these little dogs look like? Why don't we get a positive story out there to counter the neg-ative coverage that our enemies have been flooding the public with?"

Parker went into another tirade of how he knew what Proctor

wanted, and it wasn't more publicity. "You don't seem to understand, Casey," he said. "We're supposed to stop publicity, not generate it." The topic was discussed at length.

At the height of the argument, Harold Hoare arrived fresh from the golf course and proceeded to give his practical bottom-line analysis–none of this stuff affects the bottom line, and therefore it's not significant. A waste of money. Should just drop it and not worry about it anymore.

But Casey persisted. And in the end Parker and Hoare agreed that, since Philpott had hired her to help on these matters, she should present her opinion to him at the briefing scheduled for Sunday afternoon. "But," Parker had warned her, "be advised that we, Harold and I, think that what you're advocating is kind of foolish, and I for one will tell Philpott how I really feel. And the bottom line thing, too." He looked at Hoare for support, and finding it, he redoubled his resolve to state his total opposition to what she had proposed.

"I remember the last time I recommended something that I knew Proctor wouldn't like. I was right–he didn't like it and boy, oh boy, was I ever embarrassed. I mean if I could've dropped dead right on the spot, I'd have been the happiest man alive, I'll tell you." He paused and gave Casey his most earnest look. "And so I'm here to tell you, Casey, you can tell him whatever you want to; I'm telling him what I know he'll want to hear." And they headed for Philpott's office.

Thinking back on it, Casey had to laugh. Parker began the briefing by stating that Casey had a novel approach to suggest and that she would go first, before they got to the heart of the matter. Casey made her pitch for openness and for taking the offensive and, to the amazement of all, Philpott agreed. There followed a retreat the likes of which has not been seen since the First Battle of Manassas–Parker and Hoare trying to out-sprint each other in a rush to announce their support for Casey's position. They not only adopted her position but they claimed it as their own and took credit for pushing her in that direction. These guys have sure earned their nicknames, Casey thought.

The decision was made, Temeritus would issue a press release late Sunday on the break-in, and a press conference would be held Monday afternoon at which the beagles would be shown and lots of good things said about the Temeritus testing program. Casey was impressed by the precision of Proctor Philpott's decision-making and delighted that her suggestions had been accepted.

She was also surprised when Philpott asked her to remain in his office after the meeting with Parker and Hoare to discuss her project on the status of women in the company. He asked her to have a report ready for him to see by Wednesday. Although this was much sooner than the timetable she had envisioned, she agreed and spent the next two days writing her report and having it put into professional form by her staff at O'Rourke and Associates. And she was sitting now in the chilled proximity of Melville Higgins awaiting the summons into the cavernous office of Proctor Philpott.

"Mr. Philpott will see you now."

Casey went into the office and began to present her paper. The thrust of her report was simple–the status of women in the company was low because Temeritus made no attempt to recruit them and no effort to retain the ones it had. The company had no policies that would encourage women to seek it out as a potential place of employment and had created an environment that, while not hostile to women, certainly did not foster enthusiasm towards them or among them. The report listed not only Casey's findings, but also her recommendations for improvement.

These recommendations were personnel specific, listing by name the women Casey had met who appeared to be worthy of and fully prepared for advancement in the company. On this list were, among others, Liz Stokes and Melissa Fellows.

They discussed the report in detail. Philpott was effusive in his praise of her work. "Casey, this is one of the finest pieces of staff work I've ever seen. I can't tell you how much I appreciate it and how much I value its conclusions." He rose from his chair, walked around the desk and shook Casey's hand as if she had just won the Texas Lottery. "Thanks, Casey. You'll never know how grateful I am."

He placed his hand on her shoulder and escorted her to the door. "Now, if you'll excuse me, I need to prepare Mr. Timmons for the meeting tomorrow."

Casey was elated. Her report had been rushed, and she feared it might lack the depth that more time would have allowed. But he praised it, and she felt the deep satisfaction that comes with a job well done and well received. She felt almost lighthearted as she entered her office and began to prepare her report on animal testing.

Proctor Philpott closed the door to his office and returned to his desk. He picked up Casey's report and held it in front of him, staring at its cover. He riffled the pages scanning the contents of the report from back to front. A half-smile sneer crossed his face and he tossed the report into the trash can. "What a crock of shit," he said to the empty office.

Chapter 35

The first of the Senior Select to arrive for the meeting walked in about quarter till. Dewey Shivers had been there early making sure that everything was in order. By five till the room was filled with large men, most of whom looked vaguely alike, all buttoned down and in compliance with the dress code–dark pinstriped suits, white shirts, striped ties, wingtips.

By the time Casey got there, most of the attendees were already in their seats, carrying on quiet conversations, without a hint of mirth or good cheer. Casey went to the back and sat down. She got the same cold stares that she got in the lunch room. And as usual, she was the only woman in the room. She had thought that for a meeting of such magnitude–it had been explained to her as a command performance for all the Senior Select–the elusive Abigail Siefer would have flown back from her special assignment in London. But she was not there.

Casey noticed Melville Higgins standing by the door counting heads and checking the roster for Proctor Philpott.

At exactly ten o'clock, conversation ceased and Higgins took a seat against the wall, a steno pad now open on his lap while Philpott waited at the door. A funereal hush filled the room. It was common knowledge that Wilfurd Timmons did not like these things and that he was uncomfortable in groups of more than five or six people. It was his practice to come into meetings shortly after the starting time, and it was known that there was to be silence waiting for him when he arrived.

When the room had soaked in silence for thirty seconds or so, there came forth from somewhere in the middle of the seated flock the unmistakable sound of a fart escaping from one of the many tight asses gathered there. TWEEEEOOOOT. The silence was short-lived. First a twitter, as people shifted in their seats and looked embarrassedly about. A giggle here, a giggle there, then a cascade of laughter unheard in the history of Temeritus. It was as though the tension of several months had found an outlet and was now rushing forth unchecked. Casey thought she even heard Higgins laughing. And at that very moment into the room walked Wilfurd Timmons.

Timmons eased tentatively into the room, like a college professor who was not certain whether he was in the right lecture hall. By the time he reached the lectern the group had regained most of its composure. Dewey Shivers leaped to his feet and almost stumbled as he hurried to the lectern to help Timmons hook up his lapel mike.

"What in the hell is everyone laughing about?" Timmons whispered.

"I think they're just overly nervous, sir. I wouldn't worry about it."

Timmons pulled at the mike and slumped out onto the lip of the stage. He assumed his characteristic pose–hands in pockets, head down as if he had a teleprompter on his shoes, knees slightly bent–and addressed the assembled executives.

"Well, guys, it's not so often that we all get together like this. But I thought it would be appropriate today because I want to make sure that each of you gets the message straight from me. It's no secret that Temeritus is in big trouble. Our profits have been off for several years now, and we are facing the prospect of being in the red for the first time in the history of the corporation. As we used to say back when I was in college, we have been taking gas." At the word "gas" several in the room began to feel the repressed laughter of a few moments ago trying to come up for air. There was a slight stirring in the room. Timmons continued.

"Over the last few years we have seen market shares dwindle, new product lines fail to meet expectations. And the only way to sum up our condition at the present time would be to say this: it stinks."

Now the urge to laugh became almost unbearable. Harold Hoare, usually a model of controlled decorum, was among the worst. He knew he was on the verge of a fit of the giggles unmatched by anything since his college days. He couldn't believe it. Here on perhaps the bleakest day in the history of the company, he was straining like a teenager in church trying to maintain his composure. Please, God, don't let me laugh. But it was not to be. The spark applied to this tinderbox of repressed levity came from Wilfurd Timmons himself.

"Now what I want to talk about today is layoffs. We're to the point where only drastic action can save the company, and the general executive committee has decided that the company is going to have to cut a hell of a lot of people. Some of you in this room may have already gotten wind of these cuts." The spark was lighted. Almost as before–but much more quickly–wide-spread laughter broke out. First in a cough-masked explosion of air from Hoare, and then in numerous other gigglings, and finally in a torrent of laughter on the part of the Fabulous Fifty. Casey was certain this time that Melville Higgins was laughing right along with the rest.

Timmons was in shock. For the first time he raised his head, not just his eyes, and looked out over the crowd. Proctor Philpott rose from his seat in the front row and turned to the crowd, his open hands extended as if he were a preacher blessing his flock. "Men, men. We've got to get this under control. Why don't we take a ten-minute break and reconvene after we've recovered our composure?" Wilfurd Timmons agreed that this was a good idea, and the meeting stood in recess.

Timmons was furious. "What's the meaning of this, Proctor? Have things gotten so bad that we can't maintain control at a meeting of the Senior Select? I want an explanation."

Philpott put his hand on Timmons' shoulder. "Now, Wilfurd, just relax. These guys are all tensed up. Worse than you can imagine. And just before you came in someone in the room broke wind and, I don't know, it just sort of got out of control. I know it seems hard to understand but I think we'll all be better off for having had this release of tensions."

"Well, OK, I guess," Timmons said "but it's hard for me to see how this could happen with all the problems facing the company. Reschedule the meeting for two o'clock this afternoon."

Casey remained in the back of the room. Most of the men filed out with their heads down in embarrassed silence and into the reception area where the coffee had been set up. Proctor Philpott had Dewey Shivers pass the word that the meeting had been rescheduled and the Senior Select began to return to their offices.

When everyone else had departed the room, Casey got up and went back to her office, laughing all the way.

Chapter 36

Another long work week pulled to a close for Wilfurd Timmons. And a bad week it had been. All of the publicity, the boycott, the demonstrations, the violence. Now this thing at The Woodlands had caused even more publicity. As far as he was concerned, "bad publicity" was redundant–all publicity was bad publicity. It only meant sharper focus on the company's foreign ownership, and it only led to more questions from London. Wilfurd Timmons learned early in his career that publicity was to be avoided. And his general mood had not been helped by the unfortunate Senior Select incident earlier in the week. He was glad the weekend had finally arrived, and just before 7:30, a few minutes earlier than his usual quitting time, he decided to call it a day.

He tidied his desk and stuffed some small reports and memos in his briefcase. He picked up the two thick binders containing the reports he planned to study over the weekend, turned off the lights and left his office. Wilfurd Timmons' predecessor, J. Wardman Buffington, had used uniformed bodyguards whenever he left the building. Although the bodyguards came with the job, Timmons found the practice self-indulgent and actually embarrassing, and he discontinued it, preferring the anonymity of being alone. He suspected that the practice of his predecessor had its origins not in a legitimate concern for personal security, but rather in Buffington's native pleasure in the accoutrements of royalty which he layered across his presidency.

Timmons took the executive elevator to the lobby and walked to the small bank of elevators that connected the lobby with the mall and the other underground floors. The three floors under the mall level were the parking floors. The bottom two, designated as U-2 and U-3, were for the use of certain upper-middle managers who paid for the privilege and parked on a first-come, first-served basis. The prestige floor was U-1, the special parking facility where the elite of Temeritus upper management—those whose salaries were so high that the company felt compelled to provide free parking—parked their company cars in specially numbered stalls. In the days of J. Wardman Buffington, each reserved stall was emblazoned with the name and title of its occupant—J.W. BUFFINGTON, PRESIDENT AND CEO, TEMERITUS, INCORPORATED, and so on. But Timmons had discontinued this practice, along with many of the other excess excesses of the Buffington era. Ordinary excesses remained—parking stalls for overpaid upper management on U-1 were now identified only by number and the modest message, RESERVED.

Vehicular access to the underground parking areas was controlled by electronic keycard. Pedestrian access was open to anyone already in the building by using either the elevator or the stairs. Wilfurd Timmons, who usually walked the two flights to his car as part of his overall exercise program, opted for the elevator. The week had overtaken his urge to walk the stairs tonight.

Across the street and several blocks from Temeritus Tower, Nancy Wade sat at a bus stop. She had been there since 6:30 watching Timmons' office. Finally, when the light went out, she opened her cellular phone and dialed the number of the pay phone in the mall area of Temeritus Tower. Midway through the first ring Jerry Turner answered. "Lights out," she said and hung up. Turner said nothing as he replaced the handset.

At last, he thought, time to act. He walked into the hall, and down one flight to U-1. He walked past the elevators, opened the heavy glass door and walked into the parking garage. Although the awful days of full summer had ended more than a month before, the garage still felt like summer–hot and humid, with the smells of old exhaust and mildew hanging soggy in the still air.

Unlike the night before, when they had been forced to abort the operation, the garage was deserted. Only a few cars remained in the lot and no people. He walked past the blue Cadillac parked in stall thirty-six and stopped just around the corner, where he would not be seen by someone walking onto the floor from the elevator foyer.

He waited. Several minutes went by. His mouth was dry, his heart racing. And his face still hurt from shaving his beard for the first time in over ten years. I'm not so sure that this was a good idea, he thought as he stood in the stillness of the garage, braced against the wall, hoping that no one would drive by.

The operation had been planned with speed but with care. Wade knew many things about Temeritus and its executives. She had been assigned the task of gathering such intelligence for the cell in connection with its anti-Temeritus campaign. She knew Wilfurd Timmons' work habits, the layout of the parking garage, the rules concerning access to the building after hours, etc. She learned through personal reconnaissance that anyone could enter the building at any time during the day up until 7:00, when the doors were locked and a keycard was required.

Then she picked a spot outside Temeritus Tower from which she could observe Timmons' office. For two nights they had observed the light go out and measured the time it took before they saw Timmons' car emerge from the building. They conducted a "dress rehearsal," during which Turner entered the building at 6:30 wearing his blue pinstriped suit and carrying the dark leather briefcase that was the Temeritus uniform. In addition to shaving his beard and cutting his hair into a more executive-looking style, he had on a pair of tortoiseshell glasses. He went to the mall level and pretended to be talking on one of its many pay phones, holding the handset to his ear while keeping the hook depressed with his left hand.

When she saw the light go off in Timmons' office, she called Turner's pay phone, and he proceeded to U-1, where he waited in the shadows near Timmons' car. The dress rehearsal was flawless. But their first attempt at the real thing was foiled by the sudden appearance of some sycophant who had followed Timmons down from the lobby. Turner had merely walked past the two of them, blending into the background as he did with his pinstriped suit and leather briefcase.

Tonight the plan appeared to be working. He waited in the quiet, his ears straining for sound. Finally, he heard the door open . . . footsteps clipping through the nearly empty garage, louder and louder as they approached . . . silence . . . the jangling of keys–at last, his signal to act. Gripping his briefcase in his left hand he stepped out from behind the corner.

"Mr. Timmons, sir," he said, walking towards the Cadillac.

Timmons looked up from where he had just put his briefing books and briefcase in the back seat of the car. "Why, yes?" he said looking at this stranger, wondering who he was.

"You forgot something," Turner said, walking up to the car and placing the briefcase on the trunk. He opened the briefcase, grabbed the can of Mace and sprayed it straight into Timmons' startled face. Timmons coughed and sputtered and fell to the ground clutching his eyes. Turner took a loaded syringe from the briefcase and stabbed it through the luxurious fabric of a hand-tailored suit, squeezing 5 cc's of Ketamine into Timmons' thigh. Turner held him pinned to the ground, while the hypnotic drug took effect, sending Wilfurd Timmons into a deep and dreamless sleep.

Turner took the keys and opened the trunk. He returned to Timmons–stretched out unconscious on the pavement–lifted him up like he would a sleeping baby, placed him in the trunk and closed it. He walked around the car, stopping to put his briefcase in the back, and slipped onto the driver's seat. He started the engine, backed out of the stall and drove out of the building.

Nancy Wade was waiting two blocks away. He stopped and she got into the car. "Piece of cake," he smiled, as they drove towards I-45.

Chapter 37

North of Houston, north even of The Woodlands, Interstate 45 intersects with State Highway 105. Ten miles to the west is Lake Conroe, a large lake created by the Army Corps of Engineers in the early 1970s. In clusters around this lake, a number of recreational communities offer "lake houses," to which weary Houstonians can repair for a weekend away from the rigors of city life. Lake house owners will tell you that as soon as they turn off of I-45 and head west, they can feel the tensions of the week begin to slip away. This pleasant stretch of slight hills and heavy woods serves as a decompression zone for those escaping to the lake for some R&R. Such is their anticipation that they seldom notice the many little roads disappearing into woods, all but invisible to those speeding their way to the lake.

Approximately one hour after the encounter in the basement of Temeritus Tower, Wilfurd Timmons' Cadillac turned onto one of these little roads. One mile down the paved road and several hundred yards on a dirt road into the trees was the old Turner homestead, a farmhouse and barn on thirty acres of trees and open fields. Long abandoned, it was only recently being used by Jerry Turner and Nancy Wade as headquarters for what they termed "Operation Snatch."

Other than moonlight shining behind the farm house, the place was cast in darkness. They drove past the farmhouse to the barn, the Cadillac bumping and bouncing on the ruts baked into the dirt. Turner circled the car around and backed up until it almost touched the barn door. They got out and opened the trunk. Timmons was still unconscious.

"He looks like he's doing just fine," Jerry said.

"Yeah," Nancy responded. "Wouldn't want anything to go wrong with our test animal, now, would we?" She laughed.

Using a flashlight, Jerry went to the door of the barn and unlocked a heavy padlock. He swung the door open, walked inside and flicked a switch. Bright light flooded the barn, causing them to blink at the glare. As their eyes adjusted, they could see the fruit of their recent labors–the five-foot square metal cage, the steel frame bed with restraining devices and, of course, the makeshift Draize board, all designed especially for the President and Chief Executive Officer of Temeritus, Incorporated.

"It's perfect," Nancy said. "Absolutely perfect. Now, let's get him in here and let him sleep off his shot." They went back to the car and carried Timmons into the barn, Jerry holding him under the arms and Nancy holding him by the legs. They placed him on the bed, stripped him, fastened the restraining devices to his arms, turned out the lights and went to the house.

"He's going to really be surprised when he wakes up," Jerry laughed.

"Not as surprised as he's going to be when he learns what we have in store for him over the next few days," Nancy laughed even harder.

Chapter 38

"You better get over here, Larry." M was more agitated than Larry Mitchell had ever heard her. And she had never called him by his name. "We're in serious trouble and I need your help. Come to my house . . . Now!" She gave him the directions and told him to hurry.

In the thirty minutes it took him to reach her house, M had pulled her thoughts together after the phone call from Nancy Wade. She sat at her kitchen table reliving that call for Mitchell's benefit.

"A little after nine my beeper goes off and I go down to the pay phone and return the call. It's from Nancy Wade; you only know her as 'P,' the little mean one with the big eyebrows." She paused and looked across the table. "She has kidnapped Wilfurd Timmons, the CEO of Temeritus."

"What! You've got to be kidding. Why?"

"Wait till you hear. You're not going to believe it." She paced back and forth as she related what she knew. The conversation had been brief. Nancy Wade was taking over the cell—she used the word "coup"—and would make all decisions in the future. M was to give her the roster of all members and hands and, in her words, "butt out." She knew Temeritus was continuing to engage in illegal animal testing, and she was going to expose it. Timmons would be given a dose of the "humane" treatment his company regularly gave its "non-human employees" so he could see firsthand how inhumane it really was. And in the process he would tell about the secret lab. When he came clean, he would be released–but only after he promised to shut down the secret lab and stop all forms of animal testing.

"And," M said, concluding her summary of the conversation, "if I don't go along with her on this, she says she'll call the FBI and spill her guts about the cell, and we could all go to jail. I don't think she knows very much; all she has for sure is the number of my beeper. But she could sure cause trouble. And it would ruin everything we're trying to do."

"I never did like that scrawny little bitch," he said. "This is outrageous. Has she done this all by herself? How did she do it? Where does she have the guy? This is unbelievable. Do you think she's made it all up?" Mitchell was now the pacer and M was seated at the kitchen table.

"No, I don't think so. I called our most reliable Temeritus sources and they are unable to locate him. And I was assured that on a Friday night he would be at home. She has him all right, and she'll do just what she says she will. You know how wild she is at meetings. She's crazy enough to do everything she says." M went to the refrigerator and got out two small bottles of water, opened them and set them on the table. "And, she's not acting alone. T, the big guy with the red beard–Jerry Turner's his name–he's her partner in crime on this. And you know what a mean bastard he is." Mitchell rolled his eyes and groaned. "I don't know exactly what they did, but they have him and they're planning to ruin his weekend, I guarantee you that. And what a shame it is, too. Of all the people at Temeritus, they pick the one guy who is a pretty decent human being."

"Do you know him?" he asked.

"Well, our sources on Temeritus have told me a whole lot about him."

Mitchell took a long pull of the water and wiped his mouth with the back of his hand. "So what do we do now?"

"Well, I know what we have to do first. After that, who

knows? That's why I wanted you to come over. I figure that between your police background and my craftiness, we ought to be able to come up with something. And, if we're lucky, we'll have the whole weekend to work on it before anyone notices that Timmons is missing."

"Why's that?"

"Because he's a bachelor, well, technically–a widower. He lives alone. And if what she told me is true, they have his car also, got him as he was leaving work. So there is no reason anyone will even know he's missing until Monday morning."

"What about the cell?"

"I agreed on the phone to meet her tomorrow morning early and turn over the records of the cell. From then on, it's all up to her as the new leader of ALA in Houston."

"I can't believe you're going to just turn it all over to her like that." He stared at her in disbelief.

"I told her I'd turn over the roster. Nobody has said anything about turning over the real roster." And for the first time that evening M smiled. "And I'm glad you know me so well. Here's what I have in mind." M spent the next several minutes telling Mitchell her plan for the initial handling of the crisis. She would indeed turn over a roster of names and telephone numbers. But they would be pulled at random out of the phone book, with the only deciding factor being the proper initial on the name. They laughed when they thought of the conversations that would result when Nancy Wade began to rally her troops.

M also planned to call each member of the cell and each "hand." The message would be simple: There has been a serious breach in security by members P and T; your identities remain secure; however, if anyone, even another member of the cell, contacts you, do not discuss anything having to do with the cell; do not even acknowledge membership in or knowledge of ALA; do not try to contact me through the beeper; just play dumb, sit tight and wait for further instructions from me.

"Then what?" he asked.

"Don't know yet. We'll have to come up with something. But in the meantime, I have calls to make and some records to phony-up for the lovely and charming Nancy Wade. And I have two jobs for you while I'm on the phone. Call your pal at the police department and ID the phone number on my beeper. We need to know where that call came from. And then I want you to fix up one of those custom briefcases you told me about." They both smiled. She rose from the chair and walked into her office to get the files and records in shape for the delivery to Nancy Wade. "Now, come with me, Larry. I'll give you a tour of ALA Headquarters."

Chapter 39

Wilfurd Timmons awoke shortly after midnight, cold and sightless in the dark. He tried to move and found his arms bound fast. At first he thought he was in a hospital recovery room, but the restraints on his arms and the musty smell of the cold air told him that this was not a hospital.

He tried to recall what had happened, but all he could remember was gathering up his weekend reading and leaving the office. Was there something in the parking lot? He just couldn't get it into focus. What in the world is happening, he thought, as he drifted into a troubled twilight sleep. He dreamed he was dying; he dreamed he was dead; he dreamed he was visited by the Devil, he dreamed he was . . .

Footsteps. Definitely footsteps, getting closer. Closer yet. And now the screeching of a door opening. Still dark as death but now there was sound. A man close by, or was it a woman? Timmons turned his head to the side and looked in the direction of the sound. The beam of a flashlight cut through the darkness and across the floor. The flashlight itself came into view. Whoever was holding it was standing beside the bed, the light beaming into Timmons' eyes, blinding him again. Despite the cold, he could feel rivulets of sweat running down from his armpits.

"How do you feel, Mr. Timmons?" A man's voice. Timmons strained to see behind the ring of glare that was the flashlight.

"Who are you? What's going on? Where are we?"

"Relax, man. Everything's cool. Just wanted to see how you were doing. Want to make sure you get a good night's sleep. We have a busy day tomorrow." He put the flashlight on the bed next to Timmons' head so that it shone down onto his shoulders and arms. "Now, this is going to help you sleep real good," the voice said. "And don't worry. I spent four years as an Army medic; I know how to give good injection." Timmons saw a flash of metal and felt a mild sting in his right arm.

He could just barely make out the outline of the man's head in the soft gray penumbra of the flashlight's beam. Ghostlike. Oh, my God, Timmons thought, he's wearing a ski mask. His body shook in terror as the Valium began its work and within minutes, the ski mask, and the man himself, faded away as Timmons drifted into sleep.

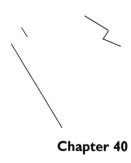

Chapter 40

On the western edge of downtown Houston is a small island of historic time-warp known as Sam Houston Park. Beginning in the 1950s with the founding of the Harris County Heritage Society, this park has become home to some of the oldest dwellings in the city, all of which have been moved to the site and restored with careful attention to historic detail. Four of the seven restored houses surround an expanse of grass at the center of which is an old-time bandstand. The park is a delightful oasis of calm in the midst of the urban chaos that is Houston, a refuge for many of the office workers in the nearby buildings and also the site of numerous festivals and musical events for which Houston is renowned. During the daylight hours any day of the year the weather allows, this little park is a haven for people to stroll and enjoy the spectacular view of the Houston skyline or to sit in peace on one of the many park benches and be alone. Early Saturday morning M sat on one of these benches waiting for Nancy Wade.

Her instructions were precise—9 a.m., Sam Houston Park, go to the first bench you come to as you walk down the path from Bagby Street into the park and wait for me there, alone; bring the ALA files in a briefcase or folder that will be easy to carry.

At 9:15, Nancy appeared, easing up behind M and sitting on the bench in one continuous movement. She wore an old army jacket that hid her scrawny frame and a pair of large plastic-rimmed sunglasses that hid her bushy eyebrows. It was an effective disguise.

"It's all in here," M said, handing her the briefcase.

"Just what exactly is it?"

"The roster of members and hands and their code names, just like you said."

"Yeah," she sneered. "I want to see it. Open it up and let me see."

M opened the briefcase and went through the contents. When she finished she said, "This is a huge mistake, and I hope you know it."

"Save your wind, bitch. I don't give a shit what you think. You're history. You're going to see me get more done in a few weeks than you dreamed of doing in a whole year. Just watch." She paused and stroked the sides of the briefcase. "And remember, don't try to interfere with what I'm doing. You stay out of it and you'll be OK. But if you get to messing with us, I'll make your life miserable. Now, I want you to just sit here for ten minutes after I leave the park. You're being watched by one of my associates, so don't even think of trying to follow me. Is that clear, bitch?" M stared at her without responding.

Nancy stood up. "And one other thing," she said sticking her finger in front of M's face. "Keep your beeper on. I may need to get in touch."

M sat on the bench and watched Nancy walk away. Yeah, she thought, I may need to get in touch with you, too.

Nancy walked out of the park and crossed the street to the Central Public Library. She walked to the elevator bank and rode to the basement parking lot. From there she walked up the entrance ramp and out onto Lamar Street to the car she had rented earlier that morning under an assumed name. She checked to make sure she was not being followed, got in and drove off.

Ten minutes later, she drove into the parking lot at the Northwest Mall where she abandoned the rental car and walked through the Mall to the parking lot on the other side. She walked to her car, which she had parked there earlier that morning before she had taken the cab to the rental agency and driven downtown to meet

M. She started the car and drove out onto the Loop.

Jerry had teased her about the elaborate precautions she was taking to assure that no one followed her but she shrugged it off. You can't be too careful, she'd said. That's one thing I've learned from M, you just can't be too careful when it comes to security. And now, feeling smug in that security, Nancy was headed back to the country and back to Wilfurd Timmons.

Ah, yes, Wilfurd Timmons, she thought, as her mind drifted back to the early morning hours in Jerry's barn. They had been up before dawn to begin the work of the day dressed in trousers, turtleneck sweaters and ski masks, all solid black. Timmons was asleep when they went into the barn. They went to the foot of Timmons' bed and awakened him by shaking his legs and shining the strong beams of their flashlights into his confused face. He strained to get a better view of his tormentors, but the restraints limited his movement and he stared, blinking into the light. Nancy handled the interrogation.

"You are Wilfurd Timmons, leader of the immoral corporation which calls itself Temeritus?" she said in her most severe voice. Timmons' eyes were opened wide, his mouth agape. He said nothing. "You will answer my questions," she said, louder, almost shouting.

"Yes, I'm Wilfurd Timmons." He paused, dropping his head back onto the bed. "And I'm the President and CEO of Temeritus." Another pause. "Who are you and what do you want?" he asked.

She raised her flashlight above her head and brought it down with all of her strength, cracking it against Timmons' knee. He cried out in pain and jerked his head up, staring in wide-eyed terror into the beam from Jerry's light. "I'll ask the questions, asshole." She refocused her light into Timmons' face and continued, "You don't know who we are. But we know you. And we know what you do to the animals in your labs. Those animals are our friends." Timmons groaned and put his head back down, resting it on the bed. "And we don't like the way you've been treating our friends."

What followed was more fun than Nancy had ever imagined. When they turned on the lights in the barn, Timmons' reaction to the sight of the two of them in the black outfits had been hilarious. And when Jerry picked up his AK-47, she thought Timmons would pass out from fear. With Jerry menacing him, Nancy placed a canvas bag over Timmons' head and removed the restraints. They told him they were going to treat him just like he treated his test animals, and since the Temeritus brochures stressed how humane it was, they were sure he would find it a pleasant experience. Then, with his hands tied behind his back, Timmons had been led to the Draize board Jerry had made earlier in the week.

It was similar to the ones used in the labs–a bottom board with a semi-circle carved out of it to make room for the neck of the test animal, and a top board also with a semi-circle in it which, when closed against the bottom board, would hold the neck of the test animal in a fixed position, not unlike the stocks of Pilgrim days. The major difference between this makeshift Draize board and the ones used in the labs at Temeritus was, of course, the species and singularity of the test animal.

Often in the lab it is necessary to prevent the test animal, usually a rabbit, from spoiling the results of a test by blinking and washing the substance being tested from the eye. This is done through the use of metal clips. The eyelid is pulled away from the eyeball and grasped in the prongs of the clip, which makes closing the eye impossible. The procedure is then repeated on the other eye and the animal left until the time needed to fully test the irritability of the test substance has elapsed.

With Timmons' head secured in the Draize board, Nancy came up behind him and pulled his head back. She pinched his left eyelid with her left thumb and forefinger, pulling it out and away from his eyeball. Then she opened the clip, which was connected to the top of the board by a wire, and placed it on the pinched fold of skin.

Timmons cried out in pain as she repeated the process on his right eyelid.

Then, with Timmons having taken on the bulge-eyed look of a man whose plastic surgery had lifted more than anticipated, she began to administer little squirts of Glitter, Temeritus' leading shampoo, directly onto the exposed eyeballs. Timmons screamed and pleaded with her to stop.

Nancy's reverie while driving back to the old Turner homestead was such that she failed to notice the dark blue 1991 Buick Skylark parked on the side of 105 just west of I-45. If she had, and if she could have looked past a hasty disguise, she might have recognized her compatriot in the animal liberation movement, the man she knew only as L–Larry Mitchell. She might also have noticed him pull onto the highway behind her, following as she led the way to her hideout. She might have; but she didn't.

She drove approximately two miles before turning left onto the side road leading into the woods where she pulled to the side and coasted to a stop. She waited several minutes. Nothing. Certain she had not been followed, she drove on making the final turn onto the dirt road leading to the farm. She sighed and congratulated herself—yep, you just can't be too careful.

Chapter 41

Larry Mitchell did not follow Nancy Wade when she turned off of
105. He didn't have to. That was the beauty of the homing device
embedded in the handle of the briefcase in which M's bogus rosters
had been delivered that morning. He knew he could delay a bit and
still pick up the signal, following close enough to remain within range
but not so close as to be observed.

When M left her house to deliver the bugged briefcase,
Mitchell drove north on I-45 to the service station identified by his
police department contact as the location from which Wade's call had
been placed–a Texaco station just west of I-45 on State Highway 105.
There he pulled to the far side of the station property and parked with
his engine running facing the highway. M's assumption–that Wade
had called from near the hideout and would return there with the
briefcase–was about to be tested. He waited. An hour of silence later,
his receiver began to pick up the signal from the tiny transmitter.
Louder. Louder yet until, just as the signal was reaching its maximum
intensity, Nancy Wade's late model blue Honda Accord, license QWK
945, sped by. Mitchell pulled out and followed for approximately two
miles until it made a left-hand turn onto a side road that went into the
woods. Two hundred yards past the side road, he turned around and
stopped.

By the time he returned to the junction of the side road and
105, the signal had dropped in intensity by about half. He proceeded

down the road into the woods. The signal began to get stronger. After about a mile it began to weaken. He turned around and went back towards 105 until the signal regained its strength–at the junction of the paved road and a narrow dirt road which led off to the right into the woods. There was no sign on the road, and it did not appear to be well-traveled. He was almost certain that the transmitter was down this road somewhere. To be sure, he drove several hundred feet down the road, and the signal got louder.

He stopped. The signal was almost at its maximum reading and it maintained a steady level, indicating the transmitter was close by and stationary. This is the place, he said to himself. He backed out to the paved road as fast as he could without stirring up dust and drove back to Houston.

" . . . And she didn't notice a thing." Larry was sitting in M's living room drinking a glass of water and telling her how he picked up Nancy Wade and followed her to what was probably the location of the hideaway.

"That's great. And it's not the only good news–we also know her phone number."

"How did we do that?" he asked.

"You remember putting that list of names and numbers together from the phone book?" Larry nodded. "Well, for the first name I used my telephone number. Just on the outside chance that she would make those calls from a phone at her hideaway. Well, the little fool didn't waste any time calling what she thought were the members of her cell. We'll have to check it and see, but there is a Conroe area telephone number on my Caller ID that came in at 11:02 and a message on the answering machine from her saying that a big meeting was set for next week. I can't believe she would be so stupid."

Another call to his friend at the HPD confirmed that the number in question was listed in Conroe to a "J. Turner." "So," he said, sitting back in his chair and smiling at their good fortune. "We have the location and phone number. What do we do now?"

Before M could answer, her pager chirped. She pulled it out of her belt and looked at the number. "What do you know. It's Nancy Wade's pay phone. Come on. Let's go down the street and call her back."

"You bitch! You scuzzy bitch!" Nancy screamed into the phone. "You gave me a phony list. Well, you think you're so goddamn smart, let me tell you what–I called that asshole who was on TV last week with those beagles and told him about what we're doing to Timmons. And I'm not going to stop until he goes on TV again and tells the world about the secret lab. And that they're going to shut it down. I told him it's a perfect deal: you close your secret lab, I'll close mine; and if you don't, you'll never see Timmons again."

"You're crazy," M said. "I know who you are and all I need to do is go to the FBI and you'll be spending the rest of your life in prison. You can't get away with this."

"Not as crazy as you are if you think I'm not going to take you down with me. If you really care about our cause, you'll butt out. Besides, if I get caught, you're dead, and you know it. So fuck off. Besides, even if I get caught, it'll be worth it just to be able to fry your big ass." Nancy paused for the first time in her Gatling gun delivery and chuckled. "But I won't get caught. So you and all of your little pals can just go fuck yourselves. Have a nice day, bitch."

M hung up the phone and turned to Larry. "Now that we know where they are, we've got to really act fast."

Chapter 42

In the Special Projects Office on the thirty-ninth floor of Temeritus Tower, an exhausted Melissa Fellows was finishing a sixth straight day of work on Proctor Philpott's "bottom fishing project." All of the lists had been compiled and all of the final versions of the notices and press releases–everything that would be needed to implement the next wave of layoffs had been prepared for Philpott's review. Melissa was going home to rest. She planned to return to the office on Sunday for one final review of the papers before she delivered them on Monday.

She pushed her chair back and took off her glasses. She raised her hands to her face, rubbing small circles on her eyes with her middle fingers and massaging her jawbones with her thumbs. She yawned, stretched and rose, walking across the hall to Philpott's office to use his private bathroom.

Philpott's was the only private bathroom in the Tower. Not even J. Wardman Buffington had felt the need for such a thing. Buffington notwithstanding, the day his promotion was announced, Philpott evicted the occupant of the adjoining office and personally supervised the design and construction of the new facility, which included a door offering direct access from his office. This facility was exclusively his. No one dared use it. In fact, its presence added new meaning to the word "throne" for those in the building who dealt with him. Despite this rigid exclusiveness, when Melissa worked late in the

Special Projects Office, she used it, relishing her sense of daring. Besides, it was the only bathroom in the Tower with linen towels and washcloths.

As she was putting her towel in the hamper, she heard voices. The cleaning crew, she thought. How embarrassing. Then she remembered–the cleaning crew doesn't work on Saturdays. Embarrassment turned to mild fear. Who would be here on a Saturday night? She turned out the light and closed the door so that it was open just a crack and waited for whoever it was to go by. To her surprise, they did not go by. They walked into the office, talking in angry tones.

" . . . since the dumb son-of-a-bitch got himself kidnapped." Melissa peeked through the cracked door and looked into the office. It was Proctor Philpott himself. And behind him like a puppy on a leash was Sam Slurry.

"I just can't believe it, Sam," Philpott yelled. "How could this happen? You're sure he isn't just out somewhere?" He went to the long low cabinet on the wall, opened one of its doors and took out a bottle of Scotch.

"Yeah, Boss, I'm sure. I went out there just like you said, and I guarantee you he hasn't been home since he came to work yesterday. His car's gone, there's two day's worth of mail in the mailbox and the papers are still on the front porch."

Philpott walked back to his desk and picked up a glass. "You want a drink?" Slurry shook his head.

"Well, I need one," he said pouring Scotch into the glass. He sat in his chair, sipped from the drink and sighed. "What about the parking garage?"

"Car's not there. He's definitely gone." Sam pulled at his collar and grimaced. "Tell me again what the lady said."

"Christ, Sam, I think you're getting feebleminded." Philpott sipped from his drink. "I told you. She said she was with some animal rights group and they've kidnapped Timmons and aren't going to release him until I go on TV and admit that we really do have a secret lab and that we're shutting it down." Philpott had risen from his seat and walked over to the window, staring out into the darkness as he talked. I guess he treats everyone the same, Melissa thought from her hiding place; he shows people his back when he talks to them.

Philpott continued, "And the strange thing is she said her group was conducting experiments on him. You know, dropping stuff in his eyes and that sort of thing. They have him in a cage of some kind. Said they wanted to give him a taste of what it's like to be a test animal."

"You gotta be kidding."

"No. And the other thing she said was, 'You close down your secret lab, I'll close down mine.'" He sipped from his drink. "'Perfect deal' is what she called it. So I guess they're really putting it to the old boy."

"And no mention of a ransom?"

"Just the lab and the testing."

"I guess you want me to call in the FBI, huh?"

At the mention of the FBI, Philpott spun around from the window. "Sam, don't you have good sense? That's the last thing I want you to do. Listen." He walked back to the desk and sat down. "We can't afford another public controversy. And this is one we can avoid. We can't be certain this crackpot is telling us the truth. And I sure as hell don't want the FBI at the lab, which is what will happen if they get involved. We've got to keep Timmons' problem under our hats for awhile. And there's no way we're going to stop the testing now that we're so close." He paused and sipped from his glass. "Speaking of which, tell me how it went when you moved those rabbits back to the green room."

Slurry reported that after the raid on the lab he had supervised the movement of the wrinkle study rabbits back into the green room after it had been refurbished, the locks repaired and the security brought in-house, under his direct supervision and utilizing hand-picked Temeritus employees. "You know, Chief, your plan was perfect. We got those rabbits out of there just in time. We'd have been in real trouble if they'd gone in there and found out what we were doing. As it turned out, they didn't find crap and those dogs came in real handy for your press conference. Gave us credibility. It was perfect. And all the while the tests on the rabbits continued."

"And what is the status of the tests?" Philpott asked.

"Well, I guess it's OK. You know, that stuff really works."

"Damn right it does. And it's going to make us both rich."

"But there's a problem starting to develop. One of our scientists keeps talking about . . . " he paused, searching for the right word. "Extrapolated, I think that's what he called it, and he seems to think there could be long-term side effects. Something about tissue breakdown. I don't know."

"I don't even want to hear about it. Scientists are always too cautious. They're worse than lawyers, always telling you what you can't do. We're on the verge of a major breakthrough in anti-aging creams, and we can't let some tight-assed scientist scare us out of it. We'll take care of him."

"Yeah, but what about Mr. Timmons?"

"Sam, some days I think you just don't understand English. Or anything else, for that matter. Here we are on the verge of literally making millions of dollars on this, and you're worried about Wilfurd Timmons. I mean, I'm real sorry about Timmons, but I'm not about to let him or anyone else stand in my way. I'm too close to having everything I want. And I'm going to have it all, Sam." Philpott stood up and returned to the window, staring out. "I'm going to have it all." After a long pause, he added, "Maybe the old fart will die. That'll solve another problem."

"Yes, sir," Slurry said, backing up a step. "But we do have to keep in mind that if the FBI gets involved, we gotta have a good story for them. It wouldn't look so good for the number two guy in the company to be sitting on his hands when he knows that the number one guy has been kidnapped."

"No problem. We just tell them we thought this was a bunch of loonies and Wilfurd was off on one of his do-not-disturb golf retreats somewhere and we didn't think much about it. We've been getting calls like these for months and they've all been phonies. How were we to know that this time the sky really was falling?"

Sam stood in silence, staring at Proctor in disbelief. "Yes, sir."

"And one other thing, Sam. I know I don't have to tell you this, but you're as deep into this as I am. And you can bet your ass if I go down, you'll go with me."

"Sure, Chief." There was a long pause during which the two men stood and looked at each other, Philpott's eye contact breaking first.

"Well, I guess that's about it," Philpott said. "Let's get out of here." He finished his drink. "Wait till I take a leak, and I'll walk down with you." Philpott put his glass on the desk and walked toward the bathroom.

Fear shot through Melissa's body. She dashed across the room, barely able to see in the dim light, and hid in the linen closet. She heard Philpott come into the bathroom, turn on the light and walk across the room to the toilet. After a brief moment of silence she heard the splashing sound of urination. Five seconds, ten seconds, fifteen seconds, more . . . God, will he ever finish? What will I do if he comes in here for a towel? But I put out a fresh towel after I used the one that was there. Thank God for that. She waited in the darkness of the linen closet, her breath keeping time with her racing heart.

"Hey, Sam," Philpott's voice boomed above the diminishing sound of his diminishing stream of water. "There's one more thing I want to do before we leave." Melissa could hear the toilet flush. A slight pause and then the water at the sink being turned on, and then off. Then Philpott's voice as he closed the door and walked back into his office. "I think we should go down to Timmons' office and put a golf outing on his schedule for next week. The Greenbrier's nice this time of year, don't you think?"

Melissa could hear Philpott laughing as they walked out of the office and into the hall, and as the sound of their voices lowered, she eased out of the closet and crept back to the bathroom door slowly opening it. The office was empty. I gotta get out of here, she thought, as she streaked for the door.

She stopped at the doorway and looked down the hall in the direction of Timmons' office. Nothing. She darted across the hall to the Special Projects Office, where she grabbed her purse and ran.

The elevator was several locked doors away, each requiring a card and a key pad number to open. She rushed to the first one, slid her security card through the reader and entered the access code. The door clicked and she pushed it open, certain she would see Philpott and Slurry coming back from Timmons' office. No, the hall was empty.

She ran to the second one and repeated the process with the same results–the hall was deserted. Maybe her luck would hold and she could get to the elevator without being caught. Just as she reached the door to the reception area and was passing her card through the reader when the door at the end of the hall opened and she saw them walk through. Her door clicked and she pushed through into the reception area.

She ran to the elevator bank and pushed the down button. She waited. Usually there was a car here. She pounded on the button, even though she knew it to be a hopeless gesture. The door she had just opened clicked behind her.

The light on the top of the elevator flashed. The bell rang, the elevator opened and Slurry burst through the door into the reception area all at the same time. She got into the car and pushed the button for the lobby. As the door was closing, she saw Slurry with Philpott close behind racing across the reception area. She wasn't certain, but she thought she saw a gun in Slurry's hand. "Hey, stop!" she heard him say as the elevator began its descent.

The elevator went nonstop to the lobby. Melissa knew she couldn't risk going to the basement for her car. She got off the elevator and walked to the security desk and as calmly as possible signed herself out. At the desk the telephone rang as she walked toward the door, and she heard the guard say "Yes, sir, Mr. Slurry. Let me see. Yes, sir. She just checked out."

Melissa pushed the security button to unlock the door. When it clicked, she pushed the door open and walked out into the cool evening air. Looking back over her shoulder, she saw the guard rise from his seat and run toward the door. She started to run. The guard opened the door and yelled out to her, "Miss Fellows! Come back. Mr. Slurry wants to talk to you."

Yeah, I bet he does, she thought as she ran across McKinney Street and into the deserted canyons of downtown Houston. I bet he does.

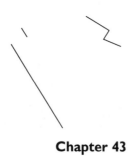

Chapter 43

Saturday was a quiet day for Casey, the beginning of what she hoped would be a quiet weekend. She spent the day in her usual manner–sleeping late, reading in bed (the latest Patricia Cornwell "Kay Scarpetta" novel) and having a relaxed breakfast.

The day continued in that fashion–quiet and semi-productive, not anything that you could write a book about, but most people's lives are like that. After a quick supper of cold chicken sandwiches and leftover bean soup, she headed for The Horse.

Jake was at the bar and Gabe was working the tables. Jake came out from behind the bar and gave her a big hug and kiss the way he always did. Casey said hello to Gabe and some of the others whom she recognized and finally sat down at the bar to enjoy a pint of Nicholas Tulrumble "Mudfog" Ale. She savored the first taste. Ah, yes, truly one of Jake's best brews, she thought.

Casey looked around the bar and her eyes stopped on a man sitting sideways on the other side of the bar. Who is that guy? she thought; he looks familiar for some reason. Maybe somebody from Temeritus . . . no, his hair is too long, hanging down like a valance around the sides of his otherwise bald head. Then she remembered–it was the guy from the animal rights group she had talked to before. Sure, it was Carl, the Mystery Man, sitting across the bar, nursing a pint of beer. Looks like he still hasn't gotten his glasses adjusted, she thought, watching him pushing his glasses up on his nose.

Almost as if her remembrance of him stirred him to action, Carl got up and walked around the bar to Casey. "Ms. O'Rourke?" He looked nervous. He sounded nervous.

"Hi, Carl, how are you?"

"I was hoping you would be here tonight. I have something very important to tell you. Can we go to a table?"

They moved to one of the open tables at the back of the room. He pushed his glasses up again and, without transition or introduction, he blurted, "There's been a stand-down." His eyes bulged and he looked at Casey as if he had just given her the formula for Coca-Cola.

"I beg your pardon?"

"A stand-down! You know, like they did in the Air Force when all the big bombers stopped flying."

"Bombers?" Casey asked. "Carl, I'm afraid you're going to have to tell me exactly what you mean."

He looked at her as if she didn't understand English. "I'm sorry." His shoulders drooped and he looked down at the table for a few moments and sighed, as if he were resigned to spending the rest of his life with such ignoramuses. "Let me begin again." He shifted in his chair and sipped at his beer.

"The last time we talked? I told you I was in a group called Animalis? And I was afraid that some of the other members were going to do something stupid?" He used the insidious new style of speech referred to by linguists as "up talk," favored by many young people and an increasing number of adults, each sentence ending in a question as if the speaker needed more than mere words to convince the listener. "And that I was concerned about the future of Temeritus?"

Casey nodded.

"Well, there isn't any problem in Animalis. I just told you that because I was scared. The group I was really talking about is the

Animal Liberation Army, the ALA. And I know you've heard of it?" Casey nodded. "Well, there's a couple of real wackos in there, just like I said. And today I got a call from the head of the group here in Houston telling me that all bets were off and we were to lay low until we heard from her again."

"Her?"

"Yeah, our leader is a woman. And she's really good. She said our security had been breached, or something like that, and we were supposed to cool it and not talk to anybody who might call from the group having to do with future activities, or anything. So the only thing I can figure is that what I predicted has come to pass. And I thought you should know about it."

"I appreciate that," Casey said. "But why do you expect me to put much faith in what you're telling me now? You just told me you didn't tell the truth the last time we talked; and some of the information you gave me last time has been proven to be false. If I recall, you said there was a secret lab, and we all know now that there wasn't. The ill-fated raid of your old group clearly showed that, didn't it?"

"Oh, no." Carl's nervousness was gone and his speech was becoming animated. "It's true. Temeritus is lying. There is a secret lab. I know because I talked to the people who were on the raid right after it was over. I drove the truck that was supposed to take the animals to the vet. And there weren't any animals to take. It wasn't the way it was reported in the papers and on TV, Casey. There were no animals in there when our people broke in. None. But there had been. They said you could see it and smell it. I don't know where those cute little beagles came from that they put on TV, but I'm here to tell you they weren't in the lab when we broke in."

"That's a serious charge, Carl. And I frankly don't believe it. I've been working on this full-time, and if what you say is true, they sure have put one over on me. And besides, how do I know you're telling me the truth this time? I thought ALA was a supersecret group and they would never divulge any of the kind of information that you're talking about right now."

"It is. And it's scary. And now that there's been this stand-down, it gives me the perfect opportunity to get out of the group. When they call me back, I'm going to tell them I can't do it anymore. I'm going to stay in my Animalis group, you know, where we can talk and not have to do anything. But the fact remains that I'm still concerned about Temeritus, and that's why I came to you with this information."

"And you're not scared of them anymore?"

"Oh, yeah, they scare me to death. But I figure that in the confusion over whatever it is that's going on, I can make a polite exit. Believe me, these people are tough. If some of them have branched out on their own, there's no telling what might happen."

He picked up his beer, his hand shaking, and finished it in a single swallow. "So, I guess that's about it. I hope they don't do anything stupid. At least you can warn the folks at Temeritus to be on guard." He stood and slinked away.

Casey related Carl's story to Jake during a lull in business, and they had a laugh at the expense of this odd little guy. But she couldn't get out of her mind the possibility there might be something going on at Temeritus that she hadn't been told. Somehow all of this didn't quite fit together.

She drank another beer and decided to go home. She was eager to find out what would happen next to Kay Scarpetta, and she figured if she went home early, she might even be able to finish the book tonight. She said her goodbyes, went to her car and drove home.

She was still thinking about her discussion with Carl when she drove into her driveway, pushed the button on her garage door opener and pulled into the garage. She closed the overhead door, locked the Jag and walked out of the garage by way of the small door leading to the walkway to the house. She closed the door and locked it. Security was a prime concern these days and, even though the exterior of her house was well lighted, this little walk from the garage to the house was the weakest link in that security. She was always wary and on the edge of nervousness when she walked from the garage to the house, especially late at night.

"Casey!" Someone called her name from the darkness just outside the reach of the overhead security lights. A stab of fear shot through her stomach. She heard the bushes rustle next to the driveway, and she turned, not certain what to expect. "Casey, it's Melissa. I need your help." And into the light came the figure of Melissa Fellows, looking haggard and scared. She ran up to Casey and hugged her, breaking into tears, sobbing without control. "Oh, Casey, I've never been so happy to see anyone in my life. I'm scared to death." She clutched at Casey as if she were a drowning swimmer.

"Melissa, you look terrible. What in the world has happened?"

"Quick, let's get inside. I think they may be after me."

Casey unlocked the door and deactivated the burglar alarm. So-So danced and barked and displayed her usual enthusiasm for Casey's reappearance in the house and for a few moments there was general pandemonium. So-So calmed down and Casey turned on the rest of the lights in the kitchen, and things began to return to normal. Although Melissa had been there before, So-So gave her a thorough sniffing and pronounced her–through the curious body language all dogs possess and all dog owners can read–to be an acceptable guest.

"My God," Casey said. "What's going on?" She went to the kitchen sink, put a hand towel under the faucet and wet it with cold water. She wrung it out and handed it to Melissa. "Here, use this on your face. It'll make you feel better."

Melissa sighed, regaining her composure. Then, twisting and untwisting the damp towel in her lap, she told Casey about the discussion she had overheard between Proctor Philpott and Sam Slurry and her terrifying dash out of Temeritus Tower.

Casey was horrified. Could this be what Carl was referring

to–that a group of dissidents from an already radical group had taken things into their own hands and kidnapped Wilfurd Timmons? Was this why the leader of the ALA had called a stand-down? Hundreds of thoughts raced through Casey's mind. But foremost in her mind was Proctor Philpott. The enormity of his behavior was beyond description. She knew of his unbridled ambition. But she would never have thought him capable of lying on such a grand scale about the lab and of sacrificing Wilfurd Timmons with such cold calculation on the altar of that ambition.

"Jesus, Melissa, this is just awful," Casey said after Melissa finished her story. "You better stay here with me tonight. I'll call Jake and ask him to come over, and then we'll decide what to do." She crossed the room to the telephone and called Jake. Well, she thought while the phone was ringing, so much for my quiet weekend.

Chapter 44

"There they are," M said, breaking a lengthy silence and bringing Larry Mitchell out of the twilight sleep he had been in since they arrived at the location almost forty-five minutes earlier. He stretched and yawned. I can't see a damn thing, he thought, staring into the darkness. He rubbed his eyes and looked again just in time to see the first sign of an approaching aircraft, just as M had said. Christ, he thought, the lady even has superhuman night vision.

Mitchell was exhausted. He had always held the highest regard for M and her stamina. But he had not seen anything until he had tried to keep up with her over the last twenty-four hours. They had returned to M's house after the brief telephone conversation with Nancy Wade and had swung into action.

First they went to the Public Library, where they studied detailed maps of the Conroe area and particularly the area surrounding the old Turner homestead. Then they returned to M's and placed a telephone call to M's contacts in London and he learned the details of her plan. As they sat on the runway waiting for the plane to land, his mind drifted back to that telephone call.

On the way back to her house, M told him she had developed a plan and had discussed parts of it with her "friends" in London. Although she had not gone into any of the details, she gave him some of the underlying philosophy. She reminded him that the credo of ALA prohibited violence to animal life of any kind. "You've heard me say it a hundred times," she said. "We can bust down doors and vandalize locks and destroy all sorts of property; but to cause serious physical pain to any living thing is contrary to the basic ideals of our movement. Nancy Wade seems to have forgotten that Wilfurd Timmons is an animal just the same as any cat or dog in a lab. How she could resort to the same thing we are all struggling to end is beyond me. And we won't let her get away with it."

She told him her contact in London was awaiting her answers to certain questions. "We have those answers," she said as they walked into the kitchen, "and if we act quickly, we can nip this thing before it ruins us all."

M went into the room that served as her office and returned with a writing tablet, some maps and a dogeared paperback book. She sat at the table, spread out the map and asked Mitchell to point out the closest airport to Conroe that could service a twin-engine Piper. He studied the map and told her that it would probably be the Montgomery County Airport near Conroe. After a brief discussion of airport procedures, she picked up the book and thumbed through it, making notes on her tablet. She put the book down, picked up the phone and placed her call to London. What followed was right out of a spy movie.

"Hello, this is Matilda Carbury calling?" Her voice rising as if it were a question. "Yes, with regard to the party we discussed? . . . That's right, the one at Beargarden. I want to confirm that there are two cakes . . . that's right, and we should be able to cater the whole thing with just three more waiters . . . and we have found room for the catering truck." M reached for the book and began, it appeared to Mitchell, to speak in tongues "eighty-three-four-seven . . . Three-twenty-five-six-five . . . four-thirty-four-seven-six . . . " Then he remembered; this was the way ALA communicates its extra-sensitive information over the telephone—spelling out the words by citing the page, line and word of a previously selected book, the first letter of each word cited being the next letter of the word being spelled. He picked up the tattered book. *The Way We Live Now*, Anthony Trollope's great novel, in the 1982 Oxford University Press edition. How literary, he thought. Much more so than the trash we have used here.

It wasn't until M had finished spelling out her message and had hung up that he began to understand what was happening. "I just gave my friends in London the location and other information about Montgomery County Airport. We're going to be having some guests later on." She laughed. "Big league guests."

"You mean these people are flying here from England in a twin-engine Piper?" Mitchell asked.

"Oh, no," M said. "That would be too complicated. No, they're flying to the U.S. on the Concorde. All rigged up in pinstriped suits and all. They could pass for British businessmen. Once they're in country, they'll hook up with the parent cell for outfitting and transportation here. You won't mistake them for British businessmen when they get here, I assure you."

"OK, let's go." M's words brought him back to the present. The plane landed and taxied to the end of the runway. Following M's instructions, Mitchell drove the car onto the apron of the runway and up to the plane. They got out of the car and ran to the plane just as the door opened and the ladder fanned out onto the tarmac.

Three people came down the steps and walked in haste towards the car. M met them halfway. "M, how are you? It's been a long time." The man gripped M's extended hand. He was dressed in green army fatigues, baggy with pockets on the sides, and combat boots. His sleeves were rolled up above his elbows, revealing lean but muscular forearms that rippled as he pumped M's hand.

"Z, meet my compatriot, L. He's my number one, and he'll brief you on our target when we get underway." Strictly business,

Mitchell thought. These people are scary. They don't even smile.

The man turned to Mitchell and extended his hand, still unsmiling. Mitchell took it and looked into the man's thin, long face, partially obscured by a full beard of dark brown, trimmed to about an inch all over, with occasional wisps of gray, his eyebrows as full and long as his beard. His eyes were a pale cold gray, with the crinkles of extreme weather and age at their sides. The Marlboro Man meets the IRA, he thought with a chuckle to himself. But when the man looked, expressionless, into his eyes, boring into them with an almost electrical charge, Mitchell felt a chill of fear. This is the big leagues, all right, he thought, as further introductions were completed.

The two people who accompanied Z opened a hatch under the belly of the plane and pulled out two large canvas duffle bags and transferred them to the opened trunk of the car. With M driving and Mitchell sitting in front where he could turn around and face the three men in the back seat and brief them on the mission, the car sped off into the night, leaving the pilot alone with the plane.

M had suspected from the study of the maps, and physical reconnaissance had confirmed, that on the far side of the Turner farmhouse, a large open field stretched to the west for several hundred yards, sloping gently all the way to the fence that marked the property line. On the other side of the fence was a dense wood of pine, oak and sweet gum from which the Turner farmhouse and its outbuildings could be observed in secret. This wood was part of a large tract surrounding a long-abandoned farmhouse accessible only by foot approximately one mile south of 105. M drove to the edge of that tract.

She turned off 105 onto the almost overgrown dirt road they discovered the night before and turned out the lights. They got out, and M opened the trunk. Z unzipped the duffle bags and under the beam of a wide-angle flashlight inspected the equipment they would use in the operation. Nested inside the first duffle, the flashlight shown on 34.21 inches of blue-black AK-47, as motionless but potentially deadly as a sleeping black mamba, 11.31 pounds when fully loaded with its box magazine of thirty rounds of 7.62 mm ammunition. He cleared the chamber and handed the rifle and magazine to one of his men. "These are mainly for show," he said to no one in particular. "But you never can tell."

He reached back into the bag and took out a canvas holster and belt. He unsnapped the holster and withdrew a Soviet-made Makarov PM. These guys don't mess around, Mitchell thought, as he looked with fascination at this weapon, so favored by terrorists in Western Europe. He had not seen one of these since he left the police force. It was a beauty–9 mm, 6.3 inches and light, a bit over one-and-a-half pounds not counting the eight-round magazine. Z held the weapon in the air with his right hand, pulled the slide to the rear and let it ride back to the front. He clicked the trigger, inserted the magazine and handed the weapon to the other man. "Don't chamber a round until we get to the fence." Even the man's voice is cold, Mitchell thought, as he listened to the emotionless British accent dispense its stingy words.

Z opened the other bag, which contained two pairs of night vision binoculars, two heavy-duty flashlights and a small canvas knapsack. He handed one pair of binoculars and a flashlight to M and kept the others for himself. He opened the knapsack and checked its contents–a small vial of Ketamine and several syringes, two pairs of handcuffs, two large cloth bags with drawstrings, several lengths of rope and five canisters of Mace.

He handed each person a canister of Mace. He removed the needle shield from one of the syringes and, holding the vial upside down, punched the tip of the needle through its rubber membrane and drew back the plunger, flooding the syringe with 5 cc's of Ketamine. He replaced the needle shield and handed the loaded syringe to M and told her to put it in the side pocket of her jacket. He repeated the process with the second syringe and put it in his pocket.

Z stood still for a moment, looking into the trunk as if he were going over a checklist in his mind. He closed the knapsack, putting his arms through the straps so that it rode high on his back. Finally, he took a small cellular phone out of the side pocket of his fatigues and handed it to Mitchell. "OK," he said. "Everyone knows the plan. Let's do it."

M and her three companions put on black ski masks and headed into the woods. Mitchell watched them disappear into the darkness, got in the car and drove out onto 105 towards the intersection of 105 and I-45, where he was instructed to make himself inconspicuous and await a call on the cellular. He drove to an all-night diner and went inside to read a newspaper and drink coffee until he was called.

While he was settling in with paper and coffee, M and friends were approaching the Turner property line. At the fence but still hidden in the woods they took out their binoculars and looked down upon the farmhouse. "This looks about the same as it did last night," M said. "They must really be giving Timmons his money's worth. See the barn over there to the right of the house? That looks like the place where they are keeping him. When they finish, they'll turn out the lights and walk back to the house. They seem to be sleeping in the back room on the right side of the house, the one that has the lights on right now."

Z kept his binoculars to his eyes and grunted a non-response to M. After several moments of silence he took the binoculars away from his eyes and said, "OK. We'll wait." And they waited. An hour, an hour fifteen, an hour thirty. Still the lights in the barn burned. At 11:30, the lights went out. M and Z picked up their binoculars and, thanks to the light-enhancing feature of these hi-tech toys, watched as Nancy Wade and Jerry Turner walked from the barn to the house.

Twenty minutes later the lights in the house went out. "Let's move," Z said. And they began to creep towards the house, spread out ten feet from each other and walking in a crouch. When they were 100 feet from the house, he motioned for them to halt. He then signaled for the man on his right, the one with the AK-47, to proceed alone. The man dropped to his belly and began to crawl forward like an alligator, with his rifle cradled in his arms, until he was underneath the side window of the bedroom. He took a tiny flashlight from his pocket and signaled back to Z–three short blinks of the light–to indicate that he was in position and that all was well.

Z then signaled for the other man to begin his approach to the house. He followed the same method as the first, but he went to the back window of the bedroom. He signaled. Everything was quiet and in place outside the bedroom. It was time for the attackers to move in. Z hoped to accomplish the mission by stealth; but if something went wrong, he wanted armed men nearby with easy access to the inside of the house.

Z and M began their approach. Slow, careful. No rush. We have all night. They passed around the left side of the house and up to the steps of the front porch. Z motioned for M to remain where she was and he began to climb the steps. As slow and as quiet as ground fog, he crept up the steps and finally stood by the front door. He motioned back to M and she began her way up the steps.

Whether it was her lack of stealth or just a quirk of the steps, she never knew. But as she placed her right foot onto the third step, it let out what seemed to her an ear-piercing squeak. She froze. Her training in England had instilled in her the reaction of freezing in this situation. You never know until you wait a moment whether you have been found out, even though the offending noise sounds like the roar of Niagara Falls to you. But if you move, you will be found out for sure. So she stood, frozen in time, every fiber of her senses tuned onto the house, expecting at any moment the light to go on . . . or worse.

But it never came and after what seemed like hours, she

resumed her trek up the steps until she was on the porch next to Z. Her breath was quick, her mouth dry, her heart racing. Z reached out and touched her shoulder. They waited while she regained her breath. Z grasped the doorknob and twisted it. Just as they had hoped, it was unlocked. He pushed the door open in slow motion and they stepped inside the house.

Nancy and Jerry had come in from the barn and gone straight to bed. Nancy, who was always horny, announced that she was hornier than ever. On these extra-specially horny nights Nancy liked to be on top controlling both speed and motion. Jerry would remain still, enjoying the practiced moves of this seasoned veteran of the sexual revolution.

Tonight her passion was so high she didn't notice the startled look on Jerry's face, as he lay beneath her writhing body, when he first saw the shadowy shapes of two masked people burst into the room with Mace canisters emptying full force.

As soon as they stepped into the house M and Z could hear the sounds of lovemaking coming from the bedroom. They crept down the hall and burst into the room. Following their plan, Z took Jerry, who was already looking at them when they entered the room, and M went for Nancy, who, after seeing Jerry's assault, turned her face directly into the first blast of Mace from M's canister.

Nancy rolled naked from the bed clutching her face; Jerry remained on the bed, writhing in pain as he too clutched his burning eyes. M took the syringe out of her pocket, ran to the side of the bed, unsheathed the needle and stabbed it into Nancy's bare buttock. At the same time, Z grabbed Jerry's left arm and twisted it so that he was forced to roll over onto his stomach. Holding Jerry's arm in a hammerlock with his left hand, he took the syringe from his pocket with his right hand, grasped the needle shield in his teeth, pulled the syringe free and slid it into the fleshy tissue of Jerry's triceps.

M and Z, both following standard procedure, fell upon their victims, holding them pinned in place until the Ketamine began to take effect. Nancy and Jerry struggled for about a minute, and then drifted into sleep. By then the other men had run into the room and were standing over the two sleeping beauties in exaggerated poses of preparedness. "That's enough, lads," Z said. "Put down your toys and give me a hand with this."

Z removed the knapsack and took out the handcuffs and head bags. And while Nancy and Jerry were being cuffed and bagged, Z pulled out his cellular phone and entered the number of Mitchell's phone.

Mitchell, waiting and worrying in the diner, read the paper three times and even tried the crossword puzzle, the word search and the anagrams, activities he usually hated. Had something gone wrong? Should he go back out there and see if there was anything he could do? No, he decided to stay put. He waited. He drank more coffee. And the night dragged by—until finally the phone rang.

His hands shook with a burst of adrenaline as he fumbled for the phone. It was Z. "A-OK. Come to the party," was all that he need-ed to hear. Ten minutes later he was driving onto the rutted dirt road to the Turner place.

M met him at the side of the house. He got out of the car and opened the trunk, and Z's men began to load Nancy and Jerry as if they were sacks of flour. Each one was bound with rope around the legs and feet and handcuffed with the hands behind the back. Capping this picture of modern terrorism were the canvas sacks that had been placed over their heads, with the drawstrings pulled tight. It'll be a long time before we see them again, M thought as she watched them being loaded into the trunk. M knew the fate of traitors like these—they would be taken to a distant city and dumped, still drugged, into an abandoned car on some back street, heads shaved and naked, without so much as a dime or an ID.

"Before we leave, we've got to check on Timmons," M said.

"Christ, woman, we ain't got time for such foolishness," Z said. "We'd best be getting on back to the plane." He glared at her as if she had just suggested that they order in a pizza.

"No," she said. "We're checking on Timmons." Even a gristly ALA radical couldn't budge M when her mind was set. M and Mitchell ran towards the barn. Z turned to the other men. "What are you lads staring at? Get the car turned around and ready to go. I think I'll have a look at the old gent myself." And he ran off in the direction of the barn.

M led the way shining her flashlight back and forth in front of them. They entered the barn, and before they could see where Timmons was, they could smell him. The barn reeked of feces and urine and vomit. They almost gagged when they entered. M walked toward the center of the barn where the bars of a cage gleamed in the light. As they approached they could see a human form curled up on the floor of the cage, on its side with its back toward them. When they got closer they could see the wounds where patches of skin had been cut away from the man's back in an apparent effort to simulate some of the skin sensitivity tests routinely run on lab animals. The sores were open and raw.

M walked around to the other side of the cage, still keeping the light on its occupant. When she got to the other side, the man raised his head and looked up at her with a look of pleading terror she had seen before–in the animals they had rescued. His eyes bulged, his mouth agape and drooling. "Please," he croaked. "Please don't hurt me any more." And his head slowly sank to the floor of the cage.

"My God," Z said.

Chapter 45

Jake rushed to the house shortly after Casey called, eager to learn the rest of the story she had begun over the phone. They talked until after two, at which time they all agreed it was time for bed.

Alone in the bedroom, Casey and Jake continued the discussion. "I don't know why you two are so hesitant," Jake said. "It seems to me the only thing to do is go to the cops. There's something really awful going on here, and I don't see how we're going to gain anything by waiting."

"Normally, I'd agree with you," Casey said. "But there's something that you don't know about yet." And she began to tell Jake the story of Melissa's affair with Proctor Philpott and of the hold he still had on her. Jake listened in silence, disgusted at what he heard. "And so," Casey concluded, "until we know more about what's really happening, all we can be sure of accomplishing if we go to the cops is destroying Melissa's career and probably her marriage. I don't see how we can do that."

"Yeah. I agree with that, for now," Jake said, rolling over and punching down the pillow. "Now, let's get some sleep."

Sleep did not come easy for Casey. Every time she was close to drifting off, she would be jarred awake by the enormity of what was happening. Finally, at dawn, she smelled coffee brewing and figured Melissa was having trouble sleeping, too. She got up, put on her robe and went into the kitchen, leaving Jake, whose sleep was never affected by anything, lost in deep slumber.

Melissa was sitting at the kitchen table, staring at the steam rising in wisps from her coffee cup. "You can't sleep, either, huh," Casey said as she walked into the room.

"Not a wink," Melissa said. "I keep thinking about all the things that could happen, and not many of them are good." Casey poured coffee and sat down at the table. "About the only thing I can say," Melissa continued, "is I'm sure glad Craig is out of town. I don't think he'd be much help in something like this."

"Yeah, you mentioned last night he was gone. But you didn't say where he was."

"He's in Midland visiting his parents. You know, don't you, he's out of work again? His company was bought out, and his job was eliminated. And he'd only been there six months since the same thing happened at MidCo. Times have been tough in the oil business, you know. Craig always lands on his feet, but the ground he seems to pick for his landings isn't ever very stable. So, he's between jobs, and he figured that with me working all hours on Proctor's project, he'd just clear out of the house and go visit his folks for a while."

They sat in silence for several minutes before Melissa continued. "And that's why I get so upset about my job, Casey. I just can't afford to lose it. There's no way I could find another one that would pay anywhere near what I'm making now. It's just awful."

"And you're still sure they saw you last night?" Casey asked.

"Yes, I'm sure," Melissa replied. "Just as I said, the security guard was talking to Slurry, and he chased me out of the building calling my name. Yeah, I'm sure about that. What I'm not sure about is what they're planning to do about it."

They spent the next several hours going over the things they had already discussed–what did it all mean, what should Melissa do, what should Casey do, and so on. At eight-fifteen, Jake joined them at the table and their plans began to crystallize.

Casey summarized the situation as she saw it. "And so what we think we know is this. First, Wilfurd Timmons has been kidnapped by a radical group of animal rights militants, most likely the dissidents that my weird little friend Carl has told me about. Second, Proctor Philpott plans to keep it a secret and even lie about Timmons' schedule in order to cover it up. And, third, all of the rumors we've been hearing about a secret lab are true. Plus we now know what they're doing there is testing some kind of skin cream."

"That sums it up, alright," Jake said. "I can believe it about the kidnapping; violence against corporate executives is becoming more and more common, unfortunately. But the other two things are truly flabbergasting. I know a lot of these folks at Temeritus from the days I was handling cases for them. And I know how overly concerned they are about short-term results. And I'm familiar with how they've cut corners on safety and staffing requirements in order to boost those results. That's why they've had so many accidents in recent years. But I would've never figured that even a sleazeball like Philpott would go to these extremes. A secret lab . . . lying about the CEO's schedule so that his kidnapping can be hidden . . . It's amazing."

"And I don't see much we can do," Casey said. "At least not today. We don't know for sure what's really going on at Temeritus. And we can't go to the police yet, not on the little bit of information we have. Philpott will be able to slip out of trouble because he really hasn't taken any action yet. I think all we'd accomplish by going to the police now would be getting Melissa fired. So we're stuck in neutral for the moment."

Casey got up and began to clear the table. "But one thing is certain, Melissa," she said. "You sure as hell can't be going to the Tower until you know more about how all of this is shaking out. And it seems to me, based on what you have told us, Melissa, that Philpott has such a death grip on the company and the people downtown that there really isn't anyone we can trust in Temeritus. The only person who can get information from inside is me; I'm the only one with access to the building who isn't being held hostage by the son-of-a-bitch. And my suggestion is that you stay right here and wait until I let you know what I'm hearing around the building tomorrow."

"Sounds good to me," she said, flashing Casey the thumbs up sign.

"Jake," Casey said, "Why don't you go over to Melissa's and see if it's staked out." Jake went to the bedroom and came back into the kitchen a few minutes later dressed in Levi's, a blue chambray work shirt and boots.

"Melissa," he said. "Are you sure you weren't followed here by Slurry or the security guard or someone else from Temeritus?"

"Pretty sure. Like I said, Slurry was on the phone to the guard when I was checking out, and I'm assuming that he was still on thirty-nine. The guard came to the door and yelled to me as I was running across the street, but I don't think he followed me. I ran down to the Four Seasons and got a cab. I definitely wasn't being chased. And all the way out here I kept looking behind me to see if I was being followed. I don't think I was. I didn't want the cabby to know where I was really going so I had him let me off three blocks from here. And believe me, I had plenty of time to observe the street in front of Casey's while I was hiding in the bushes waiting for her to get home. There was nothing suspicious."

"OK," Jake said. "And, from what you tell me, there isn't any reason to think that anyone would suspect that you're here. I mean, no one knows that you and Casey are friends." He paused while Melissa confirmed with a nod that his statement was correct. "Good, then you should be safe here."

Jake went to the refrigerator, took out the water jug and poured a glass of water. "I'll go back to The Horse to get Buzfuz. Won't hurt to have a little extra security today." He put the empty glass in the dishwasher.

"I'll drive by your house, Melissa, and see if anyone's there. Also thought I'd drive by Timmons', see if there is any activity. Should take a couple of hours or so."

Jake walked toward the front door, stopped and turned around, "One more thing, Melissa, while I'm gone to get Buzfuz, why don't you call your house and see if you have any messages?" And he was out the door.

Twenty minutes later he was back with Serjeant Buzfuz, who thought it was a regular Sunday and therefore time to romp on the lawn with So-So. To his disappointment, Jake led him directly into the house and the Sunday romp was held on the living room rug. While the dogs were still playing in the living room, Jake asked Melissa about her messages.

"Yes," she said. "There were four—two last night and two so far today. All from Slurry. You should listen to them yourself later on. His tone gets more urgent with each call. And the last one is downright panicky—'I know you're there, Melissa . . . . Please pick up the phone . . . . Things are not what you may think . . . . I have to talk to you'—that sort of thing. He obviously wants to find me real bad."

"I want to listen to them when I get back." Jake headed for the door. "Oh, Melissa, let me have your keys. I'll take in the mail and the papers and check things out for you." She got out a key ring and handed it to him. "Is there an alarm?" She told him there was not.

Jake walked to Casey and gave her a big hug and a kiss. "I love you, Case. Now try to get some sleep." Serjeant Buzfuz followed Jake to the door and stood with his nose pressed against it, whining and wishing he was with Jake in the truck.

Wilfurd Timmons lived on one of the quieter streets in River Oaks. His house sat back from the street on a wooded lot, a studied exemplar of understated opulence in this enclave of Houston's wealthiest residents. A tasteful wrought iron fence provided a physical barrier to the property, and an electronically controlled gate silently guarded access to the curved driveway. Casey had driven Jake past the house shortly after she began her job with Temeritus and had regaled him with stories she had heard about Dewey Shivers helping install a bathtub in this magnificent residence.

Jake's casual drive past Timmons' had not told him much. There had been no signs of activity, but he didn't know if that was good or bad. Just checking, Jake thought, as he left River Oaks and headed toward Bellaire.

There was a similar lack of apparent activity at the Fellows' house. The Sunday paper was still on the lawn, and the flag was up on the mailbox. But as Jake got closer to the house he saw a car–a late model Buick with a vanity plate, SLURRY-1–parked across from the house. A man wearing dark sunglasses and smoking a cigarette sat behind the wheel staring straight ahead. Gee, I wonder who that could be, Jake laughed to himself as he drove by. This guy is really crafty; those sunglasses will fool you every time. He drove until the Buick was no longer visible in his rearview mirror, turned around and headed back. When he got there, the Buick was gone.

Jake considered and then decided against taking in the mail and papers. Better to have the house look as if Melissa was out of town. Slurry would go crazy if he came back and saw that someone had been there.

Jake drove back toward Casey's, but when he got onto Bissonnet he decided to check Timmons' one more time. When he reached Kirby, he turned left and headed north, ultimately into River Oaks. As he approached the house, everything appeared to be about the same, but as he got closer he could see that the gate was opening and a car was driving into the driveway–a late model Buick, plate SLURRY-1. Well, Jake told himself as he drove out of River Oaks, life with Casey is never dull.

Casey and Melissa had managed to go back to sleep and were still sleeping when Jake returned. He went into the kitchen, called

Melissa's answering machine and listened to the messages. There were now five. And Melissa was right–they increased in urgency as they played out.

Casey and Melissa woke up and joined Jake in the kitchen later that afternoon. They spent the rest of the day sitting at the table talking about what they were going to do. Jake told them about his experience earlier in the day. " . . . and I don't know if it was Slurry himself, because I've never met the man, but it sure was his car."

"It was Slurry, alright," Melissa said. "He and Proctor are the only senior people in the company who still smoke. And you can bet that the great Proctor Philpott wouldn't be seen parked in front of my house."

By 5:30 they decided they needed a break. No one felt like cooking and they dared not risk Melissa's being seen in public by Slurry or one of his minions. So they ordered in a pizza and waited out the rest of the day watching television and pretending that the specter of Proctor Philpott had not cast its shadow on their lives.

Midway through the Sunday Night Movie, they got the call.

Chapter 46

"Casey O'Rourke, please." Oh, no, Casey thought, not another call from MCI.

"Yes, can I help you?"

"Please hear me out. I'm not trying to sell you anything or get you to make any contributions. I'm calling about Wilfurd Timmons."

Casey's stomach tightened, and she focused on the voice–a woman's, husky and strong–as it continued, "You do know Wilfurd Timmons, don't you?"

"Yes, of course. What can I do for you?"

"Wilfurd has been kidnapped. I'm going to tell you where he is so you can rescue him. Please, hear me out," the woman repeated, her voice louder and more forceful. "This is not a joke or a prank. I'm deadly serious." She sounds deadly serious, Casey thought. She motioned to Jake to get on the other line.

"OK," Casey said.

"I'm involved in the animal rights movement and in the campaign against Temeritus. That's how I know your name. We make it our business to know everything we can. We have contacts inside the company and as soon as you were hired, I knew about it." Casey felt a chill shiver across her shoulders.

"Are you with the Animal Liberation Army?" Casey asked, thinking back to her discussion with Carl last night at The Horse.

"It doesn't matter who I'm with. What matters is Timmons was kidnapped and he must be returned to safety. I tracked Timmons' kidnappers down and captured them and shipped them out of Texas. And now I'm coming to you for help."

"Why don't you go to the police?"

"I can't run that risk. This kidnapping was not committed by legitimate members of our cause, and I don't want the cause tainted by it. That's why I'm turning to you."

"What do you want me to do?" Casey said.

"I want you to go get him and take him home. No one is with him now and it will be easy, and safe for you to get him. There's a farmhouse and a barn. The lights have been left on in both. Timmons is in the barn." She paused for a moment and then continued. "He'll need clothes–a sweat suit would be ideal–but that's all. I trust you, Casey, and I know Wilfurd Timmons will trust you. You must help him."

"Where's this place located?" Casey asked. Had she heard this voice before?

"Go to your mailbox, and you'll find a map."

"But . . . " The line went dead, and Casey stood for a moment looking into the handpiece as if hoping to find an answer there. She put the handpiece back to her ear "Jake?"

"Yeah, Case, it's just me on the line now. I'll go check the mailbox."

Jake came back holding a plain white envelope with the flap tucked into the back. He opened it and removed a single piece of paper. On one side was a hand-drawn map showing the Houston Loop, with I-45 going north to Highway 105 and an arrow pointing west on 105 to a paved road labeled "ROAD TO FARM." A notation showed to the tenth of a mile the distance from I-45 to this road. On the other side of the page was a detailed map showing the rest of the way to the farm, again shown in exact distances. The map showed a farmhouse and a barn. A notation next to the barn said, "TIMMONS HERE."

"That's it?" Casey said.

"That's it," Jake said, handing her the map. Casey looked at it. If this was the woman Carl had told her about, she thought, he was right–she really is good.

"So what do we do now?" Melissa asked.

"Do we have a choice?" Casey said. "We get in the truck and go out there and see what we find."

"Why don't we just call the cops, like you wanted to before?" Melissa said.

"Because if everything really is the way she says, there is far more going on than just a kidnapping. There is the fact that Philpott is planning to lie about Timmons' whereabouts in order to get rid of him and advance his own career. And there is this thing about the secret lab. If we turn this over to the police, Philpott will be able to skate right over these problems. But, if we can get Timmons back ourselves, without Philpott knowing about it, we may be able to expose the phony bastard and catch him at his own game. I think it's worth a try. And besides, if Philpott gets away with this, it will be awful for you, Melissa, just like you said."

"Amen to that, sister," Melissa said, rolling her eyes.

"I say we recruit Gabe to go with us and head north to the farm," Casey said.

"Let's do it," Jake said.

Jake called Gabe and asked if he could come over and help them out; he'd explain the details later. He also asked Gabe to stop at The Horse and go upstairs and get the M1 rifle from the closet and the belt of loaded clips, and the service .45 in the holster next to Jake's bed, plus the belt with the extra magazines. Gabe was at Casey's in thirty minutes.

They decided to go out in Jake's truck–Jake, Casey and Gabe. Melissa would stay at Casey's. They also decided they would take So-So and Serjeant Buzfuz–they might need So-So's digging or Serjeant

Buzfuz's nose.

They put together the clothing for Timmons, checked the condition of their weapons and flashlights, got into the truck and drove away, So-So and Buzfuz with their front paws on the side-rails, ears and tongues flapping in the wind.

An hour later they were driving slowly down the paved road, just the way it was shown on the map. And sure enough, exactly where the map said it would be, a dirt road led into the woods to the right. They followed this road until it opened into a clearing in which they could see the two lighted buildings the woman caller had mentioned. At the barn, they stopped and got out.

Jake drew his pistol, inserted the magazine of seven rounds into the receiver, pulled the slide to the rear, and released it, chambering a round. Gabe did the same with the M1, inserting a clip of eight rounds into the receiver, pulling back the operating rod handle and releasing it; the operating rod flew forward, stripping the top round off the clip and locking it in place inside the chamber. CLINCH. Any old, pre-M14 Marine would recognize it, and feel a touch of nostalgia at the sound.

With Jake in front and Gabe providing cover, they crept toward the barn. Casey stayed next to the truck holding the dogs, both of whom were struggling to free themselves and join the action. Jake reached the door to the barn and signaled for Casey to release the dogs. They ran yelping and barking toward the barn. Jake wanted to be as sure as he could that there was no one waiting in ambush inside the barn, and he figured that the sudden intrusion of two yelping dogs would cause any such assassin to declare himself. The dogs raced into the barn and ran about in merry confusion.

Jake peeked around the corner and saw a large cage and the naked figure of a man on hands and knees staring out at him, terror in his eyes. Jake ran to the cage. "Don't worry. We're here to take you home. You're going to be OK." Wilfurd Timmons, who had hallucinated so many times in the last two days, didn't know whether to believe his eyes or not. But if this is a dream, he thought, it looks like it's going to be a happy one.

"OK, Gabe," Jake called out. "It's all clear. Tell Casey to come in. And bring the clothes." He went to the cage and opened it. "Jesus Christ, man. What have they done to you!" Gabe ran up to the cage and together they pulled Timmons to his feet and out of the cage.

"I don't know who you guys are, but you're the best thing I've ever seen in my life," Timmons said. Casey came in with the clothes and stared in shock at Timmons, naked and filthy in front of her, being held on his feet by Jake and Gabe. "Casey!" he said when he recognized her. And then the first hint of a smile crossed his face. "My God, Casey. I knew it was a good idea to hire you." Then, as if noticing for the first time that he was naked, Timmons asked if he could have some of the clothes he saw in her hands.

They cleaned him up as much as they could under the circumstances and headed back to Houston, Gabe driving Timmons' Cadillac. Timmons himself, saying that he had experienced all the enclosed spaces he cared to for the weekend, opted for the bed of the truck, with the dogs. "Besides," he said with a bitter laugh, "I now have a lot more in common with dogs than most people do."

Anyone driving on I-45 that night would have been treated to a rare sight indeed–a two-vehicle caravan composed of a new Cadillac and a 1949 Chevy pickup, and in the back of the truck, a reeking and battered old man in ill-fitting clothes, having the time of his life playing with a big old yellow dog and a feisty little terrier. You'd have thought for a moment it was the redeemed Ebenezer Scrooge on Christmas Morning.

Chapter 47

Wilfurd Timmons was in the shower for thirty minutes washing and scrubbing, trying to remove the filth that had encrusted his body over the two longest days of his life. Gabe dressed the wounds on Timmons' back left by the sensitivity tests, and treated with antibiotic salve the smaller but more sensitive wounds on his eyelids caused by the Draize board clips. Finally, scrubbed, shaved and dressed in an L.L. Bean chamois cloth shirt, sweat socks, soft-soled moccasins and a pair of Levi's–his first ever–Wilfurd Timmons sat at Casey's kitchen table devouring bowl after bowl of chicken soup and leftover pizza.

He looked surprisingly good, considering what he had gone through. The color had returned to his cheeks and, except for the puffiness and the cuts on his eyelids, he looked like a man just returned from a fishing trip, glad to be back indoors.

"I never knew pizza was so good," he said, as he helped himself to yet another piece. Casey, Melissa, Jake and Gabe sat around the table watching and not wanting to spoil his enjoyment by talking about any of the things they all knew had to be discussed soon. Finally, Timmons finished. He pushed his plate back and drained his glass of milk. "All right," he said. "Someone tell me what in the hell is going on."

"Before we begin," Casey said, "it would be a big help to us if you would tell us what exactly happened to you."

"Sure, but I can't really tell you much." Timmons related his departure from work on Friday and his encounter with an unknown assailant in the parking garage. "And from then on it's all a blur of nightmares and bad dreams. I thought at first I'd had a heart attack; then I thought I was dead; then I didn't know what to think. And the next thing I knew it was daylight and these people–I think there were only two of them, a man and a woman–kept telling me all the awful things the company was doing to animals. Said they wanted me to get a taste of what it was like to be a test animal."

He described how they had taken him out of the cage and fastened his head down and squirted his eyes. "They said it was Glitter. I don't know for sure, but it stung like hell. But that was nothing compared to having my eyelids clamped and pulled open. That was awful." He went on to describe how they would take him out of the cage and do something to him and then put him back in the cage and lecture him about the Temeritus animal testing program.

"They gave me shots of something when they wanted me to go to sleep. And I was having hallucinations when the stuff would begin to wear off. They told me they were going to keep me there until Temeritus announced it had a secret lab and that it was going to be shut down. Said they had called Philpott and told him that until he got on TV and made this announcement, I was theirs. They kept ranting about a secret lab. I kept telling them there is no such thing and that really made them mad. I thought they were going to kill me.

"Then, I think it was the second day, they stopped taking me out of the cage. Whatever it was they were injecting me with had made me sick and I had thrown up all over the cage. They wouldn't let me out and soon I started to mess it up real bad. They would come in and just look at me and laugh. It was the worst thing I've ever experienced, I'll tell you.

"So, when I saw you guys bust in there, I knew I was home free. Whoever these people were, they always wore ski masks and I couldn't see what they looked like. When I saw real faces, I knew that Proctor had come through for me."

The silence at the table was palpable. Casey, Melissa and Jake gaped at each other, wide-eyed with surprise. Gabe, who was not aware of the background, looked around the table wondering what had just gone wrong, everyone looked so strange. Timmons noticed it, too. "What's the matter? Did I say something wrong?"

Now it was Casey's turn. "Mr. Timmons, there is something very wrong, but it's not in anything you said." And she told him. For the next thirty minutes Wilfurd Timmons sat dumbstruck as the story spilled out. Melissa related the details of the conversation she overheard; Casey told of her discussions with Carl and with the mysterious woman from ALA; and Jake told him what he had seen at his house earlier in the day. Timmons sat with his right elbow resting on the table and his chin resting in the palm of his hand, taking it all in, listening and not responding until they had finished.

Timmons sat for a moment looking at his hands flat in front of him on the table, fingers webbed out as if he were doing some kind of isometric exercise. He raised his head and looked at each person at the table, moving his eyes from one to the other in a slow scan, still trying to decide if this was really happening. "Unbelievable," he said, just audible to the others in the room. "Just unbelievable." He rose from the table and walked to the window and stared into his reflection on the blackened pane.

Time seemed frozen as they waited to see what he would do. Finally, he spoke again, still just above a whisper. "In the cage . . . " he faltered, and began again. "In the cage I had a lot of time to think. Something I hadn't done for a while. Sounds strange, I know. Executives are supposed to always be thinking. But I mean thinking about my life and what I was doing with it and things of a more personal nature. And I thought about my beautiful Helen." He turned from the window and took his place at the table again.

"God, what a beautiful woman. Thirty-five years we were married." His eyes began to tear. "She was the joy of my life. And after she died–when the cancer finally took her–just didn't seem to care about much anymore. I moped around and went through the motions at work. But I'd really done what I've always been so critical of others for doing–I retired in place. Proctor took over more and more, and I just stood on the sidelines and watched. And I let it happen.

"Well, one of those nights in the cage, I dreamed about Helen and it was as real as if she were actually there. Feisty and ready to let me know it real quick if she thought I was doing something stupid. She was pointing that finger at me and saying, 'Wil'–that's what she always called me–'Wil, get off your butt and do something. You still have plenty of good years left, if you'll just get off your butt and stop moaning about me. I'm fine. Now you just take care of yourself.' Then she was gone." Timmons wiped his eyes with the back of his hands.

"You never realize how much you love something until it has been taken away from you. God knows that was true with my Helen. And in the cage, I became convinced that my life was about to be taken away from me, too. And I vowed to myself and to the memory of Helen that if I got out of there alive, I would start to live again. And I would retake my place as the CEO of Temeritus and start to live with gusto." Everyone at the table noticed that as he talked Timmons' voice got stronger, more animated.

"Now, if what you are telling me is true, and I have no reason to doubt it, I've been the victim of a colossal betrayal on the part of my number one man, my heir apparent, the very man I handpicked to replace me when I retire. A man who would tell people I was golfing at the Greenbrier when he knew I had been kidnapped." Timmons was now on his feet and almost shouting.

"And you know what?" He glared around the room. "That really pisses me off!" Casey thought for a moment she would stand up and cheer. But Timmons was not finished.

"And let me tell you something else. About this so-called secret lab. I'm going to find out about that, and if it's true, I'll not only fire that son-of-a-bitch, Philpott, I'll do everything within my power to put the rotten bastard in jail." Timmons was on a roll.

"And I'll tell you something else I learned in the cage. Being a laboratory animal is no fun. I didn't like it worth a damn and I doubt if the animals like it either. And as long as I'm President of Temeritus, we're not going to do it." This time they did get up and cheer. What had begun as a low volume squeak had ended as a loud roar, and they were all caught up in the enthusiasm of the moment.

"Casey," Timmons barked, "I want to go out to The Woodlands right now and check that lab. We have no time to waste. If what your friend at the bar told you is true, Philpott is pretty good at hiding these things. I want to get out there before he even knows I'm back to haunt him."

One hour later they were driving into the Temeritus facility at The Woodlands. Casey, Melissa and Wilfurd had gone together in the Cadillac so they could discuss the public relations aspects of this situation, and Jake and Gabe followed in the truck. Wilfurd insisted that they take the truck in case there were animals that needed transportation out of the lab.

Gabe discovered when he was preparing to drive the Cadillac back from the farm that Timmons' kidnappers had thrown his clothes and other personal effects into the back seat. Gabe had offered to retrieve them for Timmons so that he could put on his business suit prior to visiting a company facility. "The hell with that," Timmons had bellowed. "I wear that damn monkey suit too often as it is. And I think I'm beginning to develop a taste for these Levi's and things. But you could get my wallet for me, Gabe. I may have trouble convincing them who I am without my ID card."

The two vehicles pulled up to the front of the lab and stopped. Timmons and Casey, followed by Jake, Gabe and Melissa, barged into the reception area startling the guard who had dozed off and not heard them approach. He jumped to his feet and stared at them as if they were from outer space.

Timmons walked up to the guard and stuck his Temeritus ID card into the man's face. "Young man, my name is Wilfurd Timmons and I'm the President and Chief Executive Officer of this company. Don't let my casual attire fool you. I am who I say I am, and I'm here to go to the lab in the basement. The 'green room,' I think it's called."

The guard looked at the ID and then at Timmons, back and forth several times, until he was sure that the man was in fact who he said he was. "Yes, Mr. Timmons, sir. But, you see, I'm under strict instructions that no one gets into the green room without the prior approval of Mr. Philpott. We didn't even have a key until after the break-in."

"I see." He glared at the young man. "What's your name, son?" Timmons asked.

"Tucker, Sir. Randy Tucker."

"Well, Mr. Randy Tucker, did it ever occur to you that Proctor Philpott works for me, that he reports to me, and that, if he doesn't do what I tell him to, I can fire him?"

"Yes, sir."

"Good, I'm glad you've thought of that. And I suppose you also know that you work for me, just like every other son-of-a-bitch in the company works for me, and, that if you don't do what I tell you to, I can fire you, too?"

"Yes, sir."

"Good. Now open up the goddamn door!"

"Yes, sir." Tucker jumped to his duty. He entered the code into the control box defusing the alarm on the green room door and led them to the lab.

Timmons paced through the room looking into the cages. Inside each cage was a rabbit. Some of them appeared to be without any marks on them, but most were in some stage of testing. Most of them had large patches cut from their backs and stomachs, which were covered with gauze bandages. Timmons recognized these patches as being the same ones that his tormentors had placed on his back after shaving away the top layer of his skin. Looking at these animals caused his own wounds to pucker and hurt again.

Timmons continued to walk the length of the lab. At the very back of the room on separate steel tables were four rabbits laid out flat with their legs pulled wide apart and their paws fastened with clamps to the surface of the table. All of the top layer of skin had been removed from their stomachs and at regularly spaced intervals were the results of different substances having been applied to the raw skin, some leaving hideous ulcerations and festering sores. Timmons couldn't tell if they were still alive until he touched them to see if they moved. Just barely.

Timmons' final discovery came when he lifted the lid from a large trash can at the back of the lab and found the rotting carcasses of five or six of the rabbits who had succumbed to the rigors of the test and had escaped them through death. He wondered about the fate of the cute little beagles that had been featured in Proctor Philpott's press conference and which were now being held in cages on the main floor of the building. He also wondered why any of this was being done at all—in secret or otherwise. None of it made sense.

"That's all I needed to see," Timmons said. "Casey, I want to take the rabbits with the serious wounds with us tonight. The others can stay until tomorrow." He then turned to young Tucker, who was still quaking in fear.

"Tucker, if you breathe a word of this to anyone, I'll personally see to it that your ass is fired from this job and that you never get another one in Houston and maybe even in all of Texas; if you keep your mouth shut, I might let you keep it. This is an awful thing that has been happening down here and the people responsible for it are going to pay dearly. But if you tell anyone I was here, there's a good chance those people will go unpunished. If that were to happen because of something you did, then I'll just have to visit their punishment on you." He stuck his face right into Tucker's and snarled, "Do you understand that, Tucker?"

"Yes, sir." And everyone knew he did.

Chapter 48

"Good morning, Proctor? This is Wilfurd Timmons."

Proctor Philpott stood frozen in place by the telephone table in his bedroom. Shaving cream covered one side of his face, a towel wrapped around his trim midriff. He interrupted his shaving to take the call, expecting it to be Sam Slurry with some late breaking news on the Wilfurd Timmons matter. He never dreamed it would be Timmons himself.

"Wilfurd? . . . How are you? . . . We've been worried about you."

"Really." The word was not uttered as a question with the inflection rising at the end; it was declaratory, mocking, ironic. And it sent a chill through Proctor Philpott's testicles.

"I got this crazy call over the weekend. Something about . . . "

"Be in my office at seven-thirty. And bring Sam Slurry."

"We thought . . . "

"I do want to hear about that call, Proctor. You and Sam can tell me all about it later. Oh, and Proctor . . . ." Timmons paused for a moment. "The golf was great this weekend at The Greenbrier."

Philpott stood clutching the phone to his ear, shaving cream drying on the left side of his face, not hearing the dial tone that had replaced Wilfurd Timmons' voice on the line.

In another part of Houston, Sam Slurry was also carrying out his morning routine preparing to begin another work week. It had been a long weekend, with the Timmons thing taking up most of his time, and he was tired. He spent most of Sunday driving between River Oaks and Bellaire hoping to find some clues as to the where-abouts of Wilfurd Timmons and Melissa Fellows, but all to no avail. Now another week in the Tower was about to start and he was appre-hensive as to what it might bring.

He went into his kitchenette and made instant coffee and took it into the living room to read the newspaper and watch the early morning news. His attention was focused on the sports pages, almost blocking the TV out altogether until the word "Temeritus" pierced his concentration. He looked up and focused on the TV.

On the screen one of the morning anchors was midway through a story—"Channel 2 has learned that Temeritus, Incorporated, the Houston-based cosmetics company, has called a press conference for ten o'clock this morning to discuss what it says are matters of grave concern to the company. Company spokesperson Casey O'Rourke told Channel 2 News earlier this morning that the compa-ny's President and Chief Executive Officer, W. C. Timmons, will brief the press on recent developments in the company's long-standing dis-pute with animal rights protesters. The exact nature of these devel-opments was not disclosed. We'll be standing by live to bring you further updates on this breaking story."

"Holy shit," Slurry shouted across the room. He jumped up and dashed to the phone to call Proctor, but it rang just as he got to it. "Shit. I can't believe it." He picked up the phone after the second ring.

"What the fuck is going on?" Philpott's voice boomed over the line.

"You watching Channel 2?"

"Screw Channel 2," Philpott screamed. "I just got a call from Timmons, and he wants us in his office at seven-thirty."

Philpott told Slurry about his discussion with Timmons, and

Slurry described what he had just seen on TV. Philpott ended the conversation with what he hoped would be words of reassurance: "Don't worry, Sam. We can stonewall our way out of this. Just keep up the story that we thought it was a hoax. Couldn't do anything on it until Monday. It's no problem as long as we stick together." Sam Slurry remained unconvinced.

The Executive Floors were almost deserted when Philpott and Slurry got off the elevator on thirty-nine. None of the Senior Select came in early, except for Dewey B. Shivers, who was always in the Tower by six fixing coffee and making sure that all of the niceties he so carefully arranged for the Senior Select—the fresh-cut flowers, the fresh pastries, the early morning editions of the leading newspapers—were all properly cared for and in order by the time the first important executive arrived for the day.

They wound their way back to Timmons' office. How could things go so bad so fast, Philpott thought, from two days ago when we were in here adding an outing at The Greenbrier to Timmons' schedule? The speed at which he had descended into the metaphorical toilet remained a mystery to Philpott; but his presence there was confirmed beyond any doubt during the encounter which ensued.

Timmons was seated at his desk signing papers for John Stone, who stood next to the desk. Seated on the couch were several people Philpott had never seen before, including a uniformed policeman. Everyone stood up when Philpott and Slurry came into the room.

"Sit down. There, at the round table." They did as they were told. Am I dreaming? Philpott asked himself. He couldn't believe it. Wilfurd Timmons dressed in blue jeans and a flannel shirt, ordering me around like I was the mail boy or something. The men at the couch sat back down. Timmons remained on his feet pacing in front of the round table. No one smiled.

"This will be short." Timmons glared across at Philpott and Slurry. "You're fired, both of you. I know about your secret lab and your sleazy attempt to develop a new skin cream. And I know about your failure to come to my rescue when I was in desperate need of your help." He stopped in front of Philpott and stared at him. "Your disloyalty to me personally is really of no concern to anyone else. But what you've done to the company is unforgivable. And probably illegal."

Timmons motioned to the policeman, who stood up and nodded. "This is Deputy Chief Hillman of the Houston Police Department. You two are going with him. A warrant for your arrest has been sworn out–for abetting a kidnapping, fraud, misappropriation of corporate funds, and God knows what else–and I have pledged the total support of the resources of the company to assist in every way we can to see that the two of you are not only convicted but spend the maximum time possible in jail." As Timmons was talking, three burly Houston cops came into the room and stood looking at Philpott and Slurry with expressionless stares, their night sticks drawn and held at their sides.

Philpott jumped to his feet. "You can't do this," he said uttering the time-honored but pitiful words of the person who has just realized that the not-doable is in fact about to be done.

"You can't do this," he repeated. "Do you know who I am? I am Proctor C. Philpott, Jr. I made this company what it is. I am the company's hope for the future. I am . . . "

"Shut the fuck up, Proctor," Timmons whispered. "I haven't got time for your theatrics." He motioned to Chief Hillman. "Chief, read these thugs their rights and get 'em out of here." He glared one final time at the two men and left the room. He could hear as he left the beginnings of the Miranda warning, "You are advised that you have the right to remain silent, but . . . ."

Shortly after ten, Wilfurd Timmons, still dressed in Jake's casual clothes, stepped in front of a battery of microphones that had been set up in front of Temeritus Tower and began the press conference that Casey had arranged. He began with the remarks that Casey had prepared.

"Ladies and Gentlemen. I have asked you here today so that I can discuss with you a matter of grave concern to me and to my company. Over the weekend I learned that, contrary to what may have been stated in the past, Temeritus has been engaged in undisclosed animal testing and has been doing so in a laboratory that has been operating in secret for a number of months. This operation was carried out at the direction, and under the supervision, of a very senior executive of the company and one or more of his cohorts. These two individuals have been fired, and the matter has been turned over to the police. Temeritus pledges its total cooperation in the prosecution to the fullest extent of the law of these and any other employees or former employees who are shown to have been involved in this scheme.

"Before I take your questions, I would like to make several announcements: First, I want to announce that I am ordering an immediate cessation of all animal testing in connection with the Temeritus line of cosmetic products. Temeritus will engage in animal testing only when it is absolutely necessary to protect human health, when it is done as a part of medical research, or when it may be required by law. And in those cases where such testing is required, it will be carried out with the utmost concern for the rights of the animals involved.

"Second, I am ordering the Temeritus Foundation to begin a review of the various organizations that are active in the animal rights movement, and to contribute heavily to those we determine are most deserving of our support.

"Third, the staff reduction planned for later this year has been canceled and will not occur. As long as I am President of this company, no employee will be laid off merely to improve the bottom line for the short-term aggrandizement of the senior executives.

"Fourth, I am announcing today the closing of the Executive Dining Facility, the cancellation of all useless company memberships and the formation of a task force to study other ways of ridding the company of executive perks that bleed the company's treasury and serve only to isolate the senior management from the people who make the continued success of the company a reality–the men and women of Temeritus. Now, does anyone have any questions?"

There were lots of questions, all of which Wilfurd Timmons answered with an honesty and candor refreshing to anyone familiar with the recent history of the company. When he finished, he turned the press conference over to Casey for her further handling and returned to his office.

The entire press conference was carried live on local TV. But one event did not receive coverage until the Temeritus story was carried again on the evening news. Lost in the excitement of the live press conference, but captured on tape for later airing, were Proctor Philpott and Sam Slurry being led out of Temeritus Tower in handcuffs and being put into the back of a squad car, complete with the obligatory shot of the accompanying officer placing his hand on the back of Proctor Philpott's head and pushing it gently down so that it would not hit the door frame. This bit of the nightly news brought forth an eruption of shouts and cheers of gladness in more than a few households throughout greater Houston.

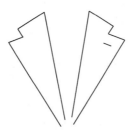

Chapter 49

One of the many Temeritus employees watching live coverage of the Wilfurd Timmons press conference was a secretary, who sat at her kitchen table riveted to the television, surprised and delighted by Timmons' announcements. When the news conference ended she went into her bedroom to begin the daily ritual of dressing for work–a meticulous process that required total concentration to every detail.

First, 100 strokes of the brush through her luxurious black hair, which she pinned into a top-knot. Then she pulled a flesh-colored rubberized hair net over her head like a swim cap providing a stable base for a hair piece–a mop of just-below-the-ears dark brown hair. Once this was in place, a thin coating of spirit gum was applied to the upper lip and eyebrows, and a dark moustache and false eyebrows were carefully affixed. Then a tight elastic wrapping, not unlike a wide Ace bandage, was pulled round and round the chest to flatten as much as possible what nature had generously provided.

The process then turned to more traditional male trappings–cotton undershirt and silk boxers; dark blue over-the-calf socks and black Johnson & Murphy wingtips; starched Egyptian cotton dress shirt with black onyx cufflinks; British regimental tie fastened in a neat four-in-hand knot; and finally, the Savile Row dark blue pinstriped suit.

At last, with the insertion of brown tinted contact lenses, Melville Higgins was ready for the office. A dog ambled over wagging its tail.

"Yeah, Patches, old buddy, you're a good old dog," Higgins said squatting down and scratching the old beagle behind his ears. "But, you, my little Nod," she said to the smallest of her three cats, picking the little creature up and nuzzling her with affection, "You're the sweetest one of all."

the end